Lady and the Pack

Line of Lilith Book Two

by

R.A. Boyd

This is a work of fiction. Names, characters, places, and incidents are either the product of the author's imagination or are used fictitiously, and any resemblance to actual persons living or dead, business establishments, events, or locales, is entirely coincidental.

Lady and the Pack

COPYRIGHT © 2019 by Roslyn Alderman-Boyd

Contact Information: info@thewildrosepress.com

Cover Art by *Debbie Taylor*

The Wild Rose Press, Inc.
PO Box 708
Adams Basin, NY 14410-0708

Visit us at www.thewildrosepress.com

Publishing History
First Scarlet Rose Edition, 2019
Print ISBN 978-1-5092-2617-7
Digital ISBN 978-1-5092-2618-4

Published in the United States of America

A shifter civil war is the perfect reason to skip class, isn't it?

"Don't you want to know what happened, Kayla?"

Shrugging, I walk to the closet and grab my clothes. Good thing yesterday was washday and I'm wearing a good bra and panty set. "I already know what happened. Low blood sugar. Nervous about my first day on the job. Getting zapped by a weird werewolf, thank you by the way. I just need to eat and calm down." And he needs to leave so I can get dressed.

I turn around to ask for privacy and run into a warm wall of man-chest. Hard, brawny, man-chest. My God, he smells awesome. I think my ovaries are going into overdrive.

Gasping, I motor backward a few paces and slam into the closet door. "You've got a real problem with personal space," I say, loving his closeness.

His full lips lift in a slow grin as he traps me between the wall and his large body, placing one palm against the wall on either side of my head. Lowering his head to meet me face-to-face, he says, "You saw it, didn't you." It's not a question.

I shiver as his warm breath caresses my face, and dang it, I can't turn my gaze away from his. "What do you…I don't—"

"Yes, you do know." His nostrils flare, and his eyes lighten to a shining caramel hue. He runs his tongue along his bottom lip. "You're already wet for me, Kayla. You smell fucking delicious."

My stars, he's right. I am wet for him, and if he keeps saying filthy things like that, I may let him have me. "You have a dirty mouth."

"A dirty mouth? Would you like to feel my mouth on you?"

Dedication

Always to my baby girl.
I love you more than tongue can tell.
Thank you, Mom! You've always been an
inspiration to me and everyone you meet.
When I grow up, I want to be just like you.
Robin, Keli, and Marie, thank you
for always being my biggest cheerleaders. You
mean more to me than you could imagine.
My husband, thanks for making it possible for
me to focus on my dreams. I appreciate you.
Charm City Writers, thanks for listening and
reading the random stuff I get ideas for.
Dianne from TWRP, thanks for taking
a chance on me and my Perry-girl.

Chapter One

"Lettie, is he dead?"

"Dead-ish. Last I checked, Ernie was still jerking around while Bertha ate him. It's gross."

I blow out a nervous breath and take my keys out of the ignition, looking around to make sure no one sees me wasting time in my car. "Well, move him before the kids come in. Don't let her gnaw on him like that. It's wrong."

"Kayla, your voice sounds muffled. Honey, I think your mouth is too close to the phone."

"Sorry." I pull the phone away from my mouth and rest it on my cheek. "Take Ernie out of the aquarium before the kids come in."

Lettie laughs. "I will. Can you bring another goldfish when you finish?"

I knew she wanted something. Lettie only calls while she's at work when she needs something. "I'm not sure how long I'll be here, but I'll try to bring you another goldfish during your lunch break. My class starts at two. You do know I work here, right?"

"I know. But if you do get off early...Pretty please?"

"I'll try."

"Thanks, Kayla. The kids don't need to learn about life and death from me." She clears her throat. "But since we're talking about life and death, can you please

1

not work there? Just quit your job, and I'll make sure the bills are paid until you find another one."

I'm already nervous, and she's making it worse. "Lettie, please. I'm not doing this with you. Again."

"Come on, Kayla. It's not safe to be around them. I saw on the news this morning that there was another murder. Mur. Der."

I don't need this crap right now. "If I get a chance, I'll bring you a goldfish."

She huffs and fumbles with the phone. "Sorry. We both know I'm a big worrier."

"Lettie, I'll be fine." Famous last words of people who are about to get eaten in the horror movies. I look out the front window of my car and see a flock of geese fly by, their honking calls reminding me of Lettie's constant griping. "Call you later."

"Damn it, Kayla. Fine. You'll be fine." Maybe she's trying to convince herself that I will be. A faint dinging noise chimes in the background behind Lettie's voice. "First bell of the school day. I have to go take Ernie out before the kids get in. I'll see you later."

Lettie and I share a two-bedroom apartment not far from our college campus. She's like a sister to me.

"Bye, Lettie." I hang up, shove the phone into my brown purse, and get out of my car. The gravel crunches beneath my feet, like an animal chewing on the bones of its latest prey. Drops of morning dew splash up onto my ankles as I step into the lush, green grass. I am calm, and I am safe. I'm not one of them, so I'm safe.

This place is beautiful. It has a wraparound porch, sits on about two hundred and fifty acres of land, and it reminds me of the manor on Tara from *Gone with the*

Wind. Lettie's words echo in my head as I grab the brass knocker on the door. She didn't have to tell me there had been another murder. I heard it on the radio on my way here this morning.

For a brief moment I think of getting back into my car, but before I get a chance to act on my second thought, the large, dark, double door on the right opens. I'm met with a kind, closed-mouth smile. I'm here assisting Kerry, opener of the door, in writing her memoirs. I'll be getting a peek into a world very few people get to witness. Even though she doesn't scream "Queen" she has an air of sovereignty. I'll get credit as co-author and write the foreword. This book is to let the world know that they are like the rest of us.

I'm happy to be here, but my brain is on high alert. Why would she pick me to do this? Me, an inexperienced college student whose only knowledge of writing anything close to a book was taking the food and drink order of a party of twenty-three. I worked in a pub.

Kerry opens the door a little farther. "Kayla, it's so good to see you." She has a natural beauty about her. She's tall with a long and lean body that's poised and strong. Her faultless short, raven-colored hair and full lips complement her small face and wide nose, but the only feature that makes me pause are her eyes. They are exquisite, but they also let me know that she's different. The golden-yellow iris contrasts severely with the pale blue of the cornea, but the friendliness of her face assures me she means no harm.

The better to see you with, my dear.

Her floor-length white skirt and gray tee-shirt fit her slim body perfectly. She's hot. She can't be older

3

than thirty. "Come," she says, stepping out of the way. "Steven has been raving about you. You're in his class this year?"

"Yes," I say, walking behind her. "I'm in his Greek and Roman Mythology class this semester."

My teacher, Steven Levay, lives here with them. After he found out I had a few short stories published and that I wanted to be an author, he introduced me to Kerry. I met with her about two weeks ago, and now I'm here for my first day of work.

"Kayla," she says, smiling softly. "Thank you for coming to the manor so early."

I'm nervous and smile too much. "It's no problem at all. I'm just happy to be here."

We walk through the living room that leads to her office, which is grand yet simple—a dark mahogany desk with a laptop, fresh flowers in a crystal vase, and a phone are all that sit on the severely neat desk.

She sits and gestures toward the chair across from her. "You can take comfort in knowing you will be completely safe here. None of my kind has ever done anything like this before, but I believe this will help humans to understand us better. All transcription will be done here at the manor. I've already recorded two tapes to start you off. There's a room set up for you to use," she says, ticking off each fact on her thin fingers. "Per our agreement, you will come here and observe at least three days a week, more if you want. My goal is to let humans know that we are no different from them. We are a family. We are Pack. Any questions, Kayla?"

I look at Kerry with calm eyes hoping my excitement and fears aren't bleeding through. This is excitement, fear, and job of a lifetime all wrapped into one little danger ball. "Will I be allowed to ask questions, or should I just hang back and wait to talk to you?" I hear a slight crack in my voice and clear my throat. I try to appear cool and pretend I am in control. Me? In control right now? Negative. I'm sitting across from the Queen and Leader of the Maryland Werewolf Pack.

"You can interact as you wish," Kerry says, clasping her hands in front of her on the desk. "There are no limitations. Ask questions. I hope eventually you will feel like part of the family. You smell anxious, but please trust me when I say there is definitely no need to be."

I gasp and feel my left eyebrow pop up in a Spock-like gesture. Lettie always pokes me in the forehead if I do it around her.

What the hell does anxious smell like? "To be honest—"

"I want nothing more than your complete honesty, Kayla. Not meaning to scare you, but I'm sure you are aware we can 'smell' emotion." She makes little bunny ears with her fingers. "It's not that we smell the emotion itself, really. It's more of how the body emits certain chemicals when a person experiences different emotions."

"Wow. Thanks for reminding me," I reply, sarcasm stinging in my voice. Just because I'm the puny human in the house doesn't mean it has to be flaunted. I smell stuff, too. "To be honest, I am a little scared. I'm the only human in a house full of werewolves, and I don't want to make the wrong impression. Humans have a history of being very biased. But I want you to know that plenty of us don't judge and are not frightened of you." Did I come across right?

She claps her hands together with a big smile. I gasp and slide back in my chair. How many frickin' teeth does she have in her mouth? "You are the right choice!" The flawless, straight, gleaming white teeth are accented by slightly larger and sharper canines.

It's unnerving. I hope she didn't see me flinch.

"I wanted someone who was open and willing to interact with us comfortably. And from what Steven says, you know a few basic things about us. That's one of the reasons I chose you. You felt like the right choice. The world will know more about us, and this is a wonderful opportunity for you as a writer." She stands up and gestures toward the door. "Come on. I'll finish showing you around and then introduce you to the pack members that live here."

So far, she has the impression that I know what I'm doing. Even though I don't. I am an English major at Perryville University. I'm of average height, average weight, and I have an average face. I'm comfortable in my deep honey-coated skin with my huge mass of curly, dark hair and child-bearing hips. There's nothing striking about me, I guess. Men don't fall over me, but I do get my fair share of dates. Cumulatively.

We walk down the stairs leading from the kitchen to the basement and it opens up into a room that runs the entire length of the house. A large family room covers a little more than half of the space, a gym area in the farthest left corner, and a gamer's heaven across from it. Chairs and couches are strategically placed so the seating doesn't overwhelm the huge space.

Humans have known about the existence of werewolves since the time of the Black Plague in

Europe. The werewolves came up with the term "Weres" in the early 1900s, hoping people would take to the term better. Werewolf sounds too scary. Deep down, most people are afraid of them, but werewolves have never caused any harm. Well, at least as of late.

There have been a few killings of werewolves over the past year, and no one understands why. At first, the murders were thought to be random until a coroner found that the same kind of blade had been used on each victim. No one knows whether or not humans are getting antsy and want to make a point, or if for some reason the wolves are killing their own.

"This is the common room. Everyone," Kerry says in a raised voice. "This is Kayla. They've been expecting you," she says to me quietly. "This is Samuel."

Samuel nods his head and gives me a closed-mouth smile that looks nothing but inviting. He's pretty tall but not intimidating, with broad shoulders and shoulder-length blond hair. He looks like a sexy Viking. And he's not wearing a shirt. And he has muscles that pop out from everywhere. Not in a gross way but in a way that makes me think he can hold me and my extra twenty pounds up against a wall and take me down to pound town. Literally. And he is looking all kinds of tasty right now. Crap. They can smell emotion. Come on, Kayla. picture Grandfather Taylor when you helped him out of the shower when he fell. Eww. Feelings of hotness for Samuel are now gone.

"This is Easay." Easay is a beautiful woman with long green hair. Awesome dye job. She has the graceful long limbs that a ballet dancer would kill for. Her creamy skin is flawless, except for a jagged scar on the right side of her neck that runs from ear to collarbone.

"It's wonderful to meet you!" Easay says with a bone-rattling handshake and a huge smile extremely occupied with shiny teeth. It must be a werewolf thing. She points to the man sitting across from us. "There is always food laid out for us, and Seeley is willing to make anything you ask for."

Seeley is sitting on the couch completely preoccupied with his colossal cold cut. The sandwich reminds me of one Scooby-Doo and Shaggy should be sharing. I'm starving. Kerry clears her throat to get his attention, and he jumps up to come and greet me. Seeley's not much taller than me, and when he speaks, it sounds like he is fresh from somewhere in Eastern Europe. I love those accents.

His baby-blue eyes match his loose-fitting shirt and faded blue jeans. "It is good to meet you, Kayla. You are hungry. I make you sandwich."

Okay. How the hell did he know I was hungry? "It's fine. I don't want to impose."

He scrunches up his face and shakes his head, giving me a "silly human" look. "Once you are finished with tour of manor, come back here and you will eat with me." He goes back to his sandwich. With large hands, he picks the huge sandwich up and takes an inhumanly large bite.

Kerry taps my arm. "Come on. I'll show you the rest of the manor." We walk through the kitchen and back to the main stairway of the house. "I love the way these stairs curve as they ascend. Beautiful, don't you think?"

"Your home is beautiful. What year was it built?"

"I had this house built back in 1959. I was only

seventeen years old, and my father was dying. He told me I was to be the next pack leader. I wanted a home where we could stay and be at peace. An area where we could run and change. Right now, seven of us live here. There are twelve rooms all together. There are two beds in most rooms." She stops talking and turns to face me. "Come on. Your emotions are pouring off of you. You're dying to know how old I am." She pauses at the platform of the stairs.

I must be doing the Spock thing again. "I'm sorry. I thought maybe you were in your late twenties. You had this house built sixty years ago." I guess I didn't ask a question.

Her smile is friendly as she shakes her head. "I'm seventy-six years old, Kayla. We age differently than humans, and if a human is affected by the lycanthropy strain, their aging process slows as well. But I do ask that you be discreet. I will put it on my recordings but in a much gentler way. Okay?"

"Oh, no. I'll keep it to myself. I appreciate your honesty. My lips are sealed." That all sounded like one big word. I'm such a dork. "I do have one question though."

She smiles like she already knows what I'm going to ask and answers before I get a chance. "Weres can live to be over two hundred years old. Though most are killed before they reach the age."

An instant wave of nausea rolls over me. I shake my head and rest my hand on my stomach. "I'm so sorry. How can humans be afraid of you? We can be so terrible."

"It's not just humans, but thank you. Many of our kind die in battles of hierarchy, mating, or just plain anger. And it's not you. You don't give off a menacing aura."

Is that good or bad? Dang it, I can be menacing.

"This room right here belongs to Patrick. He's been here since his father died some years ago. He's off handling pack business with Osai, whose room is right here." She points to the room two doors up. "There are two beds in there for when Osai's brother comes to visit from the Nigerian Pack. They both travel back and forth." Kerry steps to the side of the last door on the right and opens it. "And here is your room," she says staring at me.

"I'm sorry?" I have a room?

She shrugs one shoulder. "It's basic, but I wanted to make sure you'd be comfortable. There is a half bath in here with a shower and everything you need. Just basic stuff."

"Why do I have a room?" This is getting a little weird.

She tips her head, signaling me to go into my room. "Just in case you stay longer than expected. You have so far to drive, and I wouldn't want you driving after all the transcribing you'll be doing. Especially if you were too tired. Now, you won't feel obligated to leave."

This room is about two of my bedrooms put together. It's set up with a canopy bed and a little area in the corner with a desk and desktop computer. Everyone is being way too thoughtful toward me. Is this a set up so that I don't write the whole truth about what the hell really goes on here?

"Too much? Not enough? You seem puzzled." A line appears between her eyebrows as confusion covers her face.

"No, Kerry—the room is gorgeous. More than enough." I chew the inside of my lip, looking around the room. She doesn't even know me. "Why all of this? I'm helping you write a book, not marrying your first born. And why me? I don't know what I'm doing." I try to be as polite as possible, but the suspicion still creeps in. Does she think I'll be easily manipulated because I'm only twenty-four and she's my ticket to getting published? Maybe my age makes her think I'm carefree and don't pay attention to what's going on around me. If only I were that person.

A bit of sadness creeps into her gaze as she stares at me. Kerry folds her hands and leans against the door. "Kayla, this is a major characteristic you will learn about werewolf relationships. Packs are very close. Closer than most human families. We rely on one another, count on one another, and when we have guests, we treat them as if they were one of our own. You will be observing us and occasionally staying here. This is simply how we are."

"Oh," I say, resting my back against the wall, wishing I could disappear into it.

"You'll be integrating yourself within this pack. At least, I hope you will. You'd be treated the same whether you were a close friend, a new wolf who needed guidance, or a pack member from another area who needed shelter. Pack is family, and yes, I am well aware you are not Pack, but treating you any different than we treat our own is unheard of. Especially because you're so open to this."

I should have done more research on Weres. This could be some form of an insult. She's treating me like she would anyone else, and I'm trying to use it against her.

"Kayla, when you were anxious earlier, it didn't smell like fear. It only smelled as if you were nervous. Nervous to start anew or meet new people. You don't fear us, and for that we are…" She shrugs and looks around the room as if she's searching for the right thing to say. "I can't explain it. Most humans behave as if we need to prove ourselves to them. But you…you're interested, you're open, you are undaunted, and for that, you are a step above the average human. I saw it the moment I laid eyes on you. I felt it. Steven says the same thing." Nothing but honesty and sincerity radiate from her.

Now I feel horrible. Years of dealing with manipulative and self-serving people have left me suspicious. I feel crappy. "Thank you. That means a lot. I apologize for thinking anything less."

She looks at me like a mother who just taught her child a new lesson. If this happy-sappy "we love you for you" stuff is real, we humans should be modeling ourselves after what we call monster.

My stomach growls as we walk back toward the common room.

"I'm sure Seeley is finished preparing your meal. We eat—a lot. Our metabolism is pretty high, so we need to nourish ourselves more than humans do. Come. Seeley says your breakfast is ready."

What? I didn't hear anything.

Kerry laughs and touches my shoulder. "You are an open book. Remember, he's only downstairs, and our hearing is superb. Besides, I am Queen and pack leader. Mine is better than most."

By the time she finishes talking, we're back downstairs in the common room. Next to Seeley's plate is mine—a cold-cut sandwich with fries on the side, an iced tea, and a few cookies. I grin in spite of myself and go sit next to him. Maybe this crap really is real.

Most people think I'm crazy for doing this, but I think I'd be crazy not to. This is the opportunity of a lifetime, and no one ever got ahead by sitting on their behind. Noble words from the blonde chick in the cheerleader/bank robber movie.

I think I'll stay and finish out the day instead of leaving early.

****

"I ate with them and talked with them," I say excitedly to Lettie as we sit at the dining room table eating ice cream and popcorn. "They are literally the most considerate group of people I've ever met."

Lettie is the closest thing to family I have here in Maryland. And the ones I do call family—well, let's say I'm happy we don't live in the same state.

I've never had a significant or meaningful relationship with my mom. She left me and my dad when I was three. While growing up, I reminded my dad so much of her that he shut me out. He was angry with her, but I felt the burn.

Even now, as I'm an adult and show little interest in her, she tries to be my best friend once or twice a year. She insults me when she says I remind her of herself. I'm pretty confident that I would never abandon my child and try to be a fifty-three-year-old teenager. But to avoid pushing her farther away than she already is, I never say anything. She tires of me after a day or two and disappears until she remembers it's my birthday. Or at least until she thinks it is.

"I just don't understand how you could agree to spend so much time with them," Lettie says. She is about five foot one with dark Italian features and long, poufy dark hair. "I mean, they are animals. They're what people used to write about to scare children. You could get hurt, you know. Could be their time of the month and you're the only one in the house that smells like food."

"Lettie, that's a terrible thing to say. They were nicer to me than your family has ever been."

She glances at me sideways and laughs. "Well, you did punch my brother in the balls."

"Well, his balls were too close to me, and he grabbed my ass."

Lettie tries to stifle a laugh but only manages to spit a popcorn piece onto her arm. "Anyway, how much are you getting paid?"

"For the first six months, I get twenty-five thousand buckaronies! More than I made all of last year, I might add." If I had taken the free room and board Kerry was offering, it would have been twenty thousand, but since I love my apartment and don't loathe my short evil roommate I'm staying here with Lettie. "I was going to tell you over drinks tonight. My treat." I attempt to waggle my eyebrows, but it doesn't work out that way.

Lettie dips her finger into the sugar bowl and shoves it in her mouth. Disgusting habit. "No, Kayla, my treat. This is your dream job, *baby*! Before you graduate, you'll be co-author of the first memoirs of the Weres."

This is why Lettie is awesome. She's the most

supportive person in my life. And she's not afraid to give me her honest opinion. Even if I don't ask for it. After I told my dad I was majoring in English to be a writer, he told me my poor choice was a waste of money and time. He also told me that if I didn't go to school for nursing, he wouldn't support me financially or in any other way. I've never uttered a callous word to my dad, but when he said that to me, I almost told him to shove his financial support and go kick rocks.

So, I worked my ass off for two years waiting tables and tutoring kids from my old high school to make the move to Maryland. Alone. I'd be happy if I had a semi-decent relationship with my dad, but there is no use crying over spilled tequila.

Lettie claps her hands and stands up. "This is a night for celebration, bitches! Even though I don't agree with you spending so much time with them, I'll butt-kick the ass of anyone who tries to get in your way."

"Thank you, Lettie." She'll never know how much her threat of swift violence touches my heart. I open my eyes wide so I don't begin to tear up. I hate crying.

She sees what I'm doing and does me the honor of preoccupying herself with something else. "I'm going to take a shower." She pokes me on the forehead and walks away. Lettie is a force to be reckoned with. "Craig just pulled up," Lettie says from behind the closed bathroom door. There's a window beside the toilet.

He didn't call to say he was coming. I wait a few minutes, giving him time to walk up the two flights of stairs, and I open the door just in time to see Craig singing and shimmying to music quietly coming from his phone. He still has his chef's hat on and looks more like the Cat in the Hat than a diner cook.

Craig works at the diner. I've worked there as a waitress since I moved here.

"Hey." I smile at him and wink. "Are you singing to me again?"

He two-steps onto the top floor platform holding two large white bags. "Hey, baby. You know I sing to all my ladies. I called, but you didn't answer."

I step out of his way as he walks into the apartment and heads for the kitchen. "Is everything all right?" I ask.

He puts the two bags on the table and reaches into his back pocket. "I came to hand deliver your last paycheck, two strawberry shortcakes, and those butter rolls you love. Do you and Short Stuff still need help moving the bed in this weekend?"

Lettie's mom bought her a new headboard. One of the legs of her old headboard broke off and fell in the middle of the night. Lettie screamed bloody murder, and I came running into her room with my baseball bat that I keep under the bed.

"Yes sir, we do. Still available?"

"Of course. I'll be here Saturday morning for breakfast."

"Hell, yeah. You brought me cake, rolls, and you're helping Lettie move that thing. Of course, we'll make you breakfast. You didn't have to come all this way to bring this over. I would have come to you."

Craig has been a father figure to me since I moved to Maryland. He says I remind him of his daughter who died in a car accident eight years ago. I think he needs someone to be a father to. He says he likes helping me, so I ask him for help whenever I can. Makes him feel needed again. Even though I've only known him a few years, he's been there for me when I needed someone to play the father figure. Craig is a blessing, and I love him more than he'll ever know.

He smiles and starts backing toward the door. "I just wanted to see you after your first day and make sure you were good. You good?" He stops walking for a moment, waiting for my answer.

"I'm great. It went great."

He claps his hands together and dips his head a few times, giving me a smile I wish I could see on my father's face. "Good. I'm so proud of you. I'll see you Saturday." He walks back toward me and gives a tight hug, lingering for a moment with his chin on the top of my head. "So proud."

I rub my face against his grease-stained shirt and look up at him. "That means a lot, Craig. Thank you."

He kisses the top of my head and then walks back toward the door, opening it this time. He looks back to me and says, "You be careful around those wolves, love. Just don't get mistaken for one of them and get yourself killed."

"I'm too clumsy," I say.

"There's a killer on the loose gunning for wolves. And from what I heard on the radio earlier, a human was killed this time, too."

Chapter Two

I suck beyond the telling of it. I forgot the pin number Kerry gave me to get on the property. Practically dislocating my shoulder, I lean over my car door and hit the buzzer.

"Yes?" says a new voice.

"Hello? My name is Kayla Taylor. Kerry is expecting me."

Silence.

"Hello! Can you hear me?" Crap, I should have brought that code. He probably doesn't know who I am.

The gate slowly opens, and I pull up to the side of the house to see Kerry standing on the car-pad waiting for me with that big toothy smile. "Please tell me you didn't lose the entrance code," she says, her eyes crinkling at the corners.

Shit. I'm already making a bad impression. "I did not. I left it at home on my bed. Sorry. I was trying to figure out what I should bring with me and forgot the one thing to get me in here."

Her face relaxes. "Don't worry. It's fine."

Someone is killing the Weres. Good job, Kayla.

"I'll memorize the code and shred the letter. I'm sorry. I don't want to disappoint you." And that is the honest truth. Not because she scares me, but because I really don't want to let her down. Crap, I talked to my therapist about this—finding a motherly figure and transferring the feelings I should have had for my mom on to her.

"Think nothing of it."

I nod quickly. "Thanks, Kerry."

"We're all in the dining room eating breakfast together. Will you join us?"

"Of course. I skipped breakfast."

We walk into the dining room, and the first thing I see is Easay's bright green hair. I grin and cover it with a cough.

Kerry puts her arm around me. "Just your luck, Seeley. Kayla has not yet eaten. You can make her one of your famous omelets." She gestures to the two new guys sitting at the table. "Osai and Patrick, this is Kayla."

Osai is a little taller than me with dark skin that seems to shine from within. His eyes and smile are so bright they make me smile. He shakes my hand, and I feel a sense of power in his grasp.

"It's nice to meet you, Kayla," he says before taking a huge gulp of orange juice. His accent is thick, but he enunciates each word clearly so that I can understand him.

"You too."

Before Patrick stands up to shake my hand, he shoves a forkful of eggs and a whole piece of bacon into his mouth. As he stands to greet me, it seems like his presence unfolds from the table; as if he was keeping his very essence under control while he was sitting. He's not a large man. In fact, he's just about a head taller than me. His wide swimmer's shoulders slope slightly under his sky-blue polo shirt and lead down to a waist I'm sure has that perfect V-shape that turns me the hell on. Bad thoughts! His darker than café au lait skin fits perfectly over those muscled arms that look strong and gentle, and his close-cut hair completes his clean-cut look. The way his waist tapers inward makes his shoulders look even broader than they are.

I need to carry a picture of Grandpa Taylor around with me at all times. The Weres will think I'm a horn-dog.

Patrick wipes his hands on a napkin and talks through his food. "So sorry," he says, reaching out his hand to shake mine. "I haven't had a home-cooked meal in two weeks. Nice to meet you, Kayla." His genuine smile reaches all the way to his whiskey-brown eyes.

I lean forward, and just as our hands touch, the air surges with something akin to electricity. The fine hairs along my arms stand at attention, and when our fingers meet, I feel him go through my fingertips, up through my wrist and arm, and fill my entire body.

My heart trips over itself, literally skipping a beat, and my breath hitches in my throat. I grab the table as the room tips sideways and try to blink my way back to stability.

The forest. I can smell wind and grass. Morning dew and dirt. Patrick's nostrils flare like a new scent has invaded the room and whatever I feel, he becomes aware of it too. A vision of me and Patrick in the middle of a grassy field takes over.

Colorful wildflowers surround us and tickle my skin as he takes me from behind. His teeth bite into my shoulder as he claims me as his own, sending tendrils of passion through me and into the soft earth beneath us. The bite stings, but it adds to the warm ache of his hard cock driving into me again and again. I can feel the hard planes of his hot skin against mine as we writhe against each other. Over and over he fills a part of me that has been empty since I can remember. I give in to his dominance, I give in to his wolf, and I surrender as he takes me. I hear him whisper lovely, filthy words in my ear and feel the smile tug at my lips as he rides me.

Coming out of the delicious and unexpected vision I murmur, "Holy hell," still looking into his eyes as his large hand completely wraps around mine. I squeeze his hand and fight the oncoming orgasm whispering its way through my core. The barest of moans escapes my lips, and I look down at our still joined hands, embarrassed, as my panties flood with wet heat. What the hell just happened?

"Fuck," Patrick whispers, looking down at his growing erection that I can't keep my eyes off. He looks back up at me and involuntarily coughs eggs and bacon onto the front of my shirt, breaking the spell. Dry clean only, dang it.

"What the fuck was that?" I cry out without thinking and then follow up with slapping my left hand over my mouth. I almost came in front of a room full of people I don't know from, touching a man I just met. I let go of the table and cup my hand over the erratic beat of my heart.

"Are you all right, Kayla?" Kerry asks in a worried tone. "Patrick, when was the last time you shifted?" she scolds as I snatch my hand out of his.

"What?" He sounds just as confused as I feel. "Not since I left a few weeks ago, but—"

Kerry interrupts him. "I'm sorry, Kayla. Sometimes when we don't shift, we get a little antsy and the energy gets pent up inside us. You're the only human here. I guess it chose you as an outlet. But please believe me, you are in no danger. Come. Sit. Have a glass of juice." She apologizes and guides me to the chair next to Samuel.

Now, an air of edginess has invaded the room, and everyone is trying to ignore it. Except Patrick. He won't take his eyes off me, and every time I try to look away from him for too long, the pull of his gaze draws mine back to his. Seeley is filling my glass and asking me something that sounds like another language.

"What, Seeley? I'm sorry," I say.

"What would you like in your omelet?" he asks a bit louder.

"Umm, cheese, tomato, and broccoli, if you have any broccoli. Or spinach is better," I answer as the butterflies take over my stomach.

"I'll be back in a few minutes with your breakfast." Then he looks at Patrick the way a big brother would. He grabs Patrick's shoulder and pulls the chair from under him. "Come with me, Patrick. You've eaten. Now you shift."

"Yes, Patrick," Kerry adds indifferently. "Kayla. Are you all right?"

"I'm fine. That was just weird." My head is swimming. "Actually, may I go lie down for a moment? My head feels funny." I begin to stand before she answers.

"Of course. Samuel, would you please walk Kayla to her room." Kerry nods to Samuel. Who still doesn't have on a shirt.

I shake my head, trying not to make a big deal out of things. "No, Kerry. I'm okay. I just need to rest. He doesn't need to walk me upstairs."

"It's no problem," Samuel adds. "Don't want you to get light-headed on your way up the stairs. The ride back down would hurt a human. A lot." Poor human, he seems to imply.

"Thanks, Samuel," I say sarcastically. "Really, Kerry, I'm so sorry. Would you please tell Seeley I'd sure love that omelet a little later?"

After I start walking, my head begins to clear. I should have grabbed an apple before I left home. I'm already nervous and low blood sugar probably makes it even worse. I digress. Being zapped by a werewolf's pent-up energy probably made it even worse. This is embarrassing. I forget the code to get onto the property, and ten minutes later I take a break so I can lie down.

As we round the corner to go upstairs, I see Patrick in the kitchen being chastised by Seeley. "She's human, Patrick. You have to be careful." Seeley shakes an egg covered fork at him.

"I know. I couldn't help it. Besides," he says, shaking his head and linking his hands behind his neck, "it's not what you think. It can't be. It better not be. Someone could end up dead."

"What?" I say, holding on to the banister. Did that son of a bitch just threaten me?

Seeley goes back to beating the eggs with the fork like they owe him money, and Patrick turns to look at me and frowns. My head starts to swim again. And then the ceiling starts getting farther and farther away from my face.

"I've got her," Samuel says as I start to fall backward.

Strong arms catch me from behind, and Patrick's

voice is much closer than it should be. "Sorry, Sam, but if you touch her, I'll rip your fucking arms off." He gathers me close to his chest and picks me up. "She's mine."

"She's human."

"She's. Mine."

How the hell did he get over here so fast? What the hell does he mean?

More than anything right now, I'd love to care what all of this means. Instead, their voices get farther and farther away as I give in to the darkness.

****

It's dark. The only light that shines through sneaks in from the cracked bathroom door. I look up and try to orient myself to the dimly lit room and see the underside of the canopy bed in my part-time home. I must have passed out. In my first week of work. I didn't even have the sense to do it next week. At least they would have been used to me being here by then. Kind of. God, I suck.

My body tells me to turn over and get a few more minutes of sleep. This bed fits every contour of my body. If I ask really nicely, I wonder if Kerry would give me the bed as part of my severance package when my time here is done.

I shift to reach for a bedside lamp, and a flash of golden eyes glimmer in the darkness. "Hello? Who's there?" I silently curse myself for letting my voice go higher, the sound of fear lacing through my words.

"Do you want me to cut the light on?" a deep, melodic voice asks from the darkness. It's Patrick.

In a quick and graceless motion, I sit up in bed and run my fingers through the coily mass that is my hair and then down to my shirt to smooth it out. Patrick is sex on two legs, and I probably have the appearance of a rumpled sheet that was left in the dryer too long.

"You look perfect." His hushed voice moves through the room and caresses my skin.

"Thanks?"

He moves and his chair whispers a protest as he gets up and walks toward me.

The light blinks on. I squint my eyes as the light invades the dimness and quickly scoot backward as I realize how close Patrick's face is to mine. "Umm...I'm going to need a little space," I say, my back now pressed against the headboard.

Like a little mechanical animal, he ticks his head to the side as if thinking over my request. After a few moments of us staring at each other almost nose to nose, he moves back and sits on the bed near my feet.

"How's your head?" he asks, hand reaching forward as if to touch my face. He seems to think better of it and pulls away.

Without even thinking of it, I'd started to move toward his hand to accept his comfort. His retreat almost breaks my heart. "It's fine. Clear." I chew my bottom lip and watch him as he studies me.

His gaze is disarming. Whiskey-brown eyes stare back at me, and my cheeks warm at the thought of his undivided attention. My mind is flung back to the image of us making love in a field. I let out a steadying breath and clench the soft sheets against my palms, as if holding on to something will stop the tumbling magnetism that's pulling me to him. I'm no psychic, but I'd bet this sweet comfortable bed that Patrick is experiencing the same rollercoaster ride of emotions that I am. Where my feelings are making me unsure and apprehensive, Patrick seems more intrigued and pissed off.

"Do you have any Weres in your family?" he asks, crossing his arms against his broad chest as he leans back against the bedpost.

That's a weird question. "What?"

"Do you. Have. Any. Weres. In your family?" he asks again, accentuating the words with a derisive smile to his lips.

This bastard is being rude. How dare he? I read that it was discourteous to ask a person if they were a Were, and if they were it was rude to ask what kind.

I flip him the finger. "First off, screw you for being a smartass, and secondly, no, I don't." I start to get out of bed, but then I remember Ash. "Wait. I do. Second cousin on my dad's side. She was bitten, not born. Her husband turned her on their first wedding anniversary." They had a small gathering at her husband's parents' house right after she was registered as a wolf. "What time is it?" I ask, realizing that no natural light filters into the room from the blinds. It looks dark outside.

"Almost nine," he says. "You should lie back down. I don't want you to faint again."

I stand up and take a few steps. "Thanks for your concern, but see"—I point at myself—"I'm good. And I'm wearing pajamas?" I distinctly remember having on my own clothes before I got up close and personal with the carpet.

Patrick runs his thumbnail across his chin a few times before he answers. "After you were out for about an hour, I changed your clothes. Just in case you didn't wake until morning. They are hanging in the closest. I had your shirt dry cleaned." He points toward the closet door, never taking his eyes off me. "Don't you want to know what happened, Kayla?"

Shrugging, I walk to the closet and grab my clothes. Good thing yesterday was wash day and I'm wearing a good bra and panty set. "I already know what happened. Low blood sugar. Nervous about my first day on the job. Getting zapped by a weird werewolf, thank you by the way. I just need to eat and calm down." And he needs to leave so I can get dressed.

I turn around to ask for privacy and run into a warm wall of man-chest. Hard, brawny man-chest. My God, he smells awesome. I think my ovaries are going into overdrive.

Gasping, I motor backward a few paces and slam into the closet door. "You've got a real problem with personal space," I say, loving his closeness.

His full lips lift in a slow grin as he traps me between the wall and his large body, placing one palm against the wall on either side of my head. Lowering his head to meet me face-to-face he says, "You saw it, didn't you." It's not a question.

I shiver as his warm breath caresses my face, and dang it, I can't turn my gaze away from his. "What do you... I don't—"

"Yes, you do know." His nostrils flare, and his eyes lighten to a shining caramel hue. He runs his tongue along his bottom lip. "You're already wet for me, Kayla. You smell fucking delicious."

My stars, he's right. I am wet for him, and if he keeps saying filthy things like that, I may let him have me. "You have a dirty mouth."

"A dirty mouth? Would you like to feel my mouth

on you? Here," he says, taking one of his hands and letting it hover over my breasts. The heat of his palm radiates through my shirt. It takes more strength than it should require for me not to push my chest forward those last few inches to have him touch me. "What about here?" he says, fingers still hovering just out of reach as he traces a line from my stomach down to the apex of my thighs. "I would love to have the scent of your passion on my face."

He moves his hips toward mine and then backs away. My hands shoot up against his chest to keep the distance, and I drop my clothes. Sweet baby Jesus, this man is dangerous. And familiar. His masculine scent, the heat emanating from his body. It's all so familiar. I finally look to his eyes and see them staring back at me, a bright yellowish-orange color that glows like a harvest moon. It frightens and excites me at the same time.

"Tell me," he says.

I shake my head and close my eyes. He couldn't have seen my completely inappropriate wet dream I had while I was wide awake in a room full of people.

He nods once. "You saw the field, felt the flowers move across your skin as I rammed my cock into you, didn't you?"

Hell yes, I did. I close my eyes and can see it again. I can almost feel it. "I need space," I murmur as I grab two handfuls of his shirt, pulling him toward me.

This is bad. In a really good way. I haven't been this close or this attracted to a man in over a year. No time for dating when my life is a routine of school and work. School and work. The feel of Patrick makes me want to throw it away and be content being taken by him, being tasted by him.

He closes the short distance between us and pushes his hips against mine, keeping them there this time. Even through his pants and my pajama bottoms, I can feel his hard length, and my stars, he his large.

"Kayla. What's the one word that comes to mind when you think of me, right now? Doesn't matter how crazy it is or how much sense it doesn't make to you. Give me one word." His tongue darts out, and he licks across the seam of my lips.

Hot, hard, sexy, stranger, sinful. "Mine." I drag out in a husky, lust-filled voice.

I'm on fire. On fire for Patrick. My skin tingles from his touch, and goose bumps erupt along every surface of my skin as that word tumbles from my lips. Mine. My breaths come in pants, drying my lips with their short bursts of air. A new wave of wet heat seeps into my panties, and if I don't slow down, if we don't slow down, I may actually orgasm this time.

Patrick smiles against my lips and says, "Open."

I open my mouth in surrender and delight in the feel of his tongue stroking against mine, exploring every inch of my mouth. The sensation of his lips against mine make an instant, arduous connection between my thighs. Just like in the vision earlier he claims me, not with his cock, but with his mouth. With his touch. He moves his head in every angle, kissing me with a passion I've only read about in erotic novels that make me touch myself. One of his hands grabs my ass and pulls my center toward his thick shaft as the other snakes its way to the base of my head and grasps a handful of my hair, forcing me to come closer to his large body. The slight pain of his fingers tugging at my hair sends exquisite prickles down my spine.

Wrapping my arms around his neck, I pull him in to me and wiggle up his body, wrapping my legs around his waist. I haven't had sex in so long, and if this is the way the streak ends, then someone deserves a cookie. Patrick is the sexiest man I've ever laid eyes on, and I get to take him for a ride.

A 1970's disco song sounds off in the room. It's Lettie's ringtone.

With the spell broken, I pull back and look at Patrick. "What the hell am I doing?" I whisper, mortified at myself. I'm wrapped around Patrick's body, and my hair is hanging in my face. "Oh, my goodness. I'm so sorry." I climb down and run my fingers through my hair to tame it.

Patrick's cocky demeanor slips, and he shakes his head. "Don't panic. This is what it's like."

He tries to keep me pinned against the wall, but I dip under his arms and pick up my clothes.

I walk across the room to where my purse sits in the corner, hands shaking as I sift through my bag to find my phone. Lettie is probably having a freaking fit. I should have been home hours ago.

"I'm not panicking. I'm just…This isn't me. I don't do stuff like this," I say with a nervous giggle. Nope. I don't usually suck face and fondle random men I just met. Except that time my freshman year. I was completely wasted. I can't even blame this on alcohol. "I have to go."

Patrick turns to face me and puts his hands up as if he's soothing a wild animal. "You need to eat."

"Not hungry."

"Low blood sugar?"

"What the hell did you do to me, Patrick?"

He takes a deep breath and shakes his head like he's trying to figure it out himself. "I don't understand how a human was chosen, but you were. Come on. You know something happened."

Do werewolves have supernatural pheromones that pull in unsuspecting, sex-deprived women?

"You happened. This is creeping me out," I say, taking off the pajama bottoms and sliding into my own pants. If he wants to keep having this conversation, then he'll have to do it while I'm on my way out. This isn't natural.

"Just like you said I was yours? I feel the exact same way. You are my mate, Kayla." He stalks toward me like the predator he is.

"Stop right there." I point at him as he takes a step toward me. I button up my pants and shove my shirt into my bag. If I take this pajama top off, I may be tempted to rip off my bra and hope that Patrick gets up close and personal with my ta-tas. "I don't know what you're talking about or what you did. Don't come closer."

"Did you hear what I said?"

"I heard you. I'm your mate?" I scoff and quickly put on my shoes.

"Yes. You're mine. I'm yours."

I feel a tightening in my chest, and dang it, his words sound like heaven. "I don't know what that means."

A smile breaks across his face, but it doesn't reach his eyes. "In human terms, we just announced our engagement."

"You're out of your Goddamned mind." I look

around for anything else I may have missed. "I just met you. This is insane. You should have waited until I was here for a few more weeks before you brought on the crazy." Now I'm starting to understand why people are afraid of them. But the thing is, I do feel something. And it's not fear.

He huffs a strained breath and then goes to stand in front of the door, my only way out of the room. I'm almost afraid to try to leave. If he tries to stop me, I may really lose my shit. And even worse, I don't want to leave.

"Look," he says, putting his hand on the door knob. "Just stay and eat. You're hungry, and I need to feed you."

I close my eyes, trying to make sense of everything he's saying. "I'm sorry, Patrick. You and I don't even know each other. I can't be your mate." Even as I say the words, something deep inside of me knows that they sound so unnatural. Everything inside of him is pulling everything inside of me. If he were to touch me right now, my head would be made clear and I could think straight again. My heart knows that if only we were to touch for just a moment, that look of fear and worry in his eyes would disappear. But I can't. This is wrong. "I'll eat, and then I have to go."

His shoulders relax, and his eyes are back to their deep brown color. He seems to think it over, and then he opens the door. "After you."

I grab my things and walk past him to get through the door. When we get to the top of the winding stairs, he takes my bag from me and then steps in front of me. I think he's afraid I'll fall down the stairs.

As we get closer to the dining room, Kerry's voice

gets louder and clearer. "We give thanks to the Goddess and Her Creator for the blessings we have received. Please bless this meal, dear Lilith, to strengthen and nourish our bodies, our minds, and our beasts. We thank you as your favored creation and as pack leader, I thank You. Blessed be."

Patrick and I walk in just as everyone follows with, "Blessed be."

Abruptly, I stop walking as everyone in the room turns to look at us. A mixture of confusion, happiness, and wariness stare back at me as I look over the table.

Apprehension from their varied gazes fills me with the cold heaviness of anxiety that roosts in the pit of my stomach. Patrick reaches behind him and settles his hand on my wrist. His touch instantly soothes me, and I let him pull me in front of him. He whispers in my ear, "It's okay. You don't have to be nervous."

I give a strained smile as Patrick leads me toward an empty chair. "Good evening," I say, taking small steps.

Samuel raises his glass in the air. "A congratulations is in order. My cousin found his mate." His smile is genuine.

Easay grins and raises her fork in the air. "Blessed be."

Am I supposed to thank them? Tell them that they are wrong, because they are *so* wrong. I don't even know where to begin. Yes, I am super attracted to Patrick. Who the hell wouldn't be?

The only one who seems to be just as unhappy and confused about this as I am is Kerry. Her lips are quirked to the side, and her eyes are pensive. She purses her lips. "What do you think, Kayla?"

I stop walking, and Patrick bumps into my back. What do I think? "I don't know, really. It can't be true. I'm human."

"Yes," she says. "You are." She studies me, looking between me and Patrick.

Patrick breaks the silence and says, "She's mine, Kerry. I know she is."

Her heavy gaze shifts to him. "You think so? She's human."

A low growl starts in Patrick's chest. He pulls me toward him and settles his arm around my waist. "I know it." His voice is deep and gravelly.

Kerry gives him a tight smile. "She's. Human. You could hurt her."

Patrick's growl grows louder, deeper, and I can feel anger and dominance seeping from him. It's heavy. It's getting harder to breathe.

"I have to go," I say, backing away from the dining room.

Kerry is Alpha, but Patrick feels big to me, almost like his emotions are a storm cloud and I'm stuck in the middle of it.

Kerry gives a humorless grin, and her eyes glow like the lightbulbs hanging above our heads. "Are you challenging me, Patrick?" She slowly stands from the table.

"Stop," I say, still moving away.

I'm so confused and scared, but more than anything I feel protective and I don't know why. If Kerry tries to hurt Patrick, I'll have to hurt her right back. She could kill me without even trying, but I can't let her hurt him. I won't let her hurt him.

"Kayla, no," Patrick says, and I switch my gaze to

him. He moves his head to the side, exposing his neck to her. He's submitting to her. "You will let what happens happen."

How the hell did he know what I was thinking? I need to leave.

Without waiting for anyone to do anything, I walk to the kitchen, grab my keys off the counter where I left them this morning, and run to my car. I'm still starving, and as I drive, I pray that whatever happened earlier that made me faint doesn't happen again while I'm behind the wheel.

They're all crazy. Them and their Goddess and Her Creator. It's madness. I don't know what's happening, but never in my life have I felt more comfortable, more myself, and more at home than I've felt here these past two days.

As I approach the gate, I am so happy someone from inside the manor has the courtesy to open it for me. I sit in the car for a moment, not driving or even breathing, trying to get myself to move farther away from here. From where I am most comfortable. And as I take my foot off the brake and ease forward, a yearning howl breaks from somewhere near the manor with a sound of pain and fear and frustration.

Something tells me that it's Patrick, and his howl reverberates inside of me. Somehow, I know deep down in my heart he's making the same sound I would make if I were him. The sound I would make if I were a wolf. Afraid the one person in the whole world who was made for me may never come back.

Chapter Three

I'd planned on sitting in my car in the parking lot of the apartment complex to think, but that idea is monkey-wrenched when I see Lettie walk out on the balcony to eat her nightly ice cream sundae. If I didn't love her so much, I'd hate her skinny ass for being able to eat everything she can get her fingers on and not gain a pound.

"I've called you at least ten times this afternoon and nothing," she yells from the balcony, slamming her hand down on the little patio table we bought last week. The spoon in her hand hits the glass and the clang rings out through the silence of the parking lot. "As we speak, my brother is searching the Internet trying to find out where the Maryland Pack house is because I was coming to get you if you didn't answer by ten." The deep concern on her face makes me feel ashamed for even thinking I didn't want to talk to her.

Slamming the car door behind me, I look up at her and sigh. "Sorry. Very, very, weird day. I haven't eaten since last night, and I'm starving. Please tell me we have something other than ice cream and cereal, or I'm heading back out for some take-out." I love her dearly, but I'm not going to argue with her right now.

The anger pinching between her eyebrows softens. She knows something is wrong. "There's pizza, and I'll make you a salad. I'll have it ready for you by the time you get settled in."

I walk up the two flights of stairs, unlock the door, and head straight for my bedroom. With my head in my hands, I sit on the edge of my bed, thinking of all the crazy I just got myself involved in. None of this makes any sense, and probably no matter how long I sit here thinking, it still won't. And the feeling growing inside of me, the sense of something for Patrick, makes me more uneasy than anything else. I just met him, and I shouldn't feel anything for him, let alone a something that I don't even understand. Maybe I should be angry, yet there's another part of me that can't refute the connection between us. That something was there when he and I first looked at each other this morning, and the feeling was solidified when we touched. So was the bacon grease stain on my dry-clean-only shirt.

Stupid stain actually came out. I can understand that. Stains on fabric and washing away stains on fabric makes sense. But me and Patrick, it's not possible. And it's bullshit. It has to be.

Lettie has to be wondering what happened. I take a quick shower and put on fresh pajamas. *My* pajamas. The feel of "I told you so" is slinking around the apartment. She was right. She'll either shove it in my face or be completely accepting. Lettie has an unusual propensity of thinking the most curious things are somehow all right. Once she gets past being pissed off about it.

Lettie sets my food down on the table, opens the kitchen window, and goes back to the counter to get my juice. "What happened? Did they hurt you?" She snatches a pepperoni off one of my slices of pizza.

I sit and then take a sip of juice. The cold liquid

sooths my parched mouth. "No. No one hurt me. Though, I do think I'm getting married. You can be the flower girl," I say with a fake smile. After I tell her the whole story through a mouth full of food, she sits and shakes her head back and forth, making her ponytail move around like a big, dark cotton ball.

"You're mated," Lettie says flatly. "He's your mate." She's not really asking a question. "And you smelled green stuff when you touched him. And got horny as hell." She nods her head. "Wow. Okay. Busy day on the job, huh?" she says, still shaking her head.

"Stop moving your head like that. You're making me dizzy with your hair." I sigh and take another sip of the bittersweet cranberry juice. "He has to be wrong. I'm not even one of his kind." Am I trying to convince myself? And was that racist?

Lettie has a look I'm not entirely comfortable with. "I've read about this," she says, wagging her finger at me. "I thought it only happened between Weres. I don't know a lot about it, but if you both felt it...Well, it's not like he's trying to okey-doke you into having sex with him. On the plus side, if sleeping with a werewolf was on your bucket list, you can scratch it off any time you want," she jokes.

I close my eyes and take a deep breath. "Focus, Lettie. Please."

She quiets for a moment and then starts drumming her fingers on her leg. She does that when she's nervous. "What are you going to do, Kayla?" She's so forward when she's not running a marathon with her lips.

"I'm taking off a day or two, and then I'm going back to work, if Kerry will have me. Then we'll sit down and talk about it. Or I'll completely ignore the whole thing. I don't know." Ignoring this crap would be easy. I'm good with ignoring my problems. Until she's at my door asking to spend the night because she's pretty sure my birthday is next week.

"Are you afraid?"

"Oddly enough, no, I'm not." I rub between my eyebrows. "He looked at me like people in the movies look at each other. He doesn't even know me, but the concern on his face was so deep. And when I left, he looked like he wanted to cry. Or help throw me and my shit off the property. He was just as confused as I am." Now I'm shaking my head, but at least the size of my ponytail won't make her want to yark. "And who says we're mated, anyway? Their Goddess? That's who they gave thanks to before dinner. I think they were praying to Lilith." I need to look her up to get more information about her.

"Who's Lilith?" Lettie asks, eyeing my pizza.

"I only know a little. I remember her name from a television show on Christian Apocrypha. Lilith was the first wife of Adam. God created Adam and Lilith at the same time. Not from Adam, but with him. Adam got kind of pissy because Lilith didn't want to submit to him. She felt like they were both made at the same time, so they were equals and he could shove his manhood up his ass—"

"I can relate."

"—so, Adam whined to God and because of Lilith's girl power she was thrown out of Eden. Then God made Eve from Adam. Lilith was cursed to walk the earth alone, becoming the first demon because she embraced her hatred for God. But I have no clue what that has to do with werewolves. And I have a great idea for a book about that, too. I dreamt about it a few weeks ago." I make a mental note to check out more about Lilith. That's where most of my ideas come from—dreams.

"Yeah, I remember. You were half asleep, and you came into my room babbling about Lilith and some angel/demon hybrid girl with an attitude problem, and a book-girl. But I digress. Back to your husband to be; what does he look like?" She rubs her hands together.

"So not the point, Lettie," I say angrily, but I know she's trying to make me feel better. It's working.

"Why do you even know that stuff about Lilith?"

Her name sounded like music when I heard it. Lilith. "I watch the History Channel."

"I'm free tomorrow evening, so we can have an insane werewolf-free day before you go back to work. By the way, why are you going back?"

It's the same question I should be asking myself, but I'm afraid that if I think about it too hard, I may come to a conclusion that I'm not comfortable with. What conclusion, you may ask? The one where wolf-boy and I could really make sense.

"I don't think I have a choice, Lettie. Everything there seems so familiar to me. And oh yeah, awesome opportunity and all. Stop eating the pepperoni off my pizza. Go get your own." I slap her hand away from my plate.

"You're right. I'll go get another slice. You want more?" She gets up from the table and walks into the kitchen.

"Of course not. But I will take some ice cream," I say, fighting the urge for another slice of pizza and then throwing some ice cream on top of it. She may have the metabolism of a race horse, but I have to watch what I eat since I'm too lazy to exercise regularly.

After Lettie and I finish talking and planning for tomorrow, and when I get into my bed, I realize how tired I am. Even though I've slept all day. Not by choice. Just to be a nuisance to my father, I should call him right now and tell him he'll be having a werewolf as a son-in-law. My mother would probably adore the notion of having "one of them" in the family. I will never understand how my parents ever started dating. She was a flower child, and he was a hippie-hater. Fantastic combination.

What the hell am I thinking? I can't believe I'm even taking this seriously. I'm not mated to anyone, my father won't be getting a new son by marriage any time soon, and my mother won't have a new plaything to toy with or another birthday to try to remember. I'll go back to work in a few days and pretend that none of this even happened. I'll get used to being around him, and he'll find a nice lady-wolf to settle down with and give him many strong, healthy cubs. Or a healthy litter. Whichever.

Before I realize what I'm doing, I already have my cell phone in my hand.

"Hello," says a sleepy voice.

"Craig? Sorry, I didn't mean to wake you. I'll call you tomorrow."

He clears his throat. "Absolutely not. What's wrong?"

How do I explain this without sounding like a crazy person? A werewolf just told me we were getting married? "I don't know if I'm cut out for this job."

He laughs. "How can you say that? You were made for this job." He yawns and clears his throat again. "Kayla, you were hungry for this, and you got it. You're doing exactly what you want to do."

I shrug and shake my head. How am I supposed to make him understand when I don't understand? I'm afraid to tell him what happened. What if it's against their rules to share this with outsiders? "They're just so different from me. This was a mistake."

"Did one of the Weres hurt you?"

Well, I did get shocked, kissed senseless, and almost had an orgasm. "No. No one hurt me."

"You can tell me anything, baby girl."

I smile at his sentiment. "No. I'm good. Just a little self-doubt, I guess."

"Just put that out of your head. You are smart and strong. You can do this."

His daughter would have grown up to be such a wonderful woman. When I think of her, I not only mourn for Craig, but for the father he would have been to her. I'm not even his flesh and blood, but since I moved here to Maryland and started working at Blue's Corner, he's been the one to call whenever I needed my father. He never makes me feel bad about it. Though, sometimes he tells me to call my father. Craig is sure that my father would want to know about my life even if he doesn't know how to ask. But I know the truth. My father was a good provider, but we never had a connection. If we ever did, it left when my mother did.

"You're right. Thanks." I'll tell him about what happened between Patrick and me when I know what happened. "Sorry I disturbed you."

"Please, that's what I'm here for. And you can talk

to me anytime, day or night. I'm sure your dad would love to hear from you, too."

"Yeah." I shake my head as the lie pours from my mouth. "I'm sure he would. Have a good night, and I'll see you later, okay."

"Okay, Kayla. I'll talk to you soon."

I watch as the screen of my phone goes blank after Craig hangs up. It would be wonderful if I could call my father and talk to him like this. If I could talk to my father, maybe I would have told him everything. Maybe if I could talk to my mom, I would have told her everything.

But I can't. I don't think I'll ever be able to.

No more thinking tonight. I'm going to sleep and then I'll get up and do something constructive with my time. Like go get ice cream and ignore any attachment I may think I have to Patrick. That sounds like an excellent plan. Probably not what's going to happen, but it still sounds like an excellent plan.

****

I've slept longer than I intended. The early morning sounds of birds chirping are replaced with the distant voices of students walking to and from class. It's just past ten and the phone is almost in my hand to call Kerry and let her know I'll be late today, but my brain dredges up the emotional mayhem that went down yesterday at the manor. I remember Patrick's face and Easay's tooth-filled grin and green hair. The feral cover of Kerry's face at Patrick's challenge worried me. Still worries me. I hope he's okay.

As I plop myself back onto my fluffy pillows, I turn over and see that Lettie has slid a note under my door before she went to work. Her notes usually consist of a market list I need to add to, or her reminding me of where we're going for drinks that night. I get up and walk across the room to investigate what odd request she has for me. I open the folded paper and realize that it's not her handwriting.

It's a letter.

Good Morning,

I hope you've slept well, and I'm sorry for any uneasiness that I've caused you. Please don't be afraid when you come into the dining room. I brought you breakfast.

Patrick

What the hell. This is taking stalking to a new level. I snatch open the door and storm down the hall into the living room to see Patrick sitting there with a somber look on his handsome face. Somber isn't the emotion that seems to be emanating from him. It's almost as if he's excited. Why the hell do I know that?

"What the hell are you doing in my apartment, and where the hell is Lettie?" If he's done anything to her, I'll shove my foot so far up his ass his teeth will look French-tipped. I'm so fricking angry my ears are on fire.

He begins to speak but then stops; a wounded look blankets his face as he averts his eyes.

"That tortured look isn't working with me today, dog boy. You've moved on from slightly strange to downright creepy."

Patrick instantly drops the façade and leans back in the chair. His forearm flexes as he reaches up and rubs the back of his head. A strip of tattooed flesh shows just above the waist of his pants. His predatory grace from that small bit of movement makes the breath hitch in my throat, and I have to force myself to look in his eyes as he speaks.

"You like looking at me, Kayla?" His full lips curve into a half smile as his eyes lighten to a bright hazel.

My mouth dries and my core tightens, but I scoff and blow a raspberry to hide the instant excitement the sight of his body and the deep timbre of his voice brings. I cross my arms in front of my chest, the brief movement causing friction between my shirt and my nipples. Shaking my head, I roll my eyes to the ceiling just to stop looking at him. "No. Don't change the subject. Answer my question."

He pulls his other arm up and stretches, his bottom two abs showing more ink. "I came in after your roommate left. Your bedroom window was open, and I knew I'd startle you if I woke you. I've been sitting here waiting for you to wake up. Seeley made you an omelet with a side of bacon, and—" He points to the kitchen. "—I also brought you some coffee from the diner around the corner. I've been waiting for you, so I haven't eaten yet."

He stares at me, his focus solely on me and nothing else. In as long as I can remember, I don't think I've ever had someone's unyielding attention. He's not looking at his phone or his watch. Not glancing at the television or out the window. Just me.

"There is only you, Kayla." His baritone slides over my skin and I fight to keep myself from jumping him. Why the hell do I feel so frisky?

"How did you—" I begin, shaking my head in disbelief. I walk over to the couch and sit next to him, giving him just as much attention as he's giving me.

"This is unreal. I don't understand."

He reaches over and strokes his fingers down the bend of my jaw, and then runs his thumb along my bottom lip. "I know your feelings, just like you know mine. You don't even know it yet, Kayla, but you own me."

I let out a shaky breath and touch his hand as he softly caresses my cheek and lips. "You don't know me." I smile, feeling a part of me fill with something that has been waiting to be taken for years. Wait. My window? "You came in through my bedroom window, and I didn't even hear you?"

The right corner of his lip twitches. The son of a bitch is trying to hide a smile. "This is a lot for you. Come on. Let me feed you. Then we talk."

He stands and pulls me up with him, holding my hand on the short walk to the kitchen. His touch sends spiraling tingles along my skin. I would give anything right now to wrap my body around his and see how high that feeling could take me.

Patrick hesitates for a moment before pulling out the kitchen chair for me. He leans over and runs his lips along my ear. "Don't know what you're thinking, but you should stop before I bend you over this table and make you forget you want to be nervous." He nips my ear, and when he pulls away to look at me, his eyes shine just as bright as the sun. "This scare you?" he asks, pointing to his eyes.

"Not so much," I whisper, hypnotized by a gaze that seems to burn only for me. My core contracts, and liquid heat dumps into my panties. This man is dangerous.

Patrick leans forward, and just before his lips touch

mine, he says, "Cream and sugar?"

I blink a few times to break the spell and let out a breath I didn't know I was holding. "No sugar. Just a healthy dose of the hazelnut creamer on the first shelf." He turns away from me and opens the refrigerator door. "Not that one," I say as he reaches for the half-and-half.

He scans the contents of the fridge again and pulls out the creamer. After he fixes my coffee and hands it to me, he goes to the microwave and heats up two white Styrofoam boxes.

Quietly, I sit at the dining room table and sip my coffee as he makes his way around the kitchen with ease. Seems as if he has already acclimated himself to our place. He goes straight for the utensil drawer and plates and then pulls out a glass from the cabinet to pour himself some orange juice.

"Been checking out the apartment while I was asleep?" I cross my arms over my chest. Crap! I'm not wearing a bra and the girls haven't sat at attention on their own since I was in high school.

"Yes." Patrick puts the omelet and bacon on a plate and then pulls the toast out of the toaster. I hadn't even realized he'd been toasting. "Butter or jelly, Kayla?"

"Butter on one and jelly on the other, please. So," I say as he sits down across from me. "You broke into my apartment to feed me and convince me of…"

He picks up a piece of bacon and points it at me while he talks. "I don't have to convince you of anything, Kayla. You already know it's true, and I'm almost sure you're pretty damned all right with it. You can't help it. You want to touch me and comfort me just as much as I want to offer the same in return."

He's right. This feels right. It feels good. But, dang

it, it doesn't feel normal.

"Why are you okay with this, Patrick?"

"I feel this"—he points at the both of us—"more than anything I've ever felt in my life. I tried to fight it—"

"Briefly."

"—but I know what would happen if I did."

"That's convenient."

"You can try to fight it, too. It'll still lead you back to me."

I scoff. "Haughty much?"

"Kayla, werewolves know when they've been bound. We can feel it. It's not something you can fight. People who go against a mating wind up becoming a miserable shell of who they were. Some even go mad and have to be put down." He shoves the entire piece of bacon into that luscious mouth and licks his lips. He notices I'm watching him and bites his bottom lip, giving me a devious smile.

Holy hell, I'm in lust.

My cheeks and belly warm at the thought of those lips on my body. I clear my throat and remember to be angry with him for breaking in. "Put down? Why?"

"We lose control of our animals. When it all boils down to it, my wolf is still a wolf. He'll fight, kill, become so territorial that anyone within killing distance is up for the hunt." He huffs a joyless laugh and shakes his head. "Hell, last night after you ran out like your ass was on fire, Kerry almost ripped me in half." He rubs his ribs.

Kerry? "Why?"

"Because my wolf challenged her for doubting our union. It pissed me off. My wolf has always been level, but the thought of Kerry even thinking of keeping us apart made me crazy."

"You attacked her?"

He barks out a laugh. "Hell no. I'm not an idiot. But my wolf tried to dominate hers. That heavy feeling you felt before you left? That was my wolf. I couldn't help it."

I get up from my chair and go around the table to him. "Let me see," I say, tugging on his shirt. He grabs my hands and pulls them to his lips.

"You don't need to see, Kayla. It's healing. I'm fine."

Taking a deep breath, I pull one of my hands out of his grasp and go for his shirt again. "Rule one—don't try to shield me from parts of your life. If you and I are going to get to know each other and are what you say we are, then there has to be full disclosure. Now come on. Let me see."

I grab the fabric and pull it up as high as he'll let me. A gasp escapes my lips before I can stop it, and I have to bite the inside of my cheek to keep from crying. Four long gashes run from under his right arm straight down to his hip. The angry red lines look weeks old. Without my permission, two fat tears trek down my face. Why would Kerry do this to him?

"Patrick, I don't understand. Why would she do that?" If these slashes look painful right now, I can only imagine what they looked like last night.

He backs up his chair and pulls me into his lap. I want to curl up inside his embrace, but I'm afraid I'll hurt him. I tuck my face into the side of his neck and inhale, breathing in the scent of his warm skin. Pulsing tingles take hold of my fingers and palm that run along his bared flesh.

"Shh," he says, rubbing his thumb along my lashes to stop more tears from falling. "Don't cry. It's healing. By tomorrow, you'll barely be able to see it."

"If you didn't attack her, why would she hurt you?"

His strong hands rub comforting circles on my back. "She had to. Don't let her sweet, calm demeanor fool you. Kerry is alpha, and a God-damned monster when provoked. When she's challenged, she has to be the one to punish and she has to do it quick. An unruly pack with a lenient alpha is dangerous. I overstepped my boundaries. I should have just waited to hear her out."

I shrug one shoulder and sit up to see his eyes. "Why didn't you? It was me who ran."

He frowns and chews on his top lip. After a moment he says, "My wolf was afraid she would try to keep us apart because you're human. A human has never been chosen as a wolf's mate. Yeah, we marry humans, but a true bonding has only ever been between shifters. My wolf went apeshit at the thought of not being able to have you. After Kerry kicked my ass, she reminded me that Lilith is not without purpose. Then she left me on the ground with my intestines trying to push their way out." His eyes dip to my lips and then to my braless ta-tas. "You're mine, Kayla, and I'm yours. Fight it all you want. You're it for me."

I worry my bottom lip and then look down at his scars again. "Patrick, I think I stopped fighting it about five minutes ago."

This is crazy, but he's mine. I won't ever doubt it again. Not because he bled for me or because his words make everything seem all right. Not because he's the sexiest man I've ever laid eyes on. It's because his touch is healing. It's because, since last night, it seems as if my heart started beating for him.

To put some distance between us I start to stand up from his lap, but his hands are fast. He cups the back of my head, his hand sliding into the coily mass of my hair, and plunges his tongue past my lips. My God, he tastes wonderful. A soft moan makes its way up my throat and I open for him. I slide my arms around his solid, wide shoulders and pull him into me. Heat spears through my body as his chest rubs against my breasts; the feel of him against my nipples is like a direct line to my core. We kiss until all time seems to stop, until nothing matters except his skin against my skin; until the vengeful, foolish thoughts I have for Kerry are nothing but a distant memory. I'm falling, and flying, and soaring. Nothing matters but him. Us.

When his kiss takes every ounce of oxygen I have left, his lips leave a hot, wet trail down my jawline, my neck, and down to my breasts. Through the fabric of my thin nightshirt his warm mouth pulls my nipple in. He sucks and teases until I feel it through my entire body, and when I think I may orgasm from this alone he fists my hair and bites down. The pleasure and pain almost send me over the edge.

"Please," I whisper to the top of his head. Please, please, please. I beg him to keep his lips on me, to keep his body against mine, to keep me feeling this way.

He stands and palms my ass, bringing me closer to his hot, muscular body. Lust, happiness, and a carnal feeling I've never felt before come crashing into me over and over again as I feel his large cock against the apex of my thighs. He sets me on the table, and I whimper as his hand caresses the skin above my pajama pants and then works its way up to my breasts. He pinches and rubs one nipple and then the other, his mouth and tongue now dominating mine. The rhythmic penetration of his tongue makes me wonder how hard and fast he could make me come with that talented mouth of his.

"You want me to make you come, Kayla?"

I pant and rub myself against him, trying to get closer to him through the clothes separating my body from his. "Yes. Yes, please."

He gives me nipping, biting kisses, and smiles against my lips. "Yeah, you do. I bet you're wet right now. I can smell your arousal. You want to come in my mouth or on my dick?"

Holy hellballs. How the hell do I answer that? "Yes, please. Both."

Reaching between our bodies, Patrick slides his hands down my pants and goes straight for my clit. I close my eyes and moan as he massages the small bundle of nerves. His name is a silent prayer on my lips, and God help me, he is worthy.

He slips one finger inside me, and then another. My body jerks and an ardent feeling coils in my center. I grab his large bicep and pull him into me, urging on his strong hands. His thick fingers work me over as his palm keeps constant, rubbing pressure on my clit.

"Fuck, you are drenched for me, Kayla."

He keeps saying my name, over and over since last night. On his tongue my name sounds like the most beautiful word ever spoken. As if he were some kind of sexual puppet master, his hands control every ounce of passion and wanting inside me. With him in control, my body surges and moves to a melodic cadence he sets.

I hold on to him as his fingers thrust into me faster, deeper, hitting the right spot with each pulse of his hand. With a heavy warmth that begins in my core and climbs to the base of my spine, an orgasm starts sending out its beautiful tendrils of pleasure.

Still gripping my hair, he twists his wrist and moves my head to the side, exposing my throat to his teeth and tongue. He licks up my throat and nips at the spot right below my ear, and it sends a bolt of lightning to my aching nipples and pussy. He bites my shoulder hard enough to leave a mark, and it sends me over the edge. A long, powerful moan breaks free from my mouth and I roll my head toward the ceiling and grind my pussy against his hand. I splinter apart over and over again as he continues to draw each aftershock of my orgasm from me.

When I'm finally able to open my eyes and look at Patrick, the brightness of his eyes is almost blinding. He slides his hand from between my legs and brings his glistening fingers to his mouth, tasting my lust.

I hesitate for a moment as he cleans his fingers. "Your eyes are beautiful, Patrick."

He smiles and blinks slowly, the lowering of his lids bringing a subtle darkness to the room. "I can usually control it, but you…" he says, looking me over. "You make my wolf want to fight its way through. You make me want to claim you so that you will never think of another man again." His face is serious. "I want to give you something."

Umm, I was promised two orgasms. One with his mouth and the other with his dick. I just came from his touch, so I've still got two more waiting for me.

Patrick smiles and my entire body goes warm with embarrassment. I have to figure out how to keep him out of my head.

"Do you want my cub, Kayla?"

"That's a premature conversation you're trying to have right now, Patrick. Why do you ask?"

He kisses my forehead and pulls me into his arms. "You want my dick but you're ovulating. I'd love to see your belly round with my cub, but I'm a wolf and already know what I want. Humans move more slowly." When he leans back to look into my eyes, he smiles. "You can have me right now, but I think you'd be getting a little more than you bargained for."

"And we're done." For now. I sigh in disappointment. "So, what do you want to show me?"

Note to self—call the doctor and get back on the pill. I haven't had sex in over a year and hadn't planned on it before last night, but if my dirtiest fantasies are going to be coming true, I need to start taking those pills yesterday. If Patrick's touch is any indication of what else he has in store for me, I'm going to be having so much sex. Weres don't get sick like we do, so the only thing I can get from Patrick besides orgasms is pregnant. I'm not ready to ride that train yet.

Patrick pulls a blue silk pouch from his back pocket. He unties the bow on the top of it and with a careful ease empties the contents into his hand. "Close your eyes while I fix it." He puts the pouch on the table behind me.

I grin and close my eyes, listening to little clinks as metal hits metal. He got me a present. The idea makes my grin turn into a full-on smile, and my shoulders shake side to side on their own accord in anticipation. Since I've been an adult, I've only had one serious boyfriend, and he bought me gifts on the major couple holidays. Roses for Valentine's Day, a gift card for Christmas and my birthday. That was it. Hell, he wasn't even a real boyfriend. I was lonely when I moved to Maryland and so was he. We were really just space fillers for each other. Someone to hold on to so we wouldn't be alone. He accepted an internship in Japan, and I bid him goodbye. I hope he's happy.

"Open." Patrick leans forward and kisses my forehead.

Not wanting the suspense to end just yet I open one eye, close it, and then open them both. "It's beautiful." I raise my hand to touch the double layered gold necklace. In the middle of the top tier hangs a small, perfectly round pearl. The bottom layer holds a sideways, gold crescent moon. "I love it."

He leans forward and puts it around my neck, closing the clasp behind me. "It was my mother's. She said I would give it to the woman made for me." With reverence he touches the pearl as it sits in the hollow of my throat, and then traces the moon that sits right above the swell of my breasts. "That's you, Kayla. You were made for me, and I was made for you. Human or not, you're my mate."

Biting my bottom lip to keep in the excitement, I grab the sides of his face and pull him closer. I kiss him, once, twice, and then once more before I let it linger while I breathe him in. He smells of clean earth and pine cones. It mixes with the fresh, masculine scent of his deodorant. "Okay, stranger mate." I pull away from him. "Let's clean up in here and then get to know each other."

After the kitchen is clean and I finally brush my teeth, Patrick grabs my hand and leads me to my bedroom. I put away a few things that I left in my laundry basket, and when I turn around to see him, he's lifting his shirt over his head.

"Holy hell," I whisper.

His muscles flex as he pulls his shirt off. His torso rolls forward, and his abs tighten, his beautiful skin rolling over the tight six-pack. I take a deep breath to steady myself. Dark ink of a ferocious wolf howling at a crescent moon covers most of the right of his torso. Curvy lines of power spew forth from the wolf's mouth and large paws. I take a step forward to touch it, but the word 'ovulating' keeps me in my place.

"Come lie down next to me. I want to spoon you while you tell me about you." He raises his hands and does a 'gimme' motion. "Don't worry. I'll be on my best behavior."

"I was born," I say, walking toward to the bed. "And now I'm awesome."

He grabs my hand and yanks me onto the bed so fast my stomach dips, and I let out a soft yelp. "Not so fast, stranger mate. I like that. Tell me everything. I already know you're awesome. Tell me how you got that way."

He tucks me into him and wraps his body around mine. The feel of his warmth against my back and his breath against my neck bring me comfort and make me realize that he's not a stranger. Not to my heart. Not to my soul. With a deep inhale and steady exhale, I spill my guts, starting with my not so affectionate dad and childish mom, right up to him coughing his breakfast on my shirt yesterday.

"Has he ever laid hands on you?" Patrick asks. The air in the room becomes heavy with his anger.

"Oh, please," I say, pushing my butt into his stomach. "Calm down, buddy. He spanked me when I deserved it, but he was never abusive—verbally or physically. I could just kind of tell he distanced himself from me because of my mom." I shrug and tuck my feet under the blanket at the bottom of the bed. "I looked like her when I was little. Still kind of do. I was a reminder of her and why she left. He was never abusive, but I've always been sure I wasn't his favorite person. After getting pregnant with me my mother accepted a proposal from my father, but after about two years of a sucky marriage she decided married with a child wasn't her thing. She left my father and me alone without any more of an explanation than she couldn't let us stop her life. Even though my dad was madly in love with her and would have given her anything he could to make her happy, she still left us."

My dad made his comments. It was okay, though. It didn't break me. It made me stronger. It also made me seek out a therapist to help me sort through the feelings of self-loathing, but that's neither here nor there. "I'm happy I have Craig."

"Who?"

"He's the cook at the diner I used to work at. When I moved here to Maryland, he kind of filled that 'daddy' void. We both filled a need for one another. His daughter died and I think he needed someone to look after. To have to look after him, too. I wish Craig would have been my dad. Maybe we can adopt each other. Deep down inside, I don't think I really want to be closer to my father. It seems like it's too late." I laugh and shake my head. When I talk about either of my parents, it usually brings on tears of sadness or feelings of being pissed off.

He pulls me closer to him. "We can go talk to him if you'd like. It's a good thing you have your roommate," he says, rubbing circles between my shoulder blades. "And now you have me. And the pack. We'll never abandon you. Once we're completely mated, every werewolf will know that you are family, that you are pack related. And when you are ready, if you ever are, I'll turn you. But even if you don't, I will love you for your entire life and for all of mine. I will be with you always."

His voice is so soft and full of love, the tears that I've been trying to hold back bully their way through. Silently, I thank him as he begins to talk about his life.

"I was a born werewolf, not turned. When I was twenty-two, I came to live here in Maryland along with my mother, Rachel. My father had just died, my mother wanted a new start, and I was happy to come with her. Jackson, my father, was killed by a human. He was shot in his wolf form while running through the city." He shakes his head and lets out a slow breath. "He wasn't a threat to anyone. This happened back in Bozeman, Montana where we used to live with the local pack. After my dad died and before we finished grieving, Samuel invited us to come and meet Kerry. So we did, and my mom was at peace here. She died about nine years ago and I just stayed on. I'm happy I did."

"How do you know Samuel?"

"He's my cousin by marriage. He's been a part of the Maryland Pack since he was a child."

"What's your last name?"

"Belman."

"How old are you?" I wait to hear a horrible age.

"Thirty-four. And you?"

I let out a sign of relief. "Twenty-four. What do you do for a living?"

"Software designer. I work mainly from home."

"Not that you and I know one another that well but that sounds like a good job for you. It fits. I'm so happy you're not like eight hundred years old or something. That would have been gross." I poke him in the stomach. Mmm, rock hard. "I'm kind of hungry again."

"My kind of woman," he says hungrily. "It could be our link. You'll probably pick up some of my characteristics as time goes on and the same will happen to me." He says it like it's nothing.

My eyelids are getting heavy. "I'm going to rest my eyes for a little while."

"Sounds good."

Lying here next to him feels easy. Listening to him breathe brings me more comfort and happiness than I've ever felt before. So, why fight it?

****

In the fuzzy haze of being half asleep, I hear a soft knock on my bedroom door.

"Honey, are you still sleeping? That werewolf must have really...Kayla Marie Taylor. What the hell?" Lettie shouts, standing in the doorway of my bedroom.

"What?" I say groggily as the short evil one stands there with her hand on her imaginary hip, interrupting a nice comfortable spooning session.

"You were supposed to be going slow, you hussy." She looks horrified, but I can see the satisfied grin peeking through.

When I check to see if Patrick is awake, he seems to be asleep. But then I notice a slight smirk on his face, and I shove my finger in his ear. "Don't you have super strength hearing and stuff?" I say crossly.

"Yes, I do. I caught her scent when she closed the apartment complex door behind her." His eyes are still closed. "I thought this would be funnier."

"Gross!" Lettie says, stomping her foot like an angry child. "I don't stink."

"You shush." I point at Lettie and slide off the bed.

"Pleasure to meet you, wolf-boy. You going to start paying rent here, too?" Lettie begins to walk from my bedroom. I think she just sniffed her armpit.

"No. I expect Kayla to start spending more time with me at the manor. Don't worry; we won't let you lose your apartment." He's goading her.

"I'm not moving in with you," I say. "We just met."

Dang it. He's putting his shirt back on!

"She's not moving in with you. She's mine," Lettie says, provoking him right back.

"Both of you, cut it out! You're acting like children and I'm the new toy. I suppose it would be cute if you were children. But since you're both adults it's just disturbing." I follow her into the kitchen.

Lettie inches closer to me as Patrick goes to get his shoes. "If you want to break our date this afternoon, I'm completely all right with drinking myself into a margarita stupor. Spend time with wolf-boy over there." Wow.

I shake my head and push her with my shoulder. "No. I'm still trying to wrap my head around this, and

I'd never break a date with you for anyone," I whisper, letting her know that she'd never come second to any guy.

"But he's your mate. I asked one of my classmates. She's a minor in Werewolf Lore and Mythology and I found out a little more about this mating business." She's whispering but I'm sure Patrick can hear her. "She said humans don't really know too much about being Bound because Weres don't openly talk about it, but from what she does know, the wolves take their bonds very seriously. Like protecting your mate till the death type stuff. She said that the instant you've met your mate you're in love and fighting the connection has serious imbalances. Only thing is—"

"Only wolves have ever been Bound. Yes, I know."

"In a creepy way I wish I could find someone like that. Human or werewolf," she says, looking off absently. She quiets her voice even more. "I'm cool if you want to cancel."

"Who the hell are you and what did you do to Lettie?" I give her the Spock look on purpose.

"Look, you, I'm trying to be understanding here." She pinches my arm.

"Oww! Stop communicating with your hands. After I walk Patrick to the door I'll get dressed and we can go."

Patrick walks in and comes to stand a little too close to me. He places a lingering kiss on my forehead. "I'll be taking my leave now. It was great to meet you, Lettie." He turns around and shakes her hand.

"You too, Patrick." She turns and walks out of the kitchen to give us privacy. What the hell was that?

"I admire your loyalty to your friend. See you tomorrow at the manor?" he asks, straightening my pajama tank top and tweaking my nipple.

I slap his hand away. "Yes."

"Good." He loops his finger around the waist band of my pajama pants and yanks me to him. He runs his nose along my neck and massages my waist with his hands.

I hold my breath and lean into him. "Stop trying to start something we can't finish. I can always see if Lettie has condoms and tell her to get the hell out."

His lips tickle the nape of my neck as he smiles. "No, you won't."

"Nope, I won't. She and I have plans."

He smiles and winks at me. "Do you need anything before I go?"

"A hug. A kiss," I tell him as I fall against his body and wrap my arms around his waist.

He gives up the goods and then leaves. I stand with the door open and watch him walk down the stairs.

"You're drooling," Lettie says as she walks up to me.

"Eww, that's gross." I go to wipe my lip. "I was not!" I yell.

"Looked like you wanted to though. Get dressed. I'm starving." She takes a sip out of a huge glass of milk. "Want some?"

"Nope. Going to get dressed now." Walking from the room, I stop just short of the hallway to confide in my best friend. "I'm scared, Lettie. I'm so happy, but I'm scared."

I feel her watching me, but she doesn't know what to say. I get the notion that she's a little afraid for me, too. And then I head for the bathroom to get ready for an evening filled with trying to stay away from and not think of the one person I recently can't seem to get enough of.

****

"I'll treat you to some sexy lingerie so you can wow him next time you two do the grown-up." Lettie attempts to wiggle her eyebrows.

"What do you mean next time? There hasn't even been a first time. We fell asleep talking this morning. We were going to do it but then he started talking about me ovulating. So, we didn't."

"Why? Condoms." It sounds like I just offended her.

I touch the soft satin of a red garter belt connected to a sexy firewoman outfit. "Because we just met, you slut. And we didn't have one."

"Oh, Kayla, you're only postponing the inevitable. So, what's the mating thing consist of?" she asks, checking out a blue satin nightgown. She picks it up and holds it to my body, checking the fit. "Too big. You need something that'll barely cover you. So, mating ritual?"

My imagination begins to get the better of me as I think of all the weird things they may want me to do. Drink blood, become a Were, make a vow to them and Lilith. "I don't know. Why are you so interested?" I ask in a guarded tone. I know she can be a little overprotective, but it's like she's pushing me to make quick decisions about me and Patrick.

"You're the only one I have to ask. I'd never have the balls to ask a werewolf all of this stuff but since you're about to shack up with one, I want to know."

"Uh-huh. There's something more here you're not telling me. Either you spit it out or I'll just figure it out eventually. But please take into consideration that I've already got a lot on my plate." Attempting to figure out what she's hiding wouldn't take very long, but I don't feel like it.

"Well, besides the fact that this shit is unbelievable, I want to know when I should start looking for another roommate."

And there it is.

"Lettie, you think I'm going to leave you, huh?" How could she really think I'd leave her?

"Let's eat at Turnip's Seafood Shack." She quickly walks out of the clothing store and toward the restaurant. She's not getting out of this that easily.

Whenever she's uncomfortable with something she tries to avoid it. As soon as we're seated with our drinks from the bar, she still tries to change the subject.

"Have you registered for fall classes yet?" Lettie takes a sip of her margarita.

"Are you trying to get rid of me, Lettie? I told you I'm not moving out. What's going on?"

She uses her finger to swipe away some of the salt on the rim of the glass and wipes it on her napkin. "While you were in the shower, I read up on werewolf relationships. Whatever the hell you want to call it—bonding, mating, who knows. Anyway, I couldn't find too much information, but what I did find says that same thing my coworker said. You can't fight this. At least you shouldn't." Lettie plays with the little charms on the bracelet her mom and dad gave her for Christmas a few years ago. Every holiday they add another charm to it that represents something significant about their family.

I look down at my bare wrist and grab my drink. "I've decided not to fight it anymore."

She looks relieved. "Good. It would be bad if you did, and I don't want you to go crazy on me, which by the way is one of the side effects of ignoring your mate. Well no crazier than you already are. He's going to be your family. His entire pack is. I want you to have that." She stops at the charm that represents friendship. Her grandmother gave her that one. "I grew up with a pretty awesome family and you didn't, so I want the whole awesome family experience for you, Kayla. Besides, I don't want to be surprised when you leave me. So, yes, my motives are selfish. But I really want you to be happy. Can we not talk about this anymore?" She lifts the drink menu to her face.

"Negative."

"Come on," she whines. "This is a sore subject."

"I told you before, I'm not leaving you. Not for a long time, at least. When he and I do move in together, trust me, I will give you lots of time to prepare. You're my family, Lettie." I take a sip of my drink and am instantly chilled by the crushed ice. "You are my honorary sister and you always will be. I'd never desert you. I know how it feels and I would never want to make anyone feel that way. Especially you. It's just not who I am. And I should kick your ass for even thinking I could do something like that."

"Are you sure?"

"Do I need a thesaurus? When did you develop this fear of abandonment?" I reach over and grab her hand.

"Fuck me—"

"No, thanks."

"How does it feel to be mated?" She pinches my arm.

"I don't know. Like it did last week."

"You don't feel in love or anything?" She bats her eyes like an idiot.

"Knock it off." I poke her on the forehead. "There's a sense of being safe. Especially when we're around each other. When I was leaving the manor the other day, you know trying to get the hell away from them, it felt like my insides were trying to pull me back to him. But I refused to go back that night."

"When are you going to have sex?" she asks bluntly.

"God, Lettie. You're crude. I don't know."

"No condom? You could have at least jumped on his face."

"Lettie, sidebar. You should see their teeth when they aren't paying attention. They were practically falling out of their heads."

"He could probably do some really kinky things with those teeth." She looks at the ceiling.

"Are you on drugs?"

"So. Sex. When?

"We haven't officially set a date, you slut."

"Oh, please. I'm not the one who was laid up this morning with a dude I've only known for two days, hussy."

I shake my head and laugh. "A slut and a hussy. We make a good partnership."

"With your ass and my tits, we'd have a profitable business," she says, trying to keep a straight face. "I just want you to be happy. That's all. Where's that freaking waiter? I'm hungry." She looks around.

"It's a buffet, genius. Come on. Let's eat." I grab my margarita and take another sip before we join the crowd at the buffet table.

Chapter Four

The morning comes too fast when you have the most wonderful bed ever. I wake up at seven twenty-seven a.m., just three minutes shy of the alarm clock screaming at me. I reach over and cut it off so that I can enjoy the sounds of morning—the birds, the crickets, the sound of the light morning wind hitting my window blinds, Lettie telling someone they have two minutes before they can bother me.

Enough bed time. The only person I can imagine being here this early in the morning without warning is my mother. Before I get a chance to sit up, I feel a little tug from my insides interrupt my thoughts. The only other time I've felt anything like it was yesterday—with Patrick.

"She's awake already. I can hear her moving around." He sounds agitated.

"Good for you, wolf-boy. Give her a minute to get herself together. You're making me late."

"You could have left fifteen minutes ago. I would have waited out here for her and let her sleep, Lettie."

"I don't want you freaking her out." She's as protective of me as I am of her.

He's beginning to sound defensive. "I do not freak her out."

I turn the corner just in time to see Lettie reaching up to wave her finger in Patrick's face. "You are Mr.

Freak Out!"

"All right, children." I interrupt before they start wrestling on the kitchen floor. "I swear you two are like brother and sister. Thank you, Lettie, for letting me sleep but you're running late. Get moving so you can pay your part of next month's rent." She hands me a cup of coffee after pouring too much cream into my pink and white striped coffee cup. Just the way I like it.

I point my cup at Patrick. "I was on my way to see you. Why are you here?" Crap, now he looks like a wounded little animal. "Not that I'm not happy to see you." I take a deep breath and check my agitation. He's not the problem. I just don't like getting up early in the morning. I change direction and try to be nice instead of the morning bitch. "Good morning, Patrick," I say sweetly.

A large smile breaks across his face as I reassure him, and with that huge smile, Lettie looks like she's clutching her pearls. She's almost sitting on the small kitchen table trying to back away from him. I don't blame her. Typical human response.

"You weren't lying about the teeth. Why don't all Weres look like their teeth are falling out of their heads when they smile?" she asks.

"He likes me." I smile at him. "He likes me a lot. Now get off the table. We eat on that, you know."

Even though he has closed his mouth and his teeth are no longer visible, Lettie still stands there staring at his face. She swallows a few times and gives a nervous smile. She's trying to control herself. "Well, I'm off to work. Have a great day and I'll see you later. I have my eye on you, wolf-boy. Make sure she has a good day." She points from her eyes to his.

69

"I will do my best. Be careful on your drive. It's busy out there." He walks closer to me and puts his arm around my waist.

"Wow," I say in a monotone tone. "That was so nice. Can you two maintain this relationship, always?"

"Probably not," Lettie says with a mock smile. "Bye, you two." She heads toward the door with her oversized red and black school bag.

I take a sip of coffee and enjoy the taste of comfort and clouds. "Though I am overjoyed to be blessed by your wonderful presence, what are you doing here? I would have met you at the manor in about two hours." I shake my head as he pulls me to him.

After planting a kiss on my forehead, he takes a sip of my coffee, grimaces, then hands it back to me. "How can you drink that crap?" he says, getting a bottle of water out of the refrigerator. "I've come to take you to work. Thought we could ride over together."

He walks over to me and I put my head on his chest, hugging him a little tighter. "How thoughtful of you."

He takes my hand and rubs it against the tent in his pants. There's a stiffness that makes me lose my breath. "I also wanted to taste you to stave off the sexual tension between us. That should help you relax."

"I thought you wanted to wait," I say in a breathless voice. My stomach does a flip. Putting my mug on the counter I ease away from Patrick.

His hand snakes around me, pulling me to him by the nape of my neck. He kisses me deeply, his tongue dancing against mine. "I do. Your ovulation is at its peak and I can't think straight."

"There goes that word again—ovulation.

Somehow, that makes me not want to have sex." I think about it for a moment and push my breasts against his chest. "But I'm willing if you are. My doctor called in a prescription for the pill. I picked them up yesterday. And, I bought condoms." I rub my hand a little harder against his bulge and feel a wet heat building between my legs.

"No." He inches away from me. I can almost see the physical strength it takes for him to resist. "I don't want anything between us when I sink my cock in you for the first time."

I shudder at the thought and growl in frustration.

"That sound was pretty pathetic. Go on," he says, turning me toward the kitchen door and slapping me on my bottom.

Once I get to my bathroom I quickly strip, turn on the cold water and step in, instantly feeling a little better. That should calm me down, but it doesn't. All I think about while I'm getting dressed is Patrick touching me, of him tasting me.

I kneel and crawl into the bottom of my closet, looking for my gray flats to match my shirt. They're one of my most comfortable pair of shoes and I want to be comfortable when we meet with the other Weres this morning. Patrick and I are going to talk about our relationship with them. I crawl backward, reach into my pocket, and pull out my lip gloss. Kneeling in front of my mirror, I apply the gloss and try to calm myself. Today is going to be awesome and they will be understanding.

"You look beautiful," Patrick says from the hallway.

I smile at him in the mirror and add a little more

gloss. "Thanks."

He walks toward me and touches my shoulder. "On your knees. With your mouth open. Absolutely beautiful."

I turn and look up at him. "I…ah. Thanks."

He hooks his finger under my chin and bends down to kiss me. "Your lips are so soft."

I grab his hand and pull myself up. We can't do this anymore. A little flirting is fine, but he doesn't know how to flirt. He's doing an opening scene of a porno. Not that I look at those things.

"Look, Patrick, let's get something straight. Either we're gonna do it or we're not. No teasing."

He bites the inside of his cheek. "You're right. I'm sorry. Finish getting ready. I told everyone to be there for breakfast so we could talk about us."

Butterflies erupt in my chest and stomach when I think about talking to Kerry.

"Stop it," he says. "You're nervous but come on. No one will act any different toward you. Relax."

"You don't know how I feel. This is new to me."

Patrick kisses my neck, rubs his hands down my bare arms, and puts my head on his shoulder. "Yeah, 'cause you did this on purpose, didn't you?"

I elbow him. "Shut up. I don't need your sarcasm."

His smile tickles my ear. "I do know how you feel because I can feel what you feel."

"Please, don't remind me." I'm still getting used to the idea. "It kind of freaks me out."

He ignores me and continues. "After you woke up and Lettie was trying to bully me, I gave you a call. Didn't you feel it?"

I did feel it. Being near Patrick makes me feel

calmer. He soothes me and makes me feel stronger. My family never made me feel like that. Being around my mother makes me tense. My father makes me want to feel stoic. But not Patrick and not the other Weres. And not Lettie.

Thinking back on it, the only time I felt peace growing up was when I was alone. In my room. Shoving food into my mouth as I tried to eat away my feelings. I'll never let anything take this away from me.

"First off, Lettie can in no way bully you. Second, yes, there was a kind of pull." This is getting freakier and freakier by the minute. And I like it. "I thought it was just your voice giving me butterflies. You did it? On purpose?"

"Yes. You moved around for a minute and then you settled back into your bed. So, I gave you a call to let you know I was here. You can do the same thing, too."

"I'll have to learn all this crap, won't I? Someone should write a book or give a class entitled 'All Things Bound' for us stupid humans." What if being human stops me from being able to do all the things werewolf mates can do?

"Babe, just take your time." His voice is reassuring. "You are the only human to be Bound to a werewolf. Mating is very serious." He tugs on my shirt. "Ready? Maybe we can actually make it through a meal without you fainting or panicking," he says with a smart-assed grin.

I stomp away from him and grab my earrings. If I think about it, seriously think about it, I can see how we would be perfect together. It doesn't make any sense, but it feels like it should.

****

"Do you remember the code?" Patrick asks as he pulls up to the gate.

"Yes. But you go ahead and enter it, since you're so much closer than I am." I refuse to admit that I don't remember the code.

"You are full of it," he says while punching in the numbers. "Press three-seven-nine-six, the star sign, and you're in."

"Why do you need a gate? It doesn't look like the entire area is fenced in." There's a reason for a gate that doesn't protect the entire perimeter.

"When humans see a blockade, it deters them." He glances in the rearview mirror as if he's making sure the gates close behind us. "Most of the time. And the parts that aren't fenced have sensors around them."

"Have you ever had any problems?"

He smiles, but it doesn't reach his eyes. "A few years ago, a few drunken human males came onto the property on the night of the full moon to hunt wolves. They thought we'd be stuck in wolf form. Before they did any damage, we got wind of their scent and found them. We turned them over to the local authorities, but nothing was ever done. So, to be nice we put the fence up."

"To be nice?"

"Yes, to be nice." He laughs. "Can you imagine the harm that would come to a human if a pack of wolves were hunting? The frenzy that would ensue? Hunting the occasional deer or fox is fun, but if we were worked up from a fresh kill and actually caught wind of human-game hunting us…We'd be the ones hunting them. But we expected something like that would happen sooner or later so, before Kerry let them go, she told them that if they ever set foot on her property again, they would be the ones being hunted."

I shake my head. "What dumb-ass would come here to hunt for werewolves?"

"Most of the time when people come to check us out, they come to the front, see a long gate, and turn around. We are very aware of anyone who comes on and off this property."

He pulls into the car port, turns off the engine, then runs around to open my door. Such a gentleman.

"There's no need to be nervous. I'll stay with you all day if you want me to." Patrick's voice is full of enthusiasm.

That would make me so happy, but I won't allow him to do it. I am more confident than that and will not allow this to stop me. Besides, I may get fired for sexually harassing him. "Nope. That will not be necessary. Just stick around during breakfast."

"Brave mate." He rubs his hands over my shoulders.

As we get closer to the door, he wraps my hand in his, raises it to his lips, and kisses my palm. A wave of nausea hits me, and I want him to let go of my hand so that I can stand up to them myself.

"I will not," he says, curling his fingers around mine more firmly.

"Stop that."

"You stop it."

"Good morning, Kayla," Kerry says as we walk into the dining room.

"Good morning, Kerry. Good morning, everyone." I can hear the apprehension in my voice. Everyone is staring at us.

Easay finally breaks the tension with her tooth-filled smile and laughter. "You want to try eating with us again?" She shoves her green hair behind her ear.

"Yes. Thanks."

"How are you feeling today?" Osai asks before shoving a sausage into his mouth.

"Better. Calmer. And you?"

"As long as I'm eating, I'm always happy," he replies with a chuckle.

Patrick leads me to a chair next to Kerry and he takes the one next to me. I'm just going to spit it out. I hadn't planned on saying anything, but I can't help myself.

"I'm sorry if I've been a nuisance. That was never my intention and I hope this doesn't cause any problems. Even though I've only been with all of you a few days, I love it here. From the first day I instantly felt like I belonged, and I think, maybe, you all felt it too. I hope that me and Patrick being whatever it is that we are doesn't disrupt that."

"We feel it, too," Easay says.

I turn to Kerry specifically. "I love this job, and I promise that nothing will affect my performance. I don't know how it happened, but I love Patrick—Wow!—and even if you fire me, he and I will be together." Do I sound like an idiot? I feel like one. Can I make everyone here like me again? They'd better! Even if they don't, it doesn't matter. I love Patrick. He loves me. I hate to admit it, but it hurts my heart to be away from him for too long. And though it bothers me to even admit it to myself, I need him. And I can feel his need for me, too. "And now I'm finished."

Everyone is silently looking at me and Kerry. Until my stomach intervenes and growls. Always at the wrong time.

"Good, because your omelet is ready." Seeley walks in the room with a spinach, tomato, and cheese omelet.

Kerry gives me a caring smile and nods her head at us. "I would never dream of firing you. We were all just taken aback by our Goddess choosing a human to be the mate of a pack member. Even if you weren't mated and you and Patrick had chosen one another, it would have been just fine. But this makes it more special, and we are so happy to have you as a part of our family. Once the ceremony is completed, you do know that you will be Pack, don't you?" Kerry asks, looking from me to Patrick.

"I've told her," Patrick says, still holding on to my hand and eyeing the sausage.

She nods at him. "Good. Kayla, if you have any questions please feel free to ask. Thank you for coming back. A few people weren't sure you would." Kerry looks at Samuel.

"You looked so freaked out I thought you'd never come back," Samuel says. And even though he still isn't wearing a shirt, I feel nothing for his muscular body.

Grandfather Taylor.

"I didn't think I would either. Until I woke up and Patrick was in my living room by way of my bedroom window. I felt angry more than anything at first, but we talked, and I don't want to stay away from him. I don't think it's possible for us to stay away from each other." I look at Patrick.

R.A. Boyd

"It'd be pretty foolish if you tried to," Easay says, unfolding her napkin and placing it in her lap. "And speaking of foolish, Kerry, we got another phone call this morning. Someone already knows."

"Knows what?" Patrick asks.

Easay looks at Kerry, who shakes her head. "Nothing. We'll speak of it later. Time to eat."

After my stomach growls again, I reach for the water and Patrick starts to put my napkin on my lap. "Your omelet is getting cold. You should eat," he says, adding breakfast meats and toast to my plate. Is he trying to fatten me up?

"Seriously, you don't have to do that." What do you want to eat? I close my eyes and think really hard.

"Are you all right, Kayla?" Easay asks.

"I was just trying something. I'm good."

Patrick grabs my hand and kisses it. "You don't have to close your eyes to do it." He grabs a little bit of everything and puts it on his plate. "And that's a horrible face." He reaches for a bagel and tries to hand it to me.

I shake my head and reach for a piece of toast.

"What did you do?" Seeley asks as he watches Patrick add the extra food to his own plate.

"I was asking Patrick what he wanted to eat. He seems to be able to read me so easily, I was trying to see if I could get something from him other than emotion. Are you seriously going to eat all of that?" I look at Patrick.

"What is it like?" Samuel asks.

Patrick closes his eyes for a second trying to think of how to put it into words. "It's not like I can read her mind or anything. I can just feel what she feels. It's hard to explain. I didn't even realize we could do it until this morning when her roommate wouldn't let me wake her up. I really wanted to see her," he says, rubbing my thigh and going farther up my leg.

He and I really need to talk about the constant touching. I like it, but we're in a room full of people.

"Yeah, it was kind of weird," I say, grabbing his hand to keep it from going any higher.

"Does she know?" Easay asks, fiddling with her hair again.

"Who? Oh, you mean Lettie? Yeah, she knows. I tell her everything. She was a bit weirded out at first, but as long as I'm good with it, and safe, she's supportive."

"We'll keep you safe," Kerry says, looking at Easay, who nods her head and looks way too serious. "You can count on that."

****

After we finish breakfast, I go up to my room to start working on the tapes that Kerry has recorded. There are another three tapes to go along with the first two. Kerry was pretty sure I was coming back. I smile despite all the typing I have ahead of me, but this is what I was originally here for.

I slide the first mini-cassette tape into the little black and gray transcribing machine and begin to concentrate on Kerry's voice. It becomes a continuous song I can't stop listening to. The story becomes so addictive that I find myself typing faster just to hear what she'll say next.

"I am a direct descendent of Lilith, Adam's first wife. When Lilith was ejected from the Garden of Eden, she wandered the Earth alone scavenging, finding just enough to survive. Many years passed and a wolf befriended her. His pack would lead her to rivers or bring her small animals to eat. And when it was cold, they allowed her to huddle with them for warmth. We don't know why the wolves were so accepting of a human, but they were. The only thing she could do to repay them was to make them more than just wolves. So, she transformed herself into a wolf to lie with the leader of the pack and gave birth to the first human-wolf hybrid. We do not know how she gained the powers to transform; we just know that she was a powerful worker of magicks. Since then, we have coexisted with humans for millions of years before letting our existence be known in the late 1300s.

"The Black Plague had claimed many lives in Europe, and when most people became infected, they died within four to seven days of exposure. There were three types of the plague that affected people differently—bubonic plague—infection of the lymph nodes; pneumonic plague—infection of the lungs; and septicemic plague—infection of the blood. The latter was the one that affected the werewolves.

"The physicians who were brave enough to stay and help the sick started noticing that it took some people up to a month to die. Some even recovered. They started separating and locking away the ones who were taking longer to die, but little did they know that the ones who were surviving were all werewolves. And that's when it happened—a few of the sick who were locked away would shift into large wolves uncontrollably. Those were the ones who recovered. Shifting allows the body of werewolves to heal.

"The doctors decided to keep and study these

subjects and came to believe that the plague itself was responsible for the shifting. That was until the families of the wolves came to get them from captivity and humans saw that there was no keeping the werewolves on the outside from getting to their kin on the inside. That's when the Line of Lilith decided it was time to come out of obscurity. They would rather try to live peacefully with humans than have mass genocide on their hands. Killing all human witnesses was not the publicity we needed to say, 'Hello humans. We come in peace!' " She laughs a little and continues.

"The werewolves who had family locked away were more than willing to kill anyone and everyone who got in their way. The only effective artillery that humans could have used was the wheeled cannon, and werewolves are much faster than any human with one of those primitive weapons. After that, there were many battles between humans and werewolves, but it all died out and now we live in peace with humans."

In my opinion I think humans just gave up. Werewolves can do everything we can do, use the same weapons that we can, except they are much faster and more durable than us.

I look up to check the time and realize that almost six hours have passed, and I've completed the first three tapes. Wow, it's four in the afternoon and I could have gone a few more hours if my bladder didn't insist on being emptied. After doing a few stretches, I go back for more, eager to learn about the werewolves. My new family.

"When my father was still alive, he let it be known that I would be his successor, and just like men from any species, it was not widely accepted. Though there have been a few female pack leaders, those who were from the Line of Lilith were always men who had been chosen. There have been five other women in all our history who were leaders from the Line of Lilith, but they fought like hell to keep their title and could rival any man who tried to take it from them. I had an older brother named Simon, but my father knew that I was the right choice. After our father died, Simon challenged me for the right to be pack leader. I defeated him. I didn't want to, but I knew I had to kill him. Anything less than that would cause division in the lineage.

"There are two other World Pack leaders that are from the Line of Lilith, and together we rule every pack member everywhere. It's almost like a company—there are three CEO's that run everything and they can only be from the Line. Then there are territory pack leaders under us, like supervisors, that report to the Line. They are there to manage what we three members from the Line can't see since we can't be everywhere at once."

I don't know how they've managed to keep things peaceful for so long, but humans should take a few pointers from them. The only real problem that the wolves have ever had was from humans. And humans have always had a problem with everyone, especially other humans."

By the time I finish most of the fourth tape, two more hours have passed, and I am now seeing double. My fingers are cramping, and my back is screaming for release. My first real day at work and I'm quite impressed with myself. Tomorrow, I will go over what I've typed and edit it. My brain has absorbed its fill. I guess it's a good thing that Kerry chose me to help with her memoirs. Since Patrick and I will go through with the mating ritual, eventually, I probably need to know all this stuff. It's a little overwhelming. Your average human knows just enough about werewolves to interact with them. It's common knowledge that the Plague brought them out of hiding. And now, most of them don't like being mistaken for a human.

Like Mr. Levay. On the first day of class, he arrived about thirty minutes late and a teacher's aide from another department was having all his students sign a sheet to say that we had been there. Mr. "Call me Steven" Levay came rushing into class looking quite frazzled and he kept apologizing to everyone for the inconvenience. The aide said, in his surfer dude voice, "Bro, you're only human. We all make mistakes." As he tried to laugh it off, he caught a look from Mr. Levay that no one in the class could see, but we could all tell from surfer-dude's face that Mr. Levay was not kosher with the comparison. In a way, I'm happy his back was to the class. The teacher's aide went pale and his sun-kissed skin turned three shades lighter. After boogie-boy high tailed it out of the classroom, Mr. Levay turned around and gave us all his award-winning, charming, closed-mouth smile. Anyone in the class with good sense knew that a werewolf had just been insulted in our presence, and none of us would ever make the same mistake.

Right before I stand to take my leave from typing for the day, I feel a little tug, and I'm surprised it took this long for him to do it.

"I'll be out after I brush my teeth." I speak as if Patrick were standing right next to me. There's no need to shout. He's already walking toward my room. Even though I haven't been able to feel him all day long, the closer he gets, the more anxious I get to be near him. I stop in mid-stretch and make it to the bathroom to fluff my coily hair and brush my teeth before he plants a kiss on me that I know he's been waiting for. As soon as I open the door, Patrick descends upon me like a pack of wolves. I love my own jokes.

"Kerry wouldn't let me bother you while you were working. She said you already had a lot on your plate and me harassing you all day long wouldn't help. I think she's already beginning to feel protective of you." He settles his face into the bend of my neck and inhales deeply.

I stroke the back of his neck and kiss his ear. "That could be true. Or she realizes that the check has already hit my bank account and there are no takesie-backsies. I'm her employee. No slacker here." But I know it's more than that. I have to be careful or I'll try to make Kerry the mother I never had.

When I first met Lettie's family, her grandmother stuck up for me when her grandson, Lettie's brother Agostino, copped a feel on my ass and I responded with violence. She's still the only one, besides the short one, that treats me like I'm an actual member of the family. I could say that it's because she's sweet and grandmotherly. Or it could be because she's slightly senile and thinks I'm her youngest sister, who died sixty years ago. Her father had a baby out of wedlock with a black woman and her mother never gave her the chance to get to know her. She doesn't really know what her half-sister would have looked like if she were my age. I suppose that when she truly allows herself to forget that her sister died when she was only eight years old, I fit the profile. It's okay, though. I don't mind but my therapist told me to knock it off.

"Kayla, you're in your head way too much."

Was he just snapping his fingers in my face?

I smile and shake my head. "Sorry. Maybe I seem okay with this on the outside, but my mind is in ten places at once."

"Don't be. I understand." He bites his lower lip and looks at the desk. "I take it back. I don't understand. But I'm here for you and if I can do anything, just let me know."

I inhale deeply and let go a bit of tension. "Thank you."

"No need to thank me. You feel tangled. That's the best way I can put it. But I'm here. And I'm hungry. Dinner is almost ready," Patrick says, as he kisses my nose.

"Sorry lover, I can't stay for dinner. Lettie and I are cooking tonight. Together. It's a girl's night thing." A few times a month, her entire family gets together and cooks dinner. It's a family bonding time and since I didn't have that growing up, she feels compelled to make me share in it with her. I like it.

"I'll be back here tomorrow, and tomorrow night can be ours. If you're not busy."

He leans in and kisses my nose again. "My schedule is always clear for you, love."

Crap he is awesome.

"Now let's go so I can say goodnight to everyone." I forgot I didn't drive here this morning. "And then you can have me all to yourself in the car ride back to the apartment."

"Before we go…" Gently and urgently he pulls me

closer to him. His strong hand on the small of my back excites me with a tender passion that makes my knees go weak. I fear I may fall, but that would never happen while he was around. He pushes me against the column of the canopy bed and pulls my legs up around his waist.

I pull him closer to me with my legs and wrap my arms around his firm shoulders to let him know that if he wants to take me right now…he's gotta stop!

He pulls away from me and looks concerned. "Kayla, what's wrong?"

"Everybody in this frickin' house has super hearing," I whisper into his ear, already feeling seven minutes past embarrassed.

The look he gives me is a mixture of surprise and annoyance. "Do you honestly think that we will have been the only ones who have ever made love in this house?"

"First off, buddy-boy, I saw that look so screw you."

"If only…"

"Shut up. And honestly, I don't care who has or hasn't, but I know I'm not going to. I already feel funny passing gas in the bathroom, hypothetically speaking because I've never done that here, but we can't do this. Not here."

I start wiggling against him to make him put me down. "Kayla, you rubbing against my cock like that is only making me hard." He wears a devilish grin and just the right amount of teeth to spark that awkward sexual interest that Lettie was talking about. "You see, you do want me. I can tell." He leans in and kisses me again.

"You're damn right I want you." They can smell emotion. "No, no, no! I can't say good-bye to everyone like this." I slap my hand over my eyes as the most horrifying thought hits me. "Especially Kerry! I know my hormones are crazy with thoughts of dirty sex, and she's going to be so disappointed," I whine.

Patrick places me back down on the floor and is trying his best not to laugh. "Kerry knows we are mates. Sex is usually a part of that."

"So not funny." Cool off, Kayla. You are not a child. And you are certainly not Kerry's child.

"Come here." He hooks his fingers into my belt loops at either side of my waist and pulls me close, then backs me against the column on the bed. "You're uptight. It's making me uptight." With deft fingers he pops the button on my pants and dips his hand beneath the thin layer of my panties. "I need to make you come."

Before I can protest Patrick cups my sex, and the feel of his strong hands sliding against my saturated folds sets me on fire. His palm brushes my clit as he slides a finger into me. My back bows against the uneven, ridged wood column on the bed.

His lips twist into a cocky, feral smile. "Think you can come quick for me?" He leans into the bend of my neck and bites my collarbone, and then soothes it with his tongue.

Come quick for him? I don't think I have a choice. The orgasm is already beginning to snake its way through me. I nod and wrap my arms around his wide shoulders and bury my face into his neck to muffle my cries of pleasure. His thick fingers are skilled at zeroing in on that sweet spot just inside me that only I and my vibrators have been able to find. I roll my hips against his hand and whisper his name as he bites my ear and then kisses it.

"I can't wait to ease my cock into you and make you scream," he says, pulling his head back so that I can meet his gaze. "Look at me, Kayla. I want to look in that beautiful face of yours while you fuck my hand."

Everything inside me is heavy and aching for his touch. My breasts, my lips, my wet slit as his touch drives me to orgasm. With his fingers still working me over like a damned professional, he pistons his hips against mine as if he were fucking me.

My eyes roll closed and Patrick grabs my hair at the nape of my neck, angling my head toward him. "Look away from me again and I won't let you come," he says, biting my chin as I concentrate to look in his eyes.

"Patrick, please." I say it over and over as warmth starts to coil out from my core. How the hell does he know my body like he's been touching it for years?

I roll my hips toward his hand and rub my chest against his to feel the heat of him on my breasts. A shudder ripples through me as a low growl vibrates in his chest. The throbbing feel of the sound rubs against the hardened peaks of my nipples. I'm lost in him. In his voice, his touch.

"You going to come for me so I can taste you on my fingers again? I know," he says with a devious grin. "Why don't you take those pants off so you can come in my mouth?"

I want to. I want to so bad. Before I get a chance to say yes to that awesome idea he says, "No. You take those pants off and feeling you dance on my tongue won't be enough. I'd have to take you. Own you. Fill you with my seed so everyone would know you were mine. Mark you with my scent from the inside and then come on your chest to mark you on the outside."

Those words and that image shoves me over the edge, and just as I cry out as the orgasm blasts through me Patrick kisses me, stealing away the screams of my pleasure. I go limp in his arms as he pulls his hand out of my pants. He raises his hand to his mouth and cleans my lust off his fingers, and then buttons my pants back up.

"I need to go clean up," I say, about to walk toward the bathroom.

"No," he says. "My scent is all over you and I want it to stay. If it makes you feel better, I'll hustle you out the door and to the car."

I take a deep breath and feel dead set against this, but I do as he asks. I need to suck this shit up if I'm going to be a part of this world.

"That's my girl," he says. "Grab your purse. Besides, you're overestimating our sensitivities. We are around humans all the time and if we let their emotions and scents rule our reactions…Well, it just wouldn't be good. Most of us have learned to block these things. You can walk out of here with dignity. It's fine."

"You're right," I say, standing up and smoothing my shirt and pants. "I'll relax. I'll grab my purse and we can head out." I hug him out of sheer comfort and kiss his neck.

As we walk down the main stairway, I am horrified to see Mr. Levay standing there talking with Easay. It's so much worse than seeing Kerry in my post-lustful state. This is just frickin' awesome.

His unkempt dark hair, routine sports jacket, and wrinkled dress shirt are overshadowed by a not so nice looking purple and orange untied tie. He takes a huge gulp of whatever he's drinking and then wipes his mouth on a napkin. "Kayla," he says a little too excitedly. It seems like a bit of nervousness is peeking through him as well. I hope this doesn't reflect badly on him since he is my teacher and was the one who suggested me to Kerry. "I just heard the wonderful news. Welcome to the family."

Mr. Levay looks like he doesn't know whether to give me a hug or shake my hand. So, to cut the strangeness I reach out my hand to shake his. "Thanks Mr. Levay. It's all still very weird but everyone has been great. Missed you in class last week. How was your lecture?"

Mr. Levay is not only the Greek and Roman Mythology professor at my school, but he also lectures on werewolves in the Medieval Era and it sometimes takes him away from class.

"Very well, thanks. I'm glad to be back home. There's nothing like a home cooked meal, and Seeley is the best when it comes to cooking. Are you staying for dinner?"

"No, sir," I say, backing away from him. "I have dinner plans. I'm finished for the day and about to head out."

Patrick walks past Mr. Levay and toward the dining room counter to grab some fruit from the table. Mr. Levay's nose twitches just a hair and then he looks from me to Patrick. I'm trying to keep a straight face, but I'm horrified and feel as though I should start explaining why my hormones are still on their way back to normal. Before I get too deep into panic mode, Patrick makes four large strides toward me, reaches out, and pulls me closer to him. And with that simple touch I am calm again. How does he do that? I smile and start to thank him, but he shoves a piece of cheese into my mouth.

Eat something, he mouths and points at the cheese and lunchmeat tray that's next to a blue and gold fruit bowel.

Mr. Levay gives us a smile. "Kayla, would you excuse Patrick and me for a moment?" He winks at me and shakes his head. "I have some news for you, Patrick, about my trip. Kerry already knows, but I thought I should give you a heads up."

As they disappear into the living room, Easay hands me a cracker. "I don't mean to pry, but you need to eat more." I look at her like she's grown an extra head. "Even though you are not a Were, you and Patrick are Bound to one another. He has to eat steady meals to keep up his strength and to be able to control himself. That may be a trait you're picking up from him. For you, it may manifest in different ways. Like being strangely nervous to be here, or anywhere else for that matter. I can sense the emotions pouring off you."

I slap my hand over my eyes. "Oh, God. This is…"

She laughs and hands me ham on a cracker. "It's not one specific emotion. It's like watching a movie that makes you laugh and cry and get angry all at the same time. It's usually not this strong with other humans, but we are so sensitive to your emotions." She screws up her face and shrugs. "Must be the bond. Anyway, I know you're leaving to have dinner with your friend, but just have a few more bites." She grabs a napkin and hands it to me, and then rubs my shoulder. "Just so you know, touching helps."

I shrug and eat another cracker. "What?"

"Patrick is always touching you. It's something wolves do to comfort one another. Makes you feel better too, doesn't it?"

"Yes." The constant touching is new for me, but it still makes me feel better.

She picks up an apple. "And do me a favor—eat snacks in between meals. Something with protein. If I'm not mistaken, you haven't eaten since this morning."

After a few bites of cheese and crackers, I do feel a little better. Weird much? "Thanks. Thank you." I grab some grapes and strawberries. "Where is everyone? I wanted to say bye before I left," I say through a mouthful of food.

She finishes her apple and points to the back of the house. "They left about twenty minutes ago for a playful hunt. Kerry got wind of a rabbit."

"Okay." I instantly feel sorry for the bunny.

Before I get a clear visual of a bunny rabbit scurrying for its dear life from huge, teeth-baring wolves, Patrick and Mr. Levay come back into the room. Patrick looks a little vexed but is able to pull it together quickly. Mr. Levay heads straight for the food. "I'll see you in class next week, Kayla. Or around the manor. Either way, it's good to see you," he says, before shoving lunch meat, cheese, and crackers into his mouth all at the same time.

Patrick grabs a banana and gives me a wink. "Are you ready to leave, love?"

Good Lord, he looks awesome. Every once in a

while, I'll look at Patrick and everything but him disappears. Watching his arms flex as he peels the banana is a turn on. He brings the fruit to his mouth and bites, smiling when he notices me looking at him.

I have to get the hell away from my teacher. "Yes. I am hungry, but I don't want to ruin my dinner." I turn to Easay and Mr. Levay. "Have a good night. See you later." I grab my bag and quickly walk to the door.

They both say, "See ya," and then go back to their snacks.

****

The ride home is filled with a game of Twenty Questions. He and I don't know very much about each other. We're almost to the apartment and Patrick still hasn't told me why he looked so sour after the talk with Mr. Levay.

I pat his leg and consider grabbing his cock but decide against it. He's driving. "All right, lover, spill it. What did he say that bothered you so much that you felt like you had to hide it?"

He sighs and tilts his head toward me. "It has to do with the Pack. Just got some unwanted news, but it's all right. What are you and Lettie cooking for dinner tonight?" he says, trying to change the subject.

"So not going to work. Maybe it will help if you talked about it. You know you want to."

He flexes his fingers on the wheel and cracks his neck. "We may be having some unwanted visitors. That's all. Steven caught up with a few people that used to stay here with our local pack. Things got a little difficult. Kerry asked them to leave."

Which probably meant, "get the fuck gone" when Kerry says it because she's the leader.

"Okay." He's still not telling me everything. "Just let me know when you're ready." I rub the side of his face and feel the muscles flex beneath my fingers as he smiles.

"It may not even be an issue. Just Steven giving me a heads-up." He touches my hand as I rub his cheek. "You don't have to worry."

We pull up to the apartment building to see Lettie and Craig standing in front of his maroon pick-up truck.

"Come meet Craig," I say to Patrick as I get out of the car.

Lettie waves. "Hey, guys. Craig helped me get the frame and headboard into the apartment. He's not going to be able to make it Saturday."

Craig gives Patrick a once over and settles in on our joined hands. His lips almost completely disappear from his face as he sucks them in and starts chewing on them. "This is new," he says, holding out his hand to shake Patrick's.

"All right, Dad," I say, mocking Craig.

I see him blush and he pulls me into a sideways hug.

"Patrick, this is Craig."

Patrick shakes his hand and smiles. "I've heard a lot about you. Nice to meet you."

I shrug. "This is new," I say, pointing to me and Patrick.

Craig puts his hands on his hips, looking like Peter Pan. "Treat my baby right. I'd hate to have to kick your ass."

Patrick clears his throat and laughs. "Sir, you have nothing to worry about."

I smile at Craig. "I thought you were coming by

tomorrow. Lettie was going to cook you breakfast."

He leans against his truck and shrugs. "Hannah asked me to come in early tomorrow. Trent pulled a muscle in his back and can't work the kitchen."

Lettie grabs my bag and starts walking toward the door. "I'm going upstairs. I left the apartment door open."

Patrick and Craig both wave to her.

Craig taps my shoulder. "Can I talk to you for a minute?"

I'm sure it has to do with me and Patrick. Craig is protective. Over the past few years, he's never seen me with a guy, and even though he's never been to school for counseling, he knows why I avoid relationships. My mother and father made each other miserable, and I don't want to do that to someone. Craig tried to pep me up once by telling me that not all relationships are like my parents'.

"Sure." I turn to Patrick. "I'll be right back."

Patrick walks toward his car and opens the trunk. Even though he's preoccupying himself, I know he can hear us talk.

"Craig, what's up?"

"I've never seen you with a guy before. Must be special?"

I laugh. "Yes, he is. We just met but—"

He looks down and steps on a bug. "You feel like you've known him longer."

I think he wants to give me a father-daughter talk but decides against it.

Shrugging, I walk closer to him and lean against his truck. "I know it sounds cheesy. But it's true."

Craig grabs my hand and kisses the back of it. "Just

be careful. The look on your face when you look at him is pure. I'm happy for you."

Feeling my cheeks warm, I lean in and give him a hug. "Thanks. I am happy, and I'm being careful."

"You remind me so much of her," he says, patting my shoulder. He clears his throat and backs away. "Got to go, Kayla. Don't be a stranger at the diner."

I sigh. "Wouldn't dare." Poor Craig. "Want to come over for dinner next week?"

He turns back to me and smiles. "I'd like that. Sounds good, baby girl. Nice meeting you, Patrick."

Patrick closes his trunk. "You too, sir. Goodnight."

We watch Craig drive away.

"He seems to really care for you." Patrick steers me toward the apartment.

When I came here to Maryland, I felt like my dad just let me go. It was almost as if he was taking a huge sigh of relief to finally have me gone, like having me around was stressful and my departure was the breath of fresh air he needed. Even if he did feel that way, I think he was too noble to say it out loud.

Patrick rubs my arm. "Now you have a lot of people to help take care of you. Do you want me pick you up in the morning?" He pulls my shirt sleeve.

"Nope. I'll drive there tomorrow. You may have stuff to do, and I happen to own a car, you know. I'll be there. Can I call you tonight before I go to sleep?"

"You don't even have to ask." He pulls me closer to him and kisses me sweetly, rubbing his lips against mine in a sweet caress.

"Yes, I do. I don't have your phone number."

****

After Lettie goes to sleep, I sit on the living room

96

couch and pull out my phone to read a new book I downloaded. It's almost midnight. I don't know if it's too late to call Patrick. He may be asleep.

A soft knock sounds at the door. Part of me hopes that it's Patrick. I pull it open with a big smile and am startled to see a tall, pale man in a baseball cap with huge biceps, and a neck thick enough to rival a wrestler. He's huge.

"Umm, hi?" I say, closing the door a little.

He smiles, but it doesn't reach his eyes. "Is Meagan home?" he asks, trying to look inside the apartment.

I close the door a little more. "Sorry, you have the wrong apartment."

He inhales deeply and cocks his head to the side. His eyes lighten a little, and for a moment, I stop breathing. He's a wolf.

Every alarm bell is going off, so I do the only thing that will take away from the appearance of my fear. But he can smell it. I smile so big he can probably see my molars.

"Meagan doesn't live here?" he asks, eyes looking me up and down.

My face hurts from smiling so wide. "Nope. Sorry. You must have the wrong address. There's no one in this building by that name." I go to close the door, but he steps toward me. If I push it any farther, I'm going to hit him. He looks like he could bring down the whole door if he tried.

"I don't mean to scare you, miss." He backs away and puts his hands in his pockets. "My little sister goes to the college down the street, and I'm here to surprise her. I must have the wrong building."

Relaxing a little, I lean on the door. "It's all right. I don't know anyone named Meagan. Sorry. Good night."

"Thanks," he says smiling, keeping his mouth closed just enough so I can't see his teeth.

I close the door and lean against it, waiting to hear him walk away. He lingers for a few seconds and then walks down the stairs. A breath I didn't even know I was holding pushes its way out and I shake my head. I'm over-reacting.

I walk back over to the couch and grab my phone. There's a missed call. From my mother. Her phone calls always mean she's planning a visit and wants us to be best girlfriends for a few days. I respect the commandment of "Honor thy mother and father," I do. But for the most part, I wish she'd just leave me alone. With my dad, it's different. It's not stressful, just strained. He dishes out his sarcastic remarks, and I try not to let them get to me. My family life is awesome!

I return the call and breathe a sigh of relief as it goes straight to her voicemail. "Hey Mom, umm, sorry I missed your call. I've been kind of busy with classes and my new job. Call me tomorrow. Hope you're well. Bye."

There was a time when I would cry when I talked to my mother, and that included leaving messages. It sucks for a child, especially a girl, to know that she was never that high on her mom's wish list. It sucks fucking donkey balls. I can't even count the number of times she told me she would take me away for the summer or come visit me on Christmas break and never came through for me. She smashed my heart into bits with her promises.

After I stare at the phone for a few minutes, I have to stop myself from going into the kitchen to grab some leftovers. I'm not hungry. Eating used to be my drug to escape the feelings of being thrown away by my mother. She would call, I'd bake an apple pie from scratch and then eat half of it. And after waiting the next day for her to call me back or come visit me like she'd promised, I'd eat the other half. This went on until I was seventeen and over two hundred pounds.

My dad had to take me to the emergency room because I was short of breath and having chest pains. The doctor told him that I was eating myself sick with afternoon and late-night runs to the nearest burger and pizza joints.

On the drive home, my father pulled over to a fast food restaurant. "I know you feel like you need your mother, Kayla. But she doesn't need or want us. And that's fine with me. But if you kill yourself because she drove you to it, I will hunt her down and kill her. You got me? I'm not the best at this, but I don't know how else to do it. If I catch you in this fast food spot or anyplace like it, I'll drag your ass out of there. I won't lose you. Do you hear me?"

That conversation was probably rotting his tongue out with all the sweet things he was saying to me. Sweet in his mind. "I love you and I need you. Start walking tomorrow and by next month you'll be jogging." Then he put the car in drive and took us home.

The next day, I walked around the block twice and thought I would pass out, but I'd made it without sitting down and I breathed more deeply than I had in years. That was the most heartfelt conversation I had ever had with my father.

His threat to kill my mother didn't really concern me. It was the fact that he did love me enough to mourn me. Sounds twisted, but that's why I give my father nothing but respect. He didn't know how to love me the way fathers do on television, if that's the right way. But we never went hungry, and I never worried whether or not we'd have a place to live. He is a man. A pretty sucky father, but a damned good man, nonetheless. And the lovely talk with him prompted me to lose sixty-three pounds, and now I'm happily a size twelve.

It's late, but I dial my dad's number. He has always been a night owl. His line rings four times, and I almost feel relieved that he doesn't answer. But no such luck.

"Yes," is all he says.

"Hey, Dad. It's me. Is this a bad time?" Please tell me it is.

"Nope."

"Okay. How was your day?"

"Fine."

This conversation is going to be awesome.

"I really didn't want too much. Just to say hello and see how you were."

"I'm fine." Wow. Two whole words. Conversations with my father have always consisted of me fishing for something to talk about and him giving me the bare minimum. When I lived at home, we either stayed away from each other or sat in an uncomfortable silence, me wanting to talk and him probably wishing I didn't.

"Umm, I have good news." I gave him the skinny on the whole book deal and being a co-author, but I leave out Patrick. I wouldn't even know where to begin.

"You're living with those…things?"

"No, I'm not living with those people. Don't be that way. They're very nice to me. And very welcoming. I thought maybe there was a small possibility that you would be happy for me. Or maybe even proud. This is a big deal." I sigh and kick the coffee table. "It's okay, though. I'm doing well, and I just wanted you to know. I'll let you know when the book comes out, and Lettie and I are still sharing the apartment so no, I'm not really living with them. If that makes you feel better." He sure knows how to ruin an already unpleasant moment. "Just giving you a heads-up. You have a good night."

"Kayla," he says with a sigh.

"Yes, Dad?" I sigh right back.

"You be careful." He says it like it almost hurt for the words to break through his teeth.

"I will."

He clears his throat. "They're getting killed."

"I'm safe, Dad. I'm not a Were."

"Humans are getting killed, too. Whoever is killing the wolves just took out their third human this morning."

He cares. "I hadn't heard. I'll be safe."

"Don't get mixed up in their affairs. Don't get yourself in trouble."

If only he knew how mixed up in their affairs I've gotten already. No need to worry him. "I won't. I'll do my job and keep my head down."

"Good. It's good. Night." And then he hangs up.

Wow. We haven't shared a heartfelt moment like that since he threatened to kill my mother. Color me surprised. "It's good." That was more than I expected. I thought he would go on and on about how dangerous they were and how a career in writing would never amount to anything. But it's good. And it makes me feel a little bit better.

It's good.

Chapter Five

Three-seven-nine-six, then star. The key code for the front gate to the manor is now forever seared on my brain. Plus, I text the code to myself and shred the paper that Kerry gave me with the numbers on it. I've made it here on my own early enough to have breakfast with everyone, and I am feeling pretty good today. No fainting for me. No stress or worry in wondering if they want me here or not. Even the thought of my mother coming to town doesn't bother me.

God, I hope she's not coming here.

I suppose having a family does help with emotional issues. I need to talk to my therapist to make sure I'm not overcompensating. Or am I even allowed to share this stuff with someone outside the pack besides Lettie?

Before my mind starts to go on a hurricane of pointless thoughts, Patrick opens the front door of the manor and walks to the car to meet me as I clear the long dirt road that leads from the main gate to the manor. His beautiful brown skin and dark hazel eyes look so warm and calming. His smile lets me know he knows I'm starting to think tasty thoughts about him. Why can't we have sex?

"What are you thinking about?" he says, opening my car door for me and giving me his hand. I didn't even notice him cover the area between the front door and my car.

"The countdown. I started the pill this morning." I smile and breathe deep as his body engulfs mine in a tender embrace that warms every part of me.

"Are you trying to get fucked right here on your car?"

Hell yes. "Not so soon, wolf-boy. You want me with nothing between us, you have to wait until the pill kicks in." I lean in closer and kiss him, but before my hormones go fanatical, I break it off and pull away.

He adjusts himself and grabs my hand. "I'm a patient man."

We walk through the double doors just as Easay turns the corner from the living room. I burst out laughing. "Do you change your hair color often, Easay?"

Her hair is pink. "Every few months I get the urge. So, I change it."

"If you don't mind me asking, what do you do for a living?" I couldn't imagine her as a lawyer or a police officer. Green and pink hair would distract everyone in the court room.

"I'm a technical writer," she says. "Freelance. Right now, I'm writing a how-to manual for under cabinet TV/DVD players. You know, the ones that hang under counters in kitchens or bathrooms?"

I nod and follow her into the dining room as she talks about the different ways to hang one of the players. Kerry walks down the stairs toward us, smiling and holding her arms open.

"Kayla," she says, pulling me to her and hugging me. "Good morning. We saved a plate for you in the microwave."

"Thanks," I say, averting my eyes.

Damn them. Having a family like this growing up would have been great. Patrick notices my discomfort and pulls me aside. "What's wrong? You're blocking me."

I give him the best tight-lipped smile I can. "Don't know how the hell I'm doing that, but I'm good," I say to him. We all have our hang-ups, and family happens to be mine.

"Kayla," Kerry says. "Did we do something wrong?"

They can all smell my emotions. I've always been great with hiding how I feel and pushing it down so far nothing can trigger it. Except something small, like the water not heating up in the bathroom fast enough, or my pen running out of ink. Yeah, my therapist has worked for her money when it comes to me.

"Nope, Kerry. I am perfect. Going to go eat before I pass out," I say as I walk away from her.

"Come to my office, please," Kerry says. It's not a question. She's already walking toward her office.

Patrick and I follow behind her. She closes the door and walks to stand in front of her desk. "Kayla, did we intrude? We only want to see you comfortable." Her voice is gentle.

I try not to make eye contact, but she keeps staring at me like she's giving me no other choice than to look at her. "No, Kerry. I'm more than comfortable. It's nothing that any of you have done. I'm sure I have lots of typing to do, so I'm going—"

Once my hand is on the doorknob, she says my name more sternly. "Kayla. Please. If it's not us, then what is it? You were happy when you came in, and then it was gone. Talk to me. I'm not just your employer anymore. You'll soon be part of this pack, and you're already a part of this family. And even if you weren't…" She doesn't complete her sentence. I guess watching me hold back the tears is enough to quell her words.

"This…" I shake my head. "I didn't have this. Shit. Sorry." I sigh, an emotional flood trying to break through. "This is brilliant. This whole thing with Patrick and getting a family is so different and wonderful, and I should be happy. I should be enjoying this and not thinking of negative stuff. But I can't help it. My mother is an immature woman who left me and my dad when I was two years old. I barely see her and when I do, she reminds me of what a mother should not be like. She breaks promises, lies, and even dated one of my classmates and one of my teachers." My voice is getting higher, but she asked for it. "My father scarcely acknowledged me growing up and most of the time when he did, it was to remind me that I was foolish for letting my mother get to me and that I was making the wrong decisions. He provided for me, but his affection was almost nonexistent."

All this shit from a message from my mother. "I should be so fucking happy that I'm here with you all now, but all it does is make me realize how sucky things were when I was growing up. My mother called me, and I know she's oozing her way here to Baltimore as we speak, and I don't want to see her. And I'm happy not seeing her, but I feel guilty for being happy that I don't want to see her!" I wipe away the tears that have already broken through and that makes me cry even more. "I'm sorry I'm not happy. But I am happy. I'm so happy and I feel so safe here that it makes me uncomfortable. Isn't that stupid? It's crazy, Kerry! Years of paying my therapist has taught me to ignore my mother and get over all that stuff. But having all of you is like—like snatching a bandage off a healing sore. And since everyone in the place can probably hear whales communicating miles away, they know I suck!" I throw my hands in the air and let them land on the top of my head. Hard.

Patrick comes and puts his hand on my shoulder. His touch vibrates down my arm and into my chest. Kerry comes and pushes my hair behind my ear and then rubs the other shoulder. Their touch is like someone taking a fifty-pound weight off my chest. How the hell did they do that?

I wipe away the remaining tears and sniff. "It's like I've been on an emotional rollercoaster these past few days with a kid sitting next to me who keeps ripping off the bandage and I keep letting him. Why can't I be happy? Why can't I be grateful? Why can't she go the fuck away and leave me alone? I'm happier than I've ever been, and I just wish she would leave. Me. Alone. I'm terrible." Crap. Now I have the hiccups, and this conversation has turned out awful. I'd slap me if I were Kerry. Kerry's so strong that maybe if she did hit me, I'd forget this entire morning.

I use my shirt sleeve to wipe away the tears and snot—eww—and turn to Kerry. "I'm sorry." Hiccup. "I shouldn't have spoken to you like that." Hiccup. "You probably think I'm damaged and disrespectful. All these years of getting over her, and just when I'm happy, she finds the biggest monkey wrench to throw at me. And she didn't even do anything but leave a message on my phone." Hiccup, hiccup.

Since my head is down, all I can see are Kerry's designer shoes. My God, those shoes are gorgeous.

"Kayla," she says. "Please look at me."

I look up to see a face I can't quite read.

"Kayla, you are neither damaged nor disrespectful. You are not terrible, and you don't suck."

"Suck" sounds so weird coming out of her mouth. Almost like hearing the British kid that plays the famous wizard say, "What up dawg?"

"She is your mother, and you cannot help but love and yearn for her." Kerry puts her hands on either side of my face. "You have a family now, and we will not leave you. We will protect you and if that means having a sit down with your mother—"

"Oh, no," I say in mortification.

She smiles. "Or not."

Patrick wipes a stray tear from my face. "If you want me to, I'll get Lettie for you."

"No, you don't have to get Lettie. You're here." His smile brightens fantastically and then he appears to remember that he's supposed to be sad and comforting.

Kerry reminds me with a slight pull that she's still holding on to my face. "Anything we can do to help, and I mean anything, just let us know. We want to take care of you. You are a part of this family and we take care of our pack." She lets go of my face and grabs my right hand. She kisses it. "I won't push you about this again. But if you ever want to talk to me, Patrick, or anyone in this house, please feel free." She turns to Patrick and motions to the door. "Please take Kayla to her room and don't dawdle too much. I don't think she wants to be crowded." Kerry smiles at me and gives Patrick a slightly sterner look.

As we walk out of Kerry's office, everyone seems to have made themselves scarce. I don't know if they're trying to make me feel comfortable or if they heard Kerry say that I didn't want to be crowded. Either way, they still heard it and they still know. I wonder if they'll act differently. Probably not. This whole "making Kayla feel comfortable and accepted" stuff is making me uncomfortable.

God, I am damaged.

****

After I get over the horrifying shock that everyone knows I'm a nutcase, Patrick leaves me to my typing. I assured him I was more than fine and felt much better after getting it all off my chest. And I really do. Especially after that touch. It was healing. Mind clearing.

Even my therapist told me it was all right to have negative feelings about my mother. But a small part of me always felt bad for not liking her. Deep down, I do love her. I just don't particularly like her. She's not a nice person. Compared to my mother, my father is a saint.

Enough thinking about my parents. Focus on Kerry. That's what I'm getting paid to do, right?

A very detailed family tree is kept for the members from the Line of Lilith. The last female to be one of the World Pack Leaders from the Line was in 1684. This was a time when women were thought to be ruled over and doted upon. But she was fierce.

Her name was Emily, and at sixteen years old, she began killing her older brothers. Since her mother died and Emily was the oldest girl, she was the one who prepared the meals. She poisoned her two oldest brothers who were twenty-two and seventeen but left the youngest children alive. Emily's mother had died giving birth to her twin siblings two years prior, so they weren't much of a threat. By the time they were old enough her father had already deemed her the next in line to rule.

Though he wasn't happy with her murderous ways, Emily had devoted her life to the protection of the World Pack. Her bid to be the next to lead by murdering the two siblings that were her biggest threat showed her cunning ways and devotion to the pack. She believed that she was a better ruler than her brothers could have been and would do everything she could to make sure the pack had nothing but the best.

Before long, my hands move across the keyboard to the rhythm of Kerry's voice. Though half of the werewolf history is very intense and somewhat violent, it seems as though no matter who was in charge, they all had the pack in mind and wanted it to succeed and stay strong. Every single person in the Line of Lilith had nothing but the best intentions and did everything they could to preserve the Line. I'm sure Kerry is leaving out most of the really unsavory details. The pack has lasted this long. They came out of hiding when they were ready. I'm sure they could have easily taken over and killed everyone in the small village who found out they were werewolves to keep their existence quiet, but when the perfect opportunity presented itself, they chose to take advantage of it.

Four hours have passed, and I've already finished one tape and am halfway through the next. This has to be the easiest job in the world. I love doing it, the pay is awesome, a hot guy and a family come with it, and I can nap as I see fit.

I wonder what Patrick is doing. His wonderful smell of earth and fresh air and the hazel shade of his eyes make me melt and want to be close to him. A touch or a word from him makes it all okay. The strength of his embrace and the feel of his breath on my neck make me shiver with just a thought. He could probably break me in half if he wanted to, but his gentle touch…I think I'm going to throw up.

"She's a human! You're covered in her scent," is all I hear just seconds before there is a knock at my door.

Seeley walks in and looks as tranquil as ever. "Patrick is fine."

"Okay, Seeley, starting a sentence like that can only make me think he's not all that great." I push past him and realize that he allowed me to get by him. If he really wanted to, he could have confined me to my room. Thank God he doesn't want to.

"What's going on?" I feel the wave of nausea again, and I stop at the top of the stairs, so I won't fall.

"We have visitors and one of them—" He breaks off. "Are you all right?" It comes out "Ar'ye alight?" and I make a mental note to ask him where he is from after I find out why Patrick is making me feel queasy.

I scamper down the stairs, trying to keep my hurling in check with Seeley fast on my heels, and hurry into Kerry's office where the yelling is coming from. Patrick is standing next to Kerry, and there's a boy with thick, dark hair sitting in the chair across from Kerry's desk with his hands on the armrests. His knuckles are white, and I can hear a light cracking of wood. From what I can see of his face, there are sweat beads gently caressing his temple that lead to an ungodly amount of hair above his left eye. I have no doubt that the one brow leads to a complete uni-brow which probably takes away from his boyish face.

There's also a bony bitch with long, thick, platinum hair that comes just shy to the middle of her back standing a little too close to my Patrick with her finger in his face. My dad always said it wasn't nice to point. Her khakis are so low I can see the top of her ass.

The pants are a little big for her. She's skinny with the perky breasts of a twenty-year-old. A navy-blue sleeveless mock turtleneck clings to her perfectly size four body—I'm only guessing here—with matching flats that complement her outfit impeccably. Her faultless skin is a few shades darker than pale, and her platinum eyebrows almost disappear on her contorted face. She looks pretty pissed off.

She sniffs the air and turns her body to completely face me. "You!" she yells at me. "You were Chosen? I don't believe it." She angrily points at me and turns back to Patrick. "That is a human, Patrick. How could you touch one of them? I come here to give…It's not possi—" She inhales again. A look of confusion blankets her face. "Human?" She sniffs again. "You smell."

I do not! "Fuck you!" I say, pointing at her.

She shakes her head, her anger seeming to melt away. "You're different from other humans. You don't…you're not…" She turns to Kerry. "You don't see it?" She looks at me again, and her eyes soften. "My—they'll find you," she whispers.

Patrick takes a step forward and stands in front of me. "Is that a fucking threat, Prudence?"

Her anger resurfaces. "You deny me for that?"

I've had enough. "Look here, Mistress Peroxide. You've got one more time to call me a 'that' and I'll kick your bony ass back to the Baby Sitters Club." I instantly remember that she is most likely a werewolf and could attack me viciously and tear me to shreds.

"Over my dead fucking body," Patrick growls, listening in on my thoughts.

So, she is a Were who can beat me silly. No matter. I've put up with a lot of crap in my life, but she is neither my mom nor dad. She hasn't earned the right to make me feel like crap.

Prudence cocks her head to the right, and her chest puffs out. She drools slightly, and I realize her teeth are growing far too big for her petite mouth. "You think you can kick my ass?" A low guttural growl escapes her lips, and I see that her eyes are getting lighter. What color were they to begin with?

Before I can come up with a poor excuse of a witty comeback, Easay and her perfectly pink hair appear out of nowhere. "She may not be able to, Prudence, but I will." Easay comes to stand next to me and points to Patrick. There's a lot of pointing going on today. "He is too much of a gentleman to ever lay hands on you, but I will merrily do it for the both of them." Easay's pointing is much more appropriate.

Patrick eyes the boy sitting in the chair. I want to touch Patrick to calm him down, but as soon as the thought morphs into my head I get a feeling from him that's like a door closing. He wants me to stay back. He's afraid for me. And afraid that he may have to hurt Prudence and this young boy sitting across from him in the sturdy mahogany chair that's beginning to splinter.

Prudence. That is my new least favorite name in the whole world.

Patrick grabs my arm above my elbow and pulls me toward Easay.

Kerry's chest puffs out—I suppose it's normal wolf aggression behavior—and she closes her eyes. "Easay, please take Kayla upstairs. I fear our young Luke is losing his composure. He's feeding off his sister's anger and is very close to Changing."

I feel a bit hesitant to leave, but if all hell breaks loose, I'd rather be exactly where Kerry says I should be.

"Prudence, you will contain yourself, or I will help you do it," is the last thing I hear Kerry say before Easay grabs my arm and yanks me out of the room.

"Oww, Easay. That won't grow back if you pull it off."

She frowns and rubs my arm. "Sorry. That's Patrick's old girlfriend. Come upstairs, and we can talk about it. Luke is only fifteen, so his Changes are very sporadic and uncontrollable. They are tied to his emotions."

"Are they going to be okay?"

Easay scoffs. "Kayla, you know Kerry is from the Line and can beat the holy hell out of every wolf in this house if the mood ever struck. She can control Luke's Change if she has to. Besides, Patrick will put him down if he gets too out of hand."

I frown and feel bad for the kid. "Put him down... He'll kill the boy?"

"He may have to. The adolescent years of Changing will affect him as an adult. If he doesn't learn to control it, he could hurt lots of people. Human and werewolf. So yeah, too out of hand means consequences for us all. Come on," she says, walking ahead of me.

On our way to the stairs, I see Samuel and Mr. Levay standing in the living room, probably waiting for things to get out of hand.

"Holy hell," I say, watching the air ripple around Mr. Levay.

His gaze is focused, and his eyes are black. Mr. Levay's stance is wide, and his shoulders look broader than they usually do.

Samuel looks as if he can't wait for things to start flying out of hand. I want to stop and get a better look, but Easay gives me a gentle tug toward the stairs.

A thought hits me. I've never seen her room before. Not that I should have and not that it matters in the least bit right now. Denial. I'm so great at it.

The room we enter looks like it should be Kerry's. It's so modern and clean, and it completely goes against what I would have thought Easay's room would look like. Everything is brown or white. A four-poster bed with blossoming flowers carved into the posts is made of a dark wood. Maybe oak. A desk, enormous bookshelf, and television stand seem to have been carved from the same wood. The white throw rug that's just slightly larger than her bed looks too soft to have ever been walked on. On her desk is a brown laptop with a white Mp3 radio stand and a stack of papers. Next to the radio is a glass vase with brown rocks in it. I would have imagined heavy metal posters and pictures of drum sets plastered everywhere with colors that would make my eyes bleed, but I suppose she's an undercover neat-freak.

She gestures toward the white wicker chair in front of her brown desk and sits down on a brown chest next to said brown desk.

"How can Kerry control someone's Change?" Ouch! She sure is strong. Easay meant business when she pulled me out of the room.

"It's because she is a direct descendant of our Creator. All of those from the Line can do it. If one of us is injured and can't make the Change on our own, one of them can bring our wolf out of us which causes us to heal quicker. Coming from Lilith is to be of royalty. To be chosen by Her. Kerry is chosen. Lilith's line holds all Weres together. Anyone from the Line that did not have true intentions were disposed of by parents or siblings. Sounds terrible, but for the greater good of the pack, it has always been done."

I shrug and sit back in the chair. "How did she and Patrick get together?"

"I don't know. Prudence was always very jealous of any woman who came in contact with Patrick. She's even gotten violent in the past with women she felt threatened by. She's off her rocker if you ask me." She glances sideways. "But since you didn't…"

I scoff. "Whatever. Keep talking."

She smiles and scoots closer to me. "That's the reason she was made to leave the manor about two years ago. Pru got out of line with Kerry. Instead of killing her, which I would have thoroughly done, Kerry made her leave and told her that if she ever challenged her in any way again, she would kill Pru."

I feel a little uneasy about what will happen when I leave here. Am I in danger? Am I putting Lettie in danger? Crazy is as insane does, and that bitch sounds loco. "Why is she here?"

"I suppose I can tell you now, since you are one of us. Kind of, at least. Do you remember the articles in the paper about Weres being killed?"

"Of course. It was rumored that humans were killing them. We do have a tendency to kill what we don't understand."

"Yes, they do," she says with an indignant look on her face. She notices my grimace. "Not all of you. But enough to get the job done if they work together. Anyway, it's not humans. It's a rogue pack of wolves that have been killing them. Their own kind, for Lilith's sake. It's unfathomable. They've been killing wolves that are with humans. Having children with or getting married to humans. They think that our bloodline is becoming weaker and want to put a stop to it."

"Shit."

"You've got that right. Pru told Steven when she met him at a lecture last week that she had information on the rogues and that she may be coming to speak with Kerry about it. Thing is, Steven didn't know if it was just a ploy to weasel her way back here to Patrick or if she had actual information."

"Why didn't someone tell me this before?" I ask, instantly wanting to go back downstairs to check on Patrick.

"I'm telling you now. We don't know who they are."

I shift uncomfortably in the chair. "Well, how do you know it's a rogue pack of werewolves? Shouldn't the police know?"

"Pack members on the police force know, and that's what is important. Someone noticed similarities

117

in the murders, and a pack member went to check it out. They noticed the same scent on the bodies. The same group of Weres are responsible." She reaches over and flicks a few pieces of lint from her bed. "And it's happened so much more than you've seen in the papers. I guess the good thing is you guys are here and so close to Kerry. She'll do everything she can to protect you. And that says a lot when it comes to one like Kerry."

I rub my arm again. Not because it hurts. I rub a little harder until the pain does resurface. It gives me something to focus on besides the worry that's blooming in my body. "None of that was in the papers."

"It's really not a concern for humans. Werewolf police officers were able to gather information and report it back to the Line. The Rogue Pack will be punished." She says "Rogue" this time as if they are not the same as the pack. "The werewolf community has been alerted. We're the ones that are in danger." She shakes her head.

"Except the last two kills. The werewolf and their humans were killed."

Easay looks at me and frowns. "I hadn't heard. It was on the news?"

"Yes." I stand up and walk toward her bed to get a closer look at the designs on the bedposts. "That means Patrick is in danger. And if the Rogues have started a new trend, I'm in danger."

She comes to stand next to me. "Kerry would never let anything happen to you or Patrick. None of us would."

I begin pacing the room. It's all I can do to not go downstairs. I could be wrong, but I don't think Easay would let me out of here as easily as Seeley did. She may like me, but Kerry told her to do something and she is following through. Even if that means breaking my arm this time.

"Sorry about your arm," Easay says, rubbing my shoulder. "I'll treat us to a spa day and get you a massage."

"Um, thanks. That's the least of my worries right now. So, Patrick could be killed because of me?"

"You and Patrick were Chosen for one another. Not that I claim to know the will of Lilith, but I don't think She would let that happen. You don't know how important it is to have someone Chosen for you. Kayla, you probably love Patrick and you don't even know why, but it still makes you happy." Her head cocks to the side like she's listening. "Kerry just made them go for a hunt to burn off some steam. Come on. Let's go check it out."

Apparently, she was listening. I wonder what else she heard. I wonder if she'll share.

Kerry is now sitting at her desk. "You know, they hadn't killed any humans before last week."

When I walk further into the office, Easay trailing behind me, Patrick surprises me from behind the door and grabs me by my waist to pull me closer to him. "Is Kayla in danger?"

Patrick puts his face into my hair and inhales. I'm thrown off for a moment by his closeness, and I want to wrap my arms around him. Easay is right. Wolf traits are starting to rub off on me.

I walk away from Patrick to clear my head. "You guys can protect yourselves. And when it comes to a werewolf who means me harm, I'm defenseless." I give him a sobering look. "You're in danger, aren't you?

Just by being with me. Because I'm human."

He moves a strand of hair behind my ear and smiles but doesn't answer. His eyes darken. "I would never let anything happen to you. What we have is not like a normal werewolf-human relationship. We are Bound."

I shake my head and laugh sarcastically. "Yeah, and just like Prudence, I don't think they'd give a shit. But hey, let's call them and see if we're the exception."

Kerry interrupts. "As of right now, it isn't an issue. You're fine."

"Except from Prudence. If she's as crazy as I think she is, I'm on her list. And true psychos go for friends and family."

Mr. Levay walks into the office and leans on Kerry's desk. His hair is messier than it usually is, and the collar of his shirt looks stretched. An uneasy air surrounds him as he looks from me to Patrick. "She probably doesn't know anything about your roommate as of yet, but she has your scent. Prudence could probably find out where you live. Do you think she would even go that far?" He turns to Kerry. "Can you order her to stay away from Kayla and her loved ones?"

Kerry shrugs and starts typing on her laptop. "I hope it doesn't come to that. We'll see what happens." Kerry seems perfectly calm. A little too calm for me.

Patrick looks slightly irritated with Kerry's complacency. "I won't leave you alone. And if we need to, we'll make sure someone will keep an eye on Lettie."

I push away from the wall and start pacing the office. "It shouldn't have to come to that. Don't get me wrong, protection is awesome, but is someone always going to follow me around to keep an eye on me? That's impractical." This time I walk closer to Patrick so I can take comfort in his touch. "What does she know about the Rogue wolves who've been doing the killing?"

Kerry shifts in her chair and gives Easay a smile that doesn't reach her eyes. "I'm glad that you were informed, Kayla, which I'm sure doesn't bring you any comfort. Besides wanting to see Patrick, she only came to offer her services. A friend of hers, Rebecca, was one of the wolves that had been killed because of her choice of a mate. Prudence didn't approve of Rebecca's selection of a human, but she didn't think her friend's death was the answer. She also hoped that any residual feelings that Patrick had for her would resurface."

I laugh. "Obviously she made him sick, because that's the only feeling I got from Patrick before I came downstairs."

"Yes," Kerry agrees. "I was not able to tell if she was lying or not. Her fury was too strong. Besides, Prudence would be of no help to anyone. She cannot control herself, and she's a poor example for her brother."

Easay clears her throat. "If I may offer a suggestion, Kerry." Kerry nods her head and Easay continues. "I think Pru and Luke are living in Maine now. Contact the pack leader there and have Luke placed in a more suitable environment. Every pack leader in every state has a sanctuary for wolves, like you do here at the mansion." She says this more for my benefit than Kerry's. "Pru may not like it, but if she cares anything about her brother, she will want him to have the proper discipline which she, herself, cannot offer."

"Yes, I will do that. It makes sense. I'll even suggest that Prudence stay with him. She may be able to learn a few things." Kerry nods.

Kerry gets up from her chair and walks toward me and Patrick. "I think Patrick should take you home now while Prudence and Luke are preoccupied. I will call the pack leader in Maine and inform them of my decision. And for good measure I'll order her to maintain my wishes of you and your friend's safety. Even your mother if you wish." I think she's joking to cheer me up.

I chuckle at Kerry's joke. "I suppose she should be kept safe. And my dad. Thank you, Kerry."

Patrick and I walk back to my room in silence to collect my backpack before we leave. I don't know what I would do if anything happened to him. I just got him, and I'm not ready to let him go. I don't think I'll ever be. That's never stopped anyone from leaving before.

Chapter Six

"I'll be fine. Steven is close by," Patrick says as I start rinsing the dishes.

"What? Has he been outside this whole time sniffing the perimeter?" It's kind of disturbing to know that my teacher is outside creeping around the apartment.

He shakes his head. "His girlfriend has an apartment two buildings over."

Oh. Well, that's not so bad. He's dating a student. These apartments are filled with us. Wow. Mr. Levay is doin' a student. That's kind of hot. For him. Not me.

"I would really like you to work on keeping some of your thoughts from me. You just related Steven to something sexual."

Am I blushing? "I wasn't thinking that he was hot. Just that the idea of him dating a student, over eighteen of course, was kind of taboo."

"Well, she's not a student. She's a teacher."

"Even hotter."

"And a wolf. If someone tries to harm us, the both of them will be here right away. Same thing goes for you and Lettie if I'm not here. You're both covered."

"Lover, you keep forgetting that 'rogue' means they don't exactly follow orders." I wipe my hands on a dishtowel and turn to see Patrick staring at me with his naughty intentions all too clear.

He's leaning against the wall with his right leg crossed over the left. His crossed arms show the flex of muscles in his chest, and he's biting his bottom lip.

"Come on, Patrick. Cut it out. You can't give me that look and expect me not to want to hop on you."

He gives me a boyish wink. "I should spank you."

"I believe you should." I shrug and start putting the dishes in the cabinet. "Wait. Not while Pix is in here. I'm sure she would have no problem with telling us to keep it down, and I'm not ready for that embarrassment."

"You're damn right I wouldn't," Lettie says, padding her bare feet into the kitchen toward the refrigerator. Her hair is puffy from her shower. Now she truly looks like a Pixie with a big bushy ponytail, an oversized tee-shirt, and gym shorts. "Sorry to interrupt. Just wanted to get a glass of wine before I was off to bed. But since you two are talking dirty, I should take the whole bottle with me to drown out whatever you do later on."

I pour myself a glass of wine before she takes the bottle into her room. "Don't worry, Lettie. We won't stick hot pokers into your ears. Goodnight."

"Goodnight, guys." Once she notices Patrick isn't paying attention, she shakes her shimmy and gives me a thumbs-up.

Like that'll happen while she's at home. *Yeah.*

****

The pink of the sunrise has already started to change to a light blue as I realize I've only gotten about two hours of sleep. Though I tried hard, kept my eyes shut, and counted way too many sheep, every sound I heard in the apartment building left me straining to listen closely. To make sure Patrick was safe. To make sure that Lettie was all right. I'm not sure how binding the warning was from Kerry for our safety, but every noise to me was Prudence stealing into our apartment and hurting Lettie; it was the Rogues picking the locks on the doors and windows to kill Patrick and me. Patrick lay next to me, so I know that anyone who got too close to this apartment was in for a world of ouch. But as that thought hits me, I realize that even though he was fast asleep, he was making sure that Lettie and I were both safe.

I hear Lettie drag her keys from their normal place on the living room table as she walks out of the door, and I decide to get out of bed. After Lettie's alarm clock woke me up an hour ago, I listened to her quietly get ready and tried to will myself back to sleep.

Patrick's stomach is already growling, and he's not even awake. I may as well get up and make breakfast for us. I turn over to look at him and realize I must have way too much on my mind. Having sex was not an option while my roomy was still home but cheese have mercy, I should have at least been staring at my lover-to-be all night. Or maybe we could have played kissy face for a few hours.

He borrowed a pair of my old gym shorts to sleep in. Old as in "sixty pounds ago and thankfully too big for me now" old. They don't fit him perfectly, but the man wearing them right now is damn near perfect—one hand is tucked under his head while the other gently rests in the gym shorts. Typical man. His chest is the color of honey and his sloping shoulders and muscles are cut as if he swims for a few hours each day. The perfect V-shape leads straight down into the oversized shorts while a burst of dark curly hair creeps out above the elastic.

As my eyes roam over his body and I look at his face, I see that he's looking at me looking at him. A few days ago, that flash of kitty-cat eyes would have had me running from the room, but right now it gives me a start that makes my heart rate speed up.

Patrick pulls his hand out of his shorts—do I really want that hand? Hell yes! —and rubs my right nipple. I want to lean away from his touch, fearing what it could incite, but my body leans into it as my thighs squeeze together unconsciously, sending light spasms through my core. He keeps drawing lovely circles with his thumb and reaches his other hand to the nape of my neck to pull me closer. Our lips stop just shy of one another and before I can get a chance to catch my breath, he flicks his tongue out and licks my top lip. I close the gap between us, and we begin to melt into each other, kissing and rubbing, biting and pinching and touching.

He rolls on top of me with gentle strength and begins to take off my nightgown, but we get a little caught up because I'm trying to take off his shorts. Once they are off, he takes my hand and wraps it around his full, thick, throbbing length as if he wants me to be the one to begin so that he has my permission. Before I can get a chance to pull him inside, he stops kissing me and pulls my left breast into his mouth, drawing a delicious shiver up my spine. My breath comes in short spurts as he softly bites my nipple and rubs circles around my inflamed clit with the head of his cock.

"Son of a bitch," he whispers. Not the words I was

expecting.

"What's wrong?" I say in a breathy voice.

"Steven's at the door."

What?

Knock, knock.

"Son of a bitch!" I say, following his choice of words.

He kisses me, jumps out of bed, and grabs the gym shorts as he opens my bedroom door. I guess I should get dressed.

After putting on a tee-shirt and shorts, I head into the living room where Patrick, Mr. Levay, and a lovely forty-something woman are sitting. Dang it, they can "smell" emotion. Well, screw it, he knocked on my door.

"Is everything all right?" I ask, getting the obvious feeling that things are not all right.

Mr. Levay speaks up. "Two Weres pulled up outside your apartment as soon as your roommate left. I didn't recognize their scent, but as soon as they caught ours, they left. I don't know if that had anything to do with you, Patrick, but I had to let you know. No one got in or out. I could smell old blood coming from the car, and Sara got the license plate number before they pulled off."

"They were temp-tags," Sara chimes in. "I don't know if they're from the Rogue Pack, but they aren't local pack members." She smiles and stands up. "I'm Sara, by the way. It's nice to meet you both."

She gently shakes my hand. Careful around the puny human.

"It's nice to meet you, too. I'm Kayla. Can I get you anything?"

"No," Patrick says shortly. "We'll get ready and head over to the manor for breakfast. Pack a bag, love. You're staying with us."

I shake my head. "No, I'm not."

A muscle flexes in his jaw, and his Adam's apple dips as he swallows back the displeasure. "Kayla, I'm not going to argue with you. Pack a bag. And let's go."

Okay. That's new. He's usually a go with the flow kind of guy. I begin to argue, but he cuts me off.

"Not today I'm not."

He's worried about my safety and I completely understand, but I can't let this interrupt my life. "I'm not leaving Lettie here by herself," I say, looking at him as if he were a sexy stranger. "And in case you didn't get it, they were probably here for you, not me. Besides, my mother is liable to pop up here at any time. She may be a pain in my ass, but I won't let her be cannon fodder," I say with finality. "Kerry may have made an order for us to be safe, but 'rogue' kind of means they don't follow the rules. If I have to tell you that again, I'm going to punch you in the face." I point to Patrick. I really won't hit him, couldn't hurt him if I tried, but I won't be moved on this. Where the hell is this aggression coming from?

Patrick's eyes flash green for a moment, and he takes a step toward me. "Kayla, I love you and I would never want to make you feel uncomfortable, but if you go against me on this, I will drag you to the car and make you stay at the manor."

If I wasn't so pissed off, I'd be turned on right now. "I'm safe; you're not. Don't threaten me."

Mr. Levay comes to stand in between us. "She's right, Patrick. Come on. We need to talk to Kerry about this. I'm going to walk Sara to class, and when I come back, you two should be ready. Settle this. I won't be far."

"It was nice to meet you, Sara." I wave at her.

"Likewise. I'm very happy that you've found your mate. It's a blessed event. Good day." She's trying to sound calm, but she's clearly embarrassed from watching us argue.

They walk out of the apartment quietly.

"Patrick—"

"Kayla. Please. It's my job to protect you. That means doing it even if you don't want me to. Lettie isn't involved with me. You are." He closes the gap between us and runs his fingers through my hair. "We'll work out the specifics later. Just come home with me, and we can figure it out. But we need to let Kerry know."

I exhale and push my cheek into his hand. We stare at each other for a few breaths. "Fine. I'll come and we'll work it out. I'm not abandoning Lettie."

"I'm not asking you to."

Patrick and I stand and stare at each other, both of us realizing that what we tried to pretend couldn't happen may have just landed at my front door.

Chapter Seven

"If those were the bad guys outside of my apartment, how did they find out about us?" My tone of voice is that of a whining child. "Everything between me and Patrick just happened within the past week. Are werewolves that into gossip that word would travel around the friggin' country in a week?" I say, spitting my omelet back onto my plate. Note to self—no forceful F words when I'm eating.

We all sit at the dining room table eating breakfast. By the time we got to the manor, breakfast was already set out. Including the omelet that Seeley made for me. I have to find out when his birthday is.

Samuel wipes his mouth with his napkin. What's with him and no shirts? "In most cases, the couples had been together for some time before the werewolf was killed. I guess it depends on how fast they find out."

Before anyone can speak, Kerry reaches over and grabs my hand. When I meet her gaze, her eyes look even more odd than they usually do. The pale blue and the golden-yellow of her irises seem to be darker. "I can only guess that they must be more interested in you two. A human has never been Chosen for a wolf. Never. I can't even say that it's a rarity because it's unheard of. I even contacted the other members of the Line to see if they've heard of anything like this, which is probably how the Rogue Pack found out about you so quickly, and for that I am sorry.

"It's not your fault." I squeeze her hand.

Kerry clears her throat. "Please don't be upset, but I did some research on your family when we found out you and Patrick were Bound." She lets go of my hand and takes a sip of her orange juice before she continues. "I thought that maybe one of your ancestors would have been linked to us. But I didn't find anything. You're human, and you've been Chosen for a wolf. That makes you different. It's a gift from Lilith, and we all covet this. You were brought to us."

Everyone at the table agrees in some way. I shrug and sip my coffee.

Kerry inhales deeply and lets it out slowly. "I could have chosen someone else to assist in my memoirs. I almost did, but it just didn't feel right. You were in Steven's class, and he just happened to think you would fare well. You. You were brought here, and we all connected with you. It was instant. I want to say that it's not natural, but how can I? It's the most natural thing that could have happened. It wouldn't have happened if it weren't true." Kerry's voice has an air of discomfort. "We can't let anything happen to you. I don't know what it is, Kayla, but this is uncommon. And I couldn't be happier to be a witness."

"It's true," Easay says. "We feel an inherent intuition to protect you. We don't know what it is. Patrick has been so wrapped up in you that he doesn't even notice it. Well, I suppose he shouldn't. He's in love with you, and every werewolf that loves, longs to protect their mate. You belong here, with us. With Patrick. We embrace you."

"You've been discussing us?" Patrick rubs the side

of his face and doesn't direct the question at anyone in particular.

"Kerry just brought it up last night," Easay says. "None of us noticed. It just felt so normal. And it is. It's normal and natural, and I hope you don't hold it against us, brother."

Patrick looks annoyed. "Come on, Easay. You know I wouldn't hold it against you. And you're right, I have been so wrapped up in Kayla that everything looks…better. And I'm putting her in danger because of my lack of focus. Fuck."

"Of course not," Kerry says with a smile. "That's what the rest of your pack is here for—to help you. The both of you. Kayla, I assume you'll be staying with us from now on."

It was more of a statement than a question. Does anyone ever burst the bubble of a pack leader? I'm about to give it a try.

"Nope. I'm staying at my apartment with Lettie." I look straight into her eyes and square my shoulders to show her that the issue is non-negotiable.

Her eyes go a little lighter, and her nostrils flare.

As Patrick tries to stand, Easay grabs his shoulder and pushes him back into his chair.

Kerry sighs with a smile and shakes her head. "It's okay, Patrick. She doesn't know, and I would never hold it against her. I'm sure you've done that to your parents while growing up, Kayla. But here, with the Pack, something like that would be seen as a challenge."

Oh shit. I suppose someone should tell me this stuff. "Then I take it back," I say quickly. "Kind of. I can't leave Lettie alone. The Rogue Pack isn't after her, but Prudence gave me the impression that she takes the thing between Patrick and me personally. She takes my presence here personally. And she probably wouldn't do anything to me for fear of having him be angry with her. I'm sorry, Kerry. I didn't know that's what I was doing."

"Think nothing of it. You wouldn't know these things. Sometimes the wolf wants to step in when she feels challenged or threatened. I understand your concern for your roommate, I really do. But some agreement must be met. Just like Easay said, I feel protective of you. We all do. This is the safest place for Patrick to be. I doubt Prudence would go against my wishes. I ordered her to stay away from you and your family, and Lettie is your family. It'll all be fine."

I hope so. Not only do we have a jealous, supernatural ex-girlfriend to deal with, but we've got psychotic rogue werewolves who are more than likely curious about me and want Patrick dead. The best week of my life has just turned into the most daunting as well. Super. Please don't let my mother come for a visit.

****

After a long and insightful day of transcribing two more cassette tapes from Kerry and finally catching up, I only have two more tapes to type instead of the eight I began with. I have to do something to keep my mind off of being hunted by stupid werewolves. And if Patrick and I are going to be with one another, I need to learn more about their rules. Challenging Kerry, unintentionally, probably won't fly well after I've done it five more times.

Patrick is beginning to behave differently. It's

subtle, but it's there. Ever since our first encounter he's been so calm. Now, at times, he may as well start beating his chest like an ape when it comes to me. I kind of like it. When it's not pissing me off.

Patrick, Mr. Levay, and I pack up our things to head back to my apartment. Mr. Levay will stay at his girlfriend's again tonight, and Patrick will stay with me.

"You guys be careful and have a good night," Easay says as she walks us to Patrick's truck. "Boss-lady said she has three more tapes in her office and should have at least one more when you come back on Monday. Unless you come by this weekend. If you visit, it should be just that—a visit. No typing." She leans in and gives me a hug.

"Will do. See you later. Tell everyone I said goodnight."

Easay gives a final wave and heads back into the manor.

With only the radio playing in the background, the ride home is rather quiet. I can't keep myself from thinking that my stubbornness may get someone hurt. The safest place for all of us is at the manor, but I refuse to give up my freedom and allow myself to be constantly babysat.

But what about Patrick? It's his home, and he's doing everything to make me happy and comfortable even though I'm the newcomer.

My phone rings, and Hannah pops up on the screen. She's my old boss from Blue's Corner.

"Kayla?" she says before I can say hello.

"Hey, Hannah."

"Honey," she says, her voice somber. "Where are you?"

Patrick goes to open his door and I pull his arm, silently asking him to give me a minute. "I just got home. Is everything all right?"

She sniffles and then I hear her take a long pull from her cigarette. "Honey, something happened—"

"Oh, no. Is Trent all right?"

"He's fine. He's good." She pauses and sniffles again. "It's Craig, baby girl. He was attacked in the woods behind his apartment complex."

No. My heart starts to hammer in my chest. "Hannah, is he all right? What hospital is he in?"

I look at Patrick and shake my head, afraid of what Hannah will say next. Maybe if I hang up on her, she won't say what my gut is telling me she'll say next.

"No, honey." She inhales another puff of her cigarette. "I've heard you shouldn't fight back when someone is trying to rob you, but he did. He—he… Craig is gone, sweetie."

Her breaths are ragged, and I can hear Trent in the background.

Lie. It's a lie. He wasn't robbed. I can feel it in my gut. "No," I whisper. "It can't…he…" I shake my head. "No."

"Sweetie, I know you loved him, and he loved you too. He thought the world of you."

I put my hand over my mouth and drop the phone. I can hear Hannah calling my name, and then I hear Trent's voice.

"Kayla," he says sternly. "Kayla, are you still there?"

Patrick reaches over and grabs the phone. "Hello? This is Kayla's boyfriend."

"Her what?" I hear Trent yell.

"She's a little…can she call you back?"

I don't hear what Trent says, but Patrick hangs up the phone.

I shake my head again and feel the tears run down my face and gather at my chin. "No. He was just here."

"It's okay." He leans over the center console and pulls me into his arms.

My heart doesn't want to accept it. Craig was there for me. He treated me like I was family. He loved me. And I loved him. More than I'll ever be able to tell him now. My chest is caving in on itself. I can't breathe. This hurts more than anything.

"Patrick, I don't know what to do."

"There's nothing you can do. Does he have any family?"

A picture of his daughter pops into my head. Craig always kept a picture of her in his wallet and would show anyone who stopped to talk to him for more than five minutes.

"His ex-wife. A brother he sometimes talks about." I shake my head. There really is no one to call.

Patrick reaches over and unlocks my door. "Come on. Let's get you upstairs."

I get out and see Lettie's car across the parking lot. Maybe she can bring back a little normalcy. Rogue wolves were waiting for me outside of our apartment. Craig is…gone. I don't think I can take anymore.

When I open the door to the building, Patrick's nose starts twitching and he pulls me back outside. "Wolf," he says, throwing the door open farther.

"What? What's wrong? Oh my God, Lettie!" If getting past a werewolf was that easy, I would have pushed my way through the door and run up the stairs.

Pushing against Patrick is like pushing a stone wall that isn't afraid to push back.

"It almost smells like Prudence but not quite. Maybe she was here earlier. Would you stay down here if I asked you nicely?" He gives me a look I don't quite understand.

"Absolutely not."

He grabs my hand and pulls me up the stairs, keeping me behind him. Once we get to the top landing, Patrick takes the keys out of my hands and opens the door. "Lettie?" He calls like he's almost certain she won't answer.

"Lettie!" I scream louder.

"Kayla," says a small voice from the kitchen.

I run into the kitchen to find Lettie sitting on the floor with a bottle of dark liquor seated between her legs. Her face is sweaty. "A boy was here. He was a werewolf." She takes a huge gulp of the liquor and then clamps her hand over her mouth like she's going to yurk it back up. When she doesn't, she takes another gulp.

Patrick puts his nose in the air and takes three quick sniffs. "Did he hurt you? Did he bite you? It was Luke."

"He knocked on the door and said he was here to talk about you, Kayla. I thought you were hurt, so I let him in." She grabs her mouth again, shaking her head as if clearing away the drunkenness that's beginning to set in and then continues. "He started asking questions about how you two could possibly be Chosen for one another. I got the feeling that he wasn't here on your behalf, so I told him to get lost." She shakes her head again and then looks at Patrick. "I didn't even curse at him. I wasn't nearly as mean as I could have been. His eyes got all funny and his face started…changing. He stepped closer to me, but then it was like something stopped him. He growled and then he started panicking, like he had to use the bathroom. Really bad. Then, he jumped out of the window!" Lettie's voice raises on a wail.

I look down and see shards of glass sprinkled on the floor. The window is completely gone.

"It was Kerry's order. No true pack member can ignore a direct order from someone from the Line. It's almost like a physical force stops you from disobeying." Patrick takes hold of Lettie's arm to help her off the floor.

"Be careful, honey," I say, grabbing her other arm. It's cold and covered in goose bumps. "Don't cut yourself."

A quick knock on the door causes Lettie and me to jump, but Patrick remains calm. Mr. Levay and Sara come hurriedly into the apartment.

Sara gives Lettie a look of pure pity when she sees her going for the bottle again. "I smelled a wolf," she says.

"No," I say to Lettie as she reaches for the bottle. "You've had enough. Come on, Pix. Let's get some of your stuff. I'm staying at the manor with you, Patrick. But only if Lettie can stay, too." I put my arm around her.

Patrick and Mr. Levay give each other a look I can't interpret, but before anyone can object, I grab Lettie by the hand and lead her toward our bedrooms. We have a few bags to pack.

"Patrick," Lettie slurs from her bedroom. "Bring

that bottle!"

We pack, and after I shove a protesting Pixie into the backseat of Patrick's black four-door pickup, I close the door and fight the urge to take a swallow from the liquor bottle she's still holding on to. A stiff drink might help me calm down a little bit. But the thing is, I'm not really worried. How careless of me. Craig is gone and Lettie was approached by Luke. "Okay" is not a word that should be used right now. We pile into Patrick's truck, minus Sara, and head over to the manor.

Craig was murdered. Was it by a Rogue? Doubt it. They wouldn't be interested in his money.

He's gone. The man I wished was my father is dead. Pain unfurls in my belly, and I hunch into myself as the feeling of loss consumes me. He's gone.

Lettie's light snores from the backseat are only interrupted when Patrick makes a sharp turn. "Too fast," she says quietly.

"You should have brought some water for her to drink. Nothing personal, but if she vomits in the car, I'm going to have to get out." Mr. Levay looks at her questioningly. Super-smelling isn't so fun all the time, eh?

I look over to Patrick to see him shake his head and I smile. "If she was going to yark, she would have started whining. She'll be fine." I look back at Lettie. She keeps rubbing her leg and tapping her finger. The last time she did that was when her dad had a few stents placed. It's a nervous tic.

"Lettie, we're almost there," I tell her. Wait a minute. "Patrick, maybe I overreacted. If a true Pack member can't go against an order from Kerry, we should be fine. Right?"

Mr. Levay laughs. "Would you want to wake up to an angry Luke or Prudence standing over your bed? They may not be able to hurt you, but still, does that sound like something you'd like to see?"

"Point taken. This is probably going to be an inconvenience for Kerry. I haven't even been around that long and I'm taking liberties with my other home." I laugh to myself.

We pull up to the gate and Patrick looks at me. "No, Patrick, I don't remember the stupid code!" He shakes his head and punches in the numbers to get us entry onto the property. One of us should have called ahead to make sure it was all right to bring Lettie along. But right about now I couldn't give less of a shit if I tried.

Instead of Patrick talking to Kerry first, he cradles Lettie in his arms like a slightly oversized, drunken child and takes her to one of the unoccupied bedrooms. As he walks up the beautifully curving stairs, I get the sudden feeling that he doesn't want to be a part of the conversation that Kerry and I are about to have. I don't know how I feel about that.

Before I even get a chance to knock on Kerry's office door, I hear her soft bedroom voice from behind me. "I'm right behind you. You can go in."

Eep! I almost turn to give her an elbow to the chest but stop just short of making contact. I don't think I would have been able to make contact anyway. "Jesus Christ! Kerry you scared the...You startled me."

Kerry grins showing very little teeth and gives me a gentle nudge into her office. "I'm sure there is a reason you brought a drunken human here." She sits on the edge of her desk.

"Yes. That's Lettie—"

"I figured."

"—and Luke paid her a visit today."

A look of annoyance flashes across her face but disappears just as quickly. "She's not in the hospital, so I assume he didn't hurt her, thank the Goddess."

I almost get the feeling that she is trying to ask, "Then why the hell is she here?"

"And the man I wished was my dad was killed. Robbery gone wrong." Tears fill my eyes, but I won't let them fall.

"Kayla, I'm so—"

"No. I can't do that right now. Can't hear it. I'll start crying and won't be able to stop. If Lettie staying here is a problem, then we can go somewhere else. I understand if I'm asking too much. I just got here, and I'm already a pain in the butt."

"No. You're part of this Pack, and she is your family. Until this is resolved, she can stay. After breakfast in the morning, the three of us will sit down and talk."

Relief fills my body. "Thank you, Kerry."

"Kayla, I'm going to show you something, but I don't want you to overreact." She pulls something from under her keyboard. It's a small sheet of paper.

She hands it to me, and I see it's a postcard. With a picture of me on the front of it. "What is this?"

Kerry wrinkles her brow. "It arrived this afternoon. Read the back."

I turn it over and see a handwritten note. *A human Bound to a wolf. What is she?* I turn it over and look at the picture again. It was taken on campus. Someone's following me.

"Oh my...I don't...Why would someone..."

Kerry walks around her desk and grabs my hand. "You are now on their radar. Not simply because you are a human who is with a werewolf. But because you were Chosen and are Bound to a werewolf."

I turn it over again and reread the writing. *What is she?* What am I? I'm human. And they want me. They weren't at the apartment for Patrick. They were there for me. Because they don't know what to make of me.

"I have no doubt that you will tell Patrick, but I ask that you keep this to yourselves. I don't want anyone to panic."

Except me. Because she showed it to me. Why wouldn't she? Holy crap. I don't know what to do. Those Weres were at my apartment for me. To take me? To kill me? To kill me and Patrick?

"Kayla, I will get to the bottom of this. You're here now. We can protect you."

"They want me. What makes me different?"

She smiles and shrugs, looking confused and happy. "I don't know. You have us and as long as you're here, you're safe. Don't worry. Don't overthink this. There is no other place on the face of this planet where you would be safer. You're home now. We'll fix this." She takes the postcard from my hand and begins to walk me to the door.

"Kerry."

"Yes."

"Tell Prudence and Luke that they owe us three hundred and fifty dollars for the broken window. We're probably going to lose our security deposit."

As I leave Kerry's office and head toward the staircase, I see Patrick standing at the top of the steps.

"What the hell is going on?" he asks.

"Not tonight. I promise we'll talk about it tomorrow."

He starts to protest, but I put my hand up. "Please. Tomorrow. But right now, show me where Lettie is."

I can tell he wants to force the issue, and I can understand why. He felt what I was feeling when Kerry showed me the picture. Fear. Anger. Hatred. And now I've managed to put them away. Wrap them in a tight little box of denial and hide it away until it's staring me in the eye. I might explode if I don't.

The past week has been an emotional rollercoaster, and I don't know what to do. I'm afraid and want to run away. I'm relieved because maybe, just maybe, Patrick is safe. But I'm not. Apparently, I'm a conundrum, and the Rogue Pack want to figure me out.

I want to call Craig. The thought almost doubles me over again and sucks the air out of me. Stumbling away from Patrick, I turn around to go back downstairs. "I have to go back to the kitchen to get Lettie some water."

"Hey," Patrick says from in front of me. He moved so fast I didn't see him take the ten steps from the top of the platform to the bottom where I am. He puts his hands on my shoulders and puts me at arm's length, looking into my eyes. "You don't have to hide from me. I know it hurts. Never hide your tears from me."

I give in to the sinking feeling in my stomach and sit down on the stairs. Patrick comes down with me and pulls me into his lap. Silent tears fall down my face and land on my shirt. He's gone. The man I wished was my dad is gone.

"It's a lie, Patrick. I don't think he was robbed. He

was killed because of me."

He shakes his head and a look of pure confusion blankets his face. "No. It's not your fault. The rogues don't kill people and cover it up. They want credit."

He's wrong. Something deep inside me is whispering the truth. Craig was killed to punish me. To show me who was in control.

"Come on," Patrick says, standing me up. "Let's get you upstairs. I already took Lettie a glass of water."

The touch of his hand on the small of my back warms me as he leads us to a room two doors away from mine. As I open the door and walk in, I see Lettie sitting on the edge of the bed struggling to put on her pajama bottoms. Except, it looks like she's fighting with them.

"You know, Pix, alcohol is very bad for hand-eye coordination."

She finally manages to get them on, inside-out, and falls back on the bed. "This house is gi-hugic. So, this is where you're going to live when you get hitched." It's more of a statement than a question.

I never really thought about it, living here with all of them. At first it seemed like a bad idea, but now it's almost a comforting thought. Then again, not so much. Patrick and I would never have sex. Everyone's hearing is too good. "Actually, no. I don't think I'd like to live here. Communal living is not in the plan." I pick up the glass of water sitting on the desk next to the door and take it over to her. "You and I are going to be staying here until stuff clears up. We're going to talk to Kerry in the morning. So, for now, sleep. The bathroom is to the left and down the hallway. Same goes for water. Get it from the bathroom. Don't wander. You'll get lost."

"What if I don't want toilet water?" Lettie says with a goofy grin.

"Then, I guess you'll have to get it out of the faucet." I smile back and grab her hand. She's been pulled into this storm, and she still looks like she's having fun. "I'm sorry I got you into this."

She turns her back to me and sinks deeper into the pillows. "Are you kidding? This is the most fun I've had in years."

"If you insist. Goodnight."

Before I get to the door, she's lightly snoring. I don't want to get off this wonderful ride, but I'd sure as shit like the spinning to stop.

When I get to my room, Patrick is lying in my bed with his shirt off with the remote in his hand changing channels. I wonder if he has on any bottoms. "Hey, this isn't your room." I hold the bedroom door open.

"Well, since you're staying here—"

"I don't care. I'd love to sleep next to you."

He pulls the covers back for me to get in. So tempting.

"Going to floss and brush first, lover. And take a shower. I feel yucky."

I head over to the bed to kiss his nose. He grabs my arm and pulls me closer to the bed. "I could come get in with you. No one would hear any sounds you'd make when I made you orgasm from my tongue."

"Liar." My voice is barely audible.

"Yes, I'm lying but—"

"Save it. Going to take a shower now. Alone."

Is it wrong to stay in the shower longer since I'm not paying the water bill? Of course, it is, but tonight I'm going to do it. I wonder how the bills work around here. Does everyone pitch in? Crap, I'm avoiding the thoughts that really want to be thought about. Okay, they don't want to be thought about, but they need to be thought about. Thinking about bills is much easier. Bill collectors don't want to kidnap and kill you and your boyfriend. They may act like they will, if you don't hand over the money you owe them, but as far as I know they haven't done it yet. Bill collectors wouldn't have caused Craig's death. No. None of that.

Maybe my mother wasn't as faithful as she let on and my father is really a Were. My real father. How dare she do that to Dad? But that's stupid. If my father was a werewolf, I'd be a werewolf.

The popular thought many years ago by lots of stupid men who claimed to know everything was that only a male werewolf could mate with a human and have a werewolf as a child. That thought was put to rest when every Were who slept with a human, man or woman, produced another werewolf. And those stupid humans did not like that one bit.

I cut the water off in the shower and stand there for a moment looking at my fingers. They're wrinkled. Yes, I'll worry about my fingers. Nothing else. Just bill collectors, my cheating mother, and my fingers.

"Your fingers are wrinkled," Patrick says as he pulls the covers back and I climb into bed.

"Yup. It happens." I'm sure he can hear the sarcasm in my voice.

"Hey." He sits up and turns toward me. "Talk to me."

Grabbing and massaging the bridge of my nose, I take a deep breath and hold it in for a moment. "I'm sorry," I whine.

He pulls the blue and beige sheet off his legs. "If you don't want me in here, then I can go back to my room," he taunts.

"No." I pull the covers back over his legs. Dang it, he is wearing pajama bottoms. "This whole thing just hurts. Craig is gone. Just gone. I'm happy to be here with you, but under these circumstances, everyone's lives are being intruded upon."

"This isn't your fault."

"I never said it was. I am not taking the blame for this, and I'm not having a pity party, just stating the facts. The people who want to kill you and probably poke at me are to blame. And so is your psycho ex-girlfriend. How could you date someone like that?"

He starts to chew on the inside of his lip and looks around the room like he's trying to put his poor decisions into words. "Pru wasn't always like that." He shakes his head. "I take that back."

"I thought you would."

"She loves hard and falls in love with the idea of things. By the end of our second year together, she loved that everyone thought we were the perfect couple even though we were constantly arguing about everything. Especially other women. Pru felt like I belonged to her, and no other woman should have any contact with me that didn't go through her. She didn't want anyone to undermine the 'perfect relationship' we had."

"Sounds like a keeper."

"I finally broke up with her because I knew I was unhappy and I could tell she was, too. But that didn't matter. She said we were good together and that we could work through our problems. I did love her, but I knew she wasn't the one for me. Things around here got pretty tense, and after we broke up, she crossed the line with Kerry." He rubs his chin and then touches my cheek.

"Easay glanced over it. Tell me."

"A group of us were out hunting deer, and Kerry tackled me, just joking around. It was rough-housing; we all do it. After shifting back to human form and coming back to the manor, Pru starting yelling at Kerry saying that she went too far by coming on to me right in front of her." He laughs and shakes his head. "And this is the kicker, Prudence said that if Kerry or Easay did anything like it again, they'd have to deal with her."

The whole scenario gives me goose bumps. Kerry is a nice person, but she's not pack leader for nothing. "I would have loved to have been a fly on that wall, or blade of grass. You were outside."

"I don't think you would have. Kerry forced her into submission, called her a few kinds of bitches—"

"Oooh, burn!"

"—almost ripped her throat out, and then sent her away the next morning. Prudence is lucky she wasn't killed."

I change the subject. "Well, Lettie and I both have class tomorrow afternoon. She doesn't go back to work until Tuesday. As of an hour ago, I live at work."

Patrick shakes his head like he's trying to clear his head of Prudence. "I'll drive you tomorrow."

I burrow deeper into the covers. "Dude, don't you have to work? I haven't seen you doing anything pertaining to designing software." Maybe I'm a doofus, but what the hell does a software designer do?

Sliding closer to me, Patrick pulls his body over

mine and sighs. The warmth of his breath and the heaviness of his body tightens my core, sending electric pulses through me. He pulls my knees up on either side of him and settles between my thighs. "Saturday classes? That sounds horrible." He kisses me, and the feel of his smile against my lips is divine.

"Not so bad."

He moans in frustration and then nuzzles my neck. "I love you, Kayla. The past twenty-four hours has reminded me just how human you are."

"Thanks?"

"It's not an insult. You and I both are mortal creatures that can be taken away at any time. I don't want that."

"I don't want that either." I open my thighs a little wider, so he'll have more space and look into his eyes.

His gaze holds me in a trance. The brown of his eyes changes, and an amber ring brightens around his irises. The low rumble of a growl vibrates through his chest. The fact that his beast is showing himself to me touches something deep inside my core.

"I love you, Kayla Taylor. You need to know that." A vise grip takes hold of my heart as his gaze bores into me, and it feels like he can see it all.

All the emotional mess that comes along with me. And it doesn't bother him. I know he loves me, and I love him, but neither of us has said it to the other. It sounds definite. And beautiful.

Pinpricks of emotion make my eyes water, and before I can attempt to blink them away, they burst through as if they want to be seen. "I love you, too Patrick. So very much."

I strain to reach up to kiss him and wrap my legs

around his waist. His kiss is possessive, rough, and hot. His tongue slips into my mouth, and a sensation of heat resonates through my body. I feel like I am a part of him, and he is a part of me. He reaches down to take off my panties, and I can feel his lips smile against mine when he realizes that I don't have any on. I sleep better going commando.

The feel of his erection pressed against my core, pulls a heavy breath from me. When I go to break our kiss so that I can pull my nightgown over my head, there's a feeling that comes over me that if we were to stop kissing it would be a sin against the both of us. But I don't have to. I hear and feel a soft rip of cotton against my skin as Patrick tears my gown down the side. He gently lifts me off the bed and pushes the gown to the floor. Both of us struggle to get his pajama bottoms off, and when we do our bodies have full contact.

In the moment that his skin connects fully with mine, an unnatural but familiar intensity rushes from him to me. My cry of his name is muffled because we are still locked in the most fervent kiss I've ever experienced. As that force runs from my body back to his, goose bumps appear all over him and tickle my skin.

"You feel that, Kayla?" he says between kisses. "That's our bond."

The knowledge that we are coming closer to each other makes my pussy slick with need. Need for him. The feel of his warm palm skimming against my flesh makes me hungry for him. Balancing his muscular body over mine with one hand, he uses the other and runs it up my thigh, up my stomach, and then stops to cup my breast. He thumbs my nipple, drawing small circles around the hardened peak. The roughness of his fingertips sends electric spasms through me. With his glowing eyes holding me to the spot, he lifts my breast and brings my nipple to his scorching mouth. The soft undulations of his tongue send a lightning bolt of pleasure to my core, making me even more wet for him than I already am.

"*Fuck*, Kayla. I love the way you taste."

He sucks my nipple into his mouth and nips the sensitive peak, drawing a needy groan from me. This is everything to me. Patrick touching me, tasting me, accepting me. All of me. Not just the best parts of me, or the parts he thinks should exist. Just me.

With his nails, he skims the tips of his fingers down the sides of my legs and then up my torso, leaving a trail of fire in his path. He kisses a line between my breasts and leads his mouth to my other breast, giving it just as much attention as he did the first. Sucking, nipping, tasting.

How did I ever live before this? How has any other man ever pleased me before Patrick's touch?

The hard rod of his cock hovers above my soaked entrance, and as he takes his teeth to my sensitive nub, he rubs his length against me, abrading my clit with the ridges of his cock. Passion radiates down my spine with the feel of his cock so close to breaching my entrance.

The walls of my aching pussy throb with need for him. "Please, Patrick," I whisper, not even knowing what I'm asking for.

"You want me inside you? Want me to fill you with my cock?"

Yes, and please.

Patrick pulls my hips closer to his and thrusts my legs open so wide that it's almost uncomfortable. His lips crash into mine, and I wrap my arms around his neck and drink him in as he does the same. He slides his thumb between our lips, still not breaking the kiss, and then pushes his hand between us and starts to rub my clit with his wet thumb. The sensation of his hard hand on my most receptive spot sends a fire down my core that makes me instantly ready for him. He rubs the swollen head of his cock against my drenched folds. I lift my hips to take him inside, but he pulls away from me.

I growl in frustration and dig my nails into his shoulders, pulling a heated snarl from his lips. With a teasing smile on his lips, he breaks the kiss and grabs my breast, sucking my nipple into his mouth. The sensation spikes my heart rate even higher. Arching my back, I push myself harder against his rolling tongue and nipping bites. A shudder runs through my body.

"Just do it already," I breathe into the top of his head and without hesitation he lets go of my breast, grabs his hot, throbbing length just as it brushes against my thigh, and thrusts every inch into me.

We both cry out at the same time, but he doesn't stop. He just keeps pushing and kissing and grabbing until every touch he makes is just this side of pain. I don't want him to stop. My pebbled nipples are so hard they are sore, and as they brush against his chest it brings on an ache that takes me so high. A soft growl rattles him, and I rub my hand across the hot skin of his chest and feel the vibration through my skin.

"I'm sorry," he says in an urgent whisper but doesn't stop pummeling his cock into me. "I don't want to hurt you, but I can't…"

"It hurts just right," I pant. "Don't stop."

And he doesn't. And he can't. I don't think either one of us could stop this even if we wanted to. He sucks my bottom lip into his mouth and just keeps pumping and pushing until a craze starts to boil inside my core and reaches through every part of my being and brings me screaming to an orgasm I've never felt with any other person. His mouth covers mine, and he swallows the sound.

Just when it seems as if my body can't take anymore, that ardent feeling starts to rise again, and I can feel my body convulsing around his cock even harder than it did before. It makes him come so hard that his fingers dig into my thighs, and he calls my name. "Kayla" has never sounded so true and welcomed and loved. Jets of liquid heat shoot into me, and I lift my hips a few more times to milk every ounce of pleasure from him.

We lie there, more a part of each other than anyone could ever be. Nothing could be more perfect than me and Patrick in this moment. It seems as though no one in the world could have ever been closer than he and I are right now, and nothing can sully it or make it seem wrong.

"Cheese and crackers!" Pant, pant. "That was my first—" I cut myself off before I say it, instantly feeling embarrassed.

His body is so covered in sweat, he can only open one eye or he'll get perspiration in the other. "What?"

"Nothing." Orgasms make me talk too much.

He grabs my torn nightgown from the floor and wipes his face with it. "Talk, woman." He falls next to me onto the pillow.

I slap my hands over my eyes, feeling like a person who's done something wrong and is afraid to admit it. "This is my first orgasm from sex." It sounds more like a whine than anything else.

"You've never had an orgasm before?"

"Yes. With my battery-operated buddies or from clitoral stimulation. I didn't think it was possible." I hope he's not staring at me.

He pulls my hands away from my eyes and wipes his face again with my nightgown. "Why are you ashamed? There are plenty of women who never have orgasms from sex. Baby, you don't have to be uncomfortable." He pulls me on top of him and nibbles my bottom lip. "You know what this means, don't you?"

"That you've been with tons of women and know how to break 'em in?" I try to take the attention away from me.

"It means that I am perfect for you."

"You got all that from one orgasm, eh?" I joke.

"I believe it was two. You felt it. I know you did. My body was made to please yours." Patrick shakes his head and begins to slide down beneath the sheets.

He's right. I could feel every part of him finding a home in me and vice versa. "We belong to each other, Patrick. That's what I think."

"Yes. You're very correct." His voice is muffled against my skin.

After he disappears beneath the sheet, I feel him slide his finger inside of me as he draws my clit into his mouth and then gently bite as I straddle his face.

To hell with everyone in this house that has ears to

hear.

Chapter Eight

"No one will say anything. They were probably asleep anyway, and even if they did hear something, no one's going to say anything."

After last night, I don't think I can face anyone at the breakfast table. "We were loud. Everyone in this place can hear everyone else."

"You're going to avoid the people who live here now? Come on, Kayla."

"I don't think I like your tone of voice, Patrick." Now, I'm being snarky because he's being condescending. Aww, our first argument.

Patrick's head cocks to the side. "Lettie's looking for you," he says as he walks toward the bedroom door and then peeks out.

God, he looks awesome in his blue and white gym shorts, blue tee-shirt, and gray running shoes. He looks all kinds of hot right now. I bite my lip and squeeze my thighs together remembering last night. I can still feel the weight of him between my legs.

"Cut it out unless you want me to fuck you against the door," he says, smiling at me wickedly.

"—freaking maze. Are you all right?" Lettie says as she walks into my bedroom.

Blasted dirty words! I didn't hear what she said. "What?"

"I said I had to get directions from a dude who

should never wear shirts and lucky for me, he didn't have one on. This place is a freaking maze." She crosses her eyes slightly and then chews on her lip. "And then I asked if you were all right. Morning, Patrick."

"Good morning, Lettie. Kerry wants to talk to you and Kayla after breakfast."

"Is she mad at you guys for bringing me here?"

Patrick puts his hand on her shoulder and smiles. "Not at all. She said you can stay here with us until everything blows over. After you two finish at school, I'll run you past the apartment to get more clothes. Sound good?"

She looks as if she's going to protest, but I interrupt her before she starts yapping. "Of course, it sounds good. Awesomely free food, huge mansion. You're okay with it," I tell her.

"If breakfast tastes as good as it smells, I am so okay with it," she declares with a nervous laugh.

"Come on, Pix. Let's eat breakfast." Lettie seems as if she's trying not to be nervous about everything that's going on. So, I'll suck it up and go have breakfast with the all-hearing werewolves if that will make her feel even the tiniest bit better.

We walk into the dining room and everyone turns to look at us. "Hey, everyone, this is Lettie." Even Osai is here today. Lord, I hope he wasn't here last night. At least there could be one person who doesn't think I'm a Jezebel.

Lettie seems to shrink about two sizes next to me. "Fuck that," she whispers. Never one to make herself appear smaller despite her tiny size, she stands a little taller and squares her shoulders. "Hi. It's nice to meet you all."

Everyone goes around the table to introduce themselves. Even Patrick.

"Sorry you got 'changed on'. I don't think anyone has had the pleasure of Luke losing control on them. At least I hope not." Easay winks.

"Eww, you make it sound so dirty." Lettie laughs a little and then walks toward the two empty seats between Patrick and Samuel.

"I am starving," Patrick says, grabbing pancakes and toast.

"Didn't you eat enough last night? Sure as shit sounded like you did." Samuel punches Patrick in the arm.

"Oh, God," I say, lowering my face to my hands just after Patrick shoves Samuel's head.

Easay pokes his hand with her fork. "Knock it off, you." Her voice is stern, but she's smiling.

Lettie tells her story to everyone and seems to lighten up a bit. I can tell she's starting to feel comfortable when she drops the F-bomb and doesn't even realize it.

Apprehension starts to settle in when breakfast is over. It's time to talk to Kerry. Even though I've been assured it's no problem that Lettie stays here, Kerry did refer to her as the "drunken human." When she said it last night, it sounded as if she'd tasted something too tangy.

As we round the corner to Kerry's office, Mr. Levay catches up to us. "I'll be tagging along with you two this afternoon on campus. I have papers to check."

I scrunch my face and look at the ceiling. "I guess that's werewolf speak for 'I'll make sure you don't get kidnapped and poked at.' "

He smiles and winks at Lettie. "Yes, Kayla, that's exactly what that means. Whenever Patrick leaves the manor, one of us will be on his heels. Yours, too. See you guys later."

"Come on in and have a seat, you two," Kerry says from her office.

We walk in, and Lettie looks as if she doesn't know where to sit until I shove her into the mahogany chair across from Kerry. If there is a Goddess, please help Lettie to keep her tongue. She curses when she's nervous. Or scared. Or if the sun or moon are in the sky.

Lettie instantly starts talking. "I understand if you want me to leave. I'm sure my family would be more than happy to let me stay with them. Besides, there's probably no need for me to even be here." Lettie starts tapping her leg with her fingers.

Kerry gives a brief shake of her head, brushing off Lettie's words. "Absolutely not. I don't believe you are in any danger, but just to be safe you should stay here. You're Kayla's family. And now she's our family, which means you're an in-law." Kerry smiles lightly and shakes her head. A joke.

Lettie and I both laugh with her. We know when we should laugh at someone's joke. Even if it's not that funny.

Lettie looks at her with caution. "But do you really think it's necessary? I don't want to impose."

"Luke is just a boy, and he's not yet in control of his emotions." Kerry tilts her head back and takes a slow, measured breath as if the stress of this whole thing is starting to get to her.

Lettie turns in her chair to face me. "Are you okay with this?"

"What? Why would you ask that? Why wouldn't I be okay with you staying here to be, you know, safe?"

She looks uncomfortable and then gestures to Kerry.

I turn in the chair to face her. "Don't look at her, Pix. Spit it out."

"I—I don't want to intrude. This is your area. Your...I don't even have the right words. I don't want to impose on your space."

My mouth is open so wide that flies and other flying creatures are probably on their way in. "Are you serious? Why would you be intruding? How could you think I would think that? You take me around your psychotic family all the time."

"My mom is happy that you have this going on, but she told me to keep my distance. Thought you might get territorial."

"And what did you think? Oh, never mind, I know what you thought."

Before I can stay angry at her, her eyes start to water. "I was so scared last night. I thought he was going to hurt me. I called my mom this morning and told her everything, and she told me to let your family protect you and for me to come home." No tears have fallen yet, but I can see her struggling to keep them at bay.

"Curse your mother's lips! Come on, Pix. Did you really think I'd be that way?"

She slaps her hand over her mouth. "No. Buh I dnt—"

"Move your hand, honey. I can't understand you."

She sniffs and moves her hand. "No. But I didn't want to seem selfish and have you think I was trying to keep you with me, since you feel guilty for wanting to move out. I don't want to hold you back. I just want what's best for you."

I shake my head and stand up so that I can hug her. "You are a dummy, do you know that? Lettie, you are the least selfish person I know, especially when it comes to me. You want me to be happy, and I adore you for that. And you're being really girly right now, so knock it off." I want to cheer her up.

Kerry clears her throat. Oh, right—she's still here in her office. "Good. I'm happy you both cleared that up. We wouldn't want any bad blood between you two, now would we? Lettie, if there is anything, you'd like to add to the grocery list, it's on the counter by the refrigerator. And I hope you don't mind, but I contacted two teachers at your school who are a part of the Maryland Pack. If anything happens while you're at work, they will be more than willing to assist you." She smiles sweetly.

Lettie's confused face almost makes me laugh. "How did you—"

"I told you," Kerry says with a triumphant smile. "We protect our family. What time will you two be leaving for class? Prudence will be coming over so that I can let her know what will not be permitted."

"We're leaving at eleven. Class starts at twelve." My voice is flat. Kerry didn't look too happy when she referred to Prudence. She looks pretty pissed off at the mere thought of that cow. Better her than me.

Chapter Nine

As the next couple of weeks go by, Lettie and I are treated as if we've always lived here and it's starting to feel as if we have. My mom called to let me know that she wasn't going to make it into town this month. Her current boyfriend surprised her with a vacation to some resort in Utah. "Have fun. See you whenever you're available, Mom." Yay for me. I don't think she would have fared well, if I told her not to visit because things were kind of weird. I think I was afraid that if I did tell her to stay away because I was in danger, she really would have.

We all fall into a steady routine. Watching Lettie try not to look at Samuel is more entertaining than she would like it to be. This all feels more like a rerun of some apple pie family that used to be on television in the 1950s and '60s. Not the home of werewolves.

It's almost easy to forget that I attended Craig's funeral two weeks ago, that his ex-wife told Hannah that she always believed they would get back together again, after they had both finished grieving for their daughter. I watched her tuck a small picture of their daughter into his jacket pocket.

I decided to leave those memories behind me at the church where his funeral service was held. Nothing would take away from the person he was. Craig was good to me. And that's all that matters. That's all I ever need to remember.

Every once in a while, I grab my phone to call him. A crippling pain decimates my heart, but I remind myself that he wouldn't want that for me. He wanted me to be happy.

It was easy to forget that Patrick and I are being guarded constantly when we're not at the manor or that Lettie is staying here to avoid any unwanted visits from psycho-boy Luke who is now calmly learning how not to be crazy—I mean impulsive—somewhere in Maine.

Most of my days are spent transcribing the tapes Kerry gives me, studying for school, or spending every moment being careful to divide my time between Patrick and Lettie. He's always telling me to make sure she's all right, and she's always telling me to go spend time with him. What other time Patrick and I are willing to sacrifice is spent listening to Kerry and Mr. Levay tell us about the mating ceremony we've chosen to go through. It's pretty much like a regular wedding ceremony, except you're taking vows before God and Lilith, the Goddess and creator of the werewolves.

We also "unite ourselves unto one another with the earth that is eternal," which means we get a thrice-blessed white ribbon soaked in our blood to wrap around our joined hands during the hand-tying ceremony. Our blood is then allowed to fall to the earth where we are united until death us do part. Kerry wants us to do a few of the older ceremonies since I'm human. She wants to make sure the bonding sticks. Apparently, there's an old wolf ritual where we mix our blood in a thrice-blessed chalice with other herbs and sacred red wine—where the hell would we get this wine?—let it sit under the full moon, and once the moon sets we drink it. I vetoed that idea right after the words finished flying from Kerry's lips. She looked a little disappointed.

For the first time in a long time, I'm alone. Lettie is visiting her parents, and Patrick is with Samuel and Seeley hunting deer. Poor Bambi.

I'm sitting in a small clearing on the property, reading my book and letting my toes dig into the lush green grass. My small, round bug repellant fan is whirring, and a warm breeze tickles my nose. It's quiet. I haven't had quiet in a long time.

Up until I met Patrick, I hated sitting in the grass. It made me itch, and mud makes me uncomfortable. It's messy. But now, it seems to talk to me. The earth whispers to me, telling me that this is my space now. It makes me feel alive and energized. Almost as if the sun shining on it brings oxygen forth just for me. It makes me feel powerful.

The rustling of bushes a few feet away pulls me from my thoughts. I close my book, uncross my legs, and stand up, hoping it's not someone from the Rogue Pack coming to kill us.

But there is no attacker. Only a huge brown and white wolf with black speckles across his back. The tips of his ears and the tip of his tail are black, and his beautiful hazel eyes glow like the afternoon sun. As he stands on all fours, his massive shoulders are high enough to reach mine while I'm standing.

Patrick.

"I've never seen you in wolf form. You're beautiful. And very big."

The wolf's tongue lolls out of his mouth and his eyes cross. I laugh and fall down to both knees. Patrick walks up to me and drops his pointed muzzle in my lap. I rub his warm, soft fur and scratch behind his ears. This is weird.

"Did you eat a poor defenseless deer?"

He shakes his head and sits down on his hind legs.

"A bunny?"

He makes a soft whining sound and then licks his lips.

"Poor bunny." I laugh and shake my head at the thought of a rabbit running for its life. "I'm sure it felt good to run free."

His head bounces a few times as he nods "yes."

"Well, you run around some more, and I'm going to head back to the manor. I'm sleepy."

Patrick sits up, points his muzzle toward the manor, and licks my face.

"Eww, don't do that. Go. Run. Have fun."

He gives a low guttural grunt and begins walking toward the manor.

"Such a perfect gentleman. I can make it back there all by myself you…"

He growls softly, circles around me, and gives me a push toward the house.

"All right, no need to be pushy."

If I didn't know it was Patrick, I'd be frightened. Werewolves, in their wolf form, stay away from public places, and I can see why. They are huge.

Kerry leans against one of the white columns under the back porch as Patrick and I approach the manor. Patrick grunts a "hello" at her, then trots back the way we came.

"How are you, Kerry?" I sit on the steps leading to the porch.

She rubs her arms and lifts her head to the sky. "I'm well. Still trying to figure out how to sort all of this out."

I shrug. "You will. I have faith in you."

Kerry turns to face me. "You do." It's more of a statement than a question. "You and Patrick have been brought together for a reason. And it's not for either of you to be killed. Of that I know."

"You've been worrying. I can see it. It'll work out."

She smiles. "And how do you know this, Kayla?"

"Like I said, I have faith in you." I touch her arm. "You are a descendant of Lilith. She was pretty badass. You are too."

I smile at her and walk into the manor, happy that amidst this chaos, our house is still our sanctuary.

****

We all sit on the porch after everyone, minus me and Lettie, went for a two-hour romp around the property. "Do you feel that?" I whisper to Patrick.

I know he hears me. Patrick and the rest of the Weres have gone tense, and their eyes are locked on Kerry, whose eyes have gone from their usual striking gold-yellow and pale blue to a deep black that reveals no iris.

I grab Lettie's hand and pull her toward the door. I don't know what's going on, but we can find out later.

A bone-chilling growl makes its way up Kerry's throat. It's deafening and makes every hair on my body stand at attention. "Son of a whore!" Kerry yells.

Lettie's hand tightens on mine as I pull harder. "Pix, let's skadoodle. Something's wrong."

Kerry continues to yell. "How fucking dare they

threaten me and my people!" She stands up, and a letter falls from her hands. She grabs the pillow-covered iron chair she was sitting on and throws it across the yard just before Lettie and I make it into the foyer.

She just dropped the F-bomb. Wow. Kerry is pissed, and I'm a little scared.

"They will have to go through my dead, putrid carcass if they think they will ever lay hands on you or Patrick," Kerry says, pointing at me.

"Umm…Thanks?" I'm almost afraid to speak. "We're going inside."

As Kerry begins to protest, Lettie and I hightail it to the kitchen.

I can hear Kerry yell, and I get the gist of what just happened. The Rogues sent a letter saying that they don't believe Patrick and I are really Bound to one another by Lilith, that us being Chosen for one another is a rumor that Kerry started to keep us safe. No human has ever been Chosen by Lilith. And if we are supposed to be together, they want to know why and they will find out, even if that means coming here to take me.

And now alone in the kitchen, Lettie and I wait for someone to tell us what to do next. We may talk a lot of shit, but when a queen and stoic pack leader gets furious, it's time to shut up and wait for instructions.

"Happy-fun life go poof," Lettie says in a squeaky voice. "At least for you two. They never even mentioned me. I'm cool sailing." She pretends to wipe sweat from her brow.

"This is serious, Lettie."

"I know. I was just trying to make you feel better." She gets up and starts rummaging around the kitchen for her nightly banana split. Lettie takes out two clear bowls to make me one too.

"Extra chocolate sauce and strawberries, please."

"*Oh*, living dangerously, eh?" She pulls more strawberries out of the refrigerator. "I'll take some extra with you. We can be unhealthy and gain weight together."

"I don't like dangerous, Lettie. Denial is always fun, and I've enjoyed doing it these past few weeks. They want me." I busy my shaking hands and start cutting up a banana.

"I'm going to ask Samuel out on a date when this is all over," she blurts out before shoveling a large spoonful of ice cream into her mouth.

"Okay. When did you decide he was more than just fun to look at? Has he, you know, shown interest, or are you just going to hop on his face as fast as you can?"

Taking the chocolate sauce, Lettie pours it right in her mouth. "We've been talking, usually when you and Patrick go do your dirties in your room, which by the way, you guys sound like a porno and I want to have sex like that at least once in my life. He taught me to play chess, and I've taught him how to play Phase Ten. I know this sounds crazy, but he's been putting on shirts the last few nights. I think it's his form of 'dressing up' for me." She wipes away chocolate sauce from her chin and stares at the chocolate. "Let's not eat all of the chocolate sauce. He and I might use it later. Ow, ow, ow, ow!" She jumps up and does a sexy dance and then sits back down.

"You're a mental case. Why don't you ask him tonight?"

"Because Queen Kerry seems off her rocker, and we all need to get serious and talk about you and

Patrick. So, what do you think is going to happen?"

Too many questions over banana splits. "Wait for Kerry to tell us what to do? Or stay holed up in here until those cattle-rapists have been caught. I really don't know, Pix."

"She'll figure it out. I'm sure the werewolves have ways of dealing with this stuff. We've got more talking to do, and I just finished my ice cream. I'll make another banana split and we can share it." She grabs another banana.

"Dude, make it a double. I feel the need to overeat tonight."

Samuel and Patrick come in with wary looks. Lettie manages to keep scooping ice cream from the container without looking at Samuel. I should have known.

Samuel goes and stands just this side of too close behind Lettie. "Can you make me one, too?" He smiles faintly and pulls the chocolate sauce out of her reach. "You can save that for later. Extra whipped cream please."

Lettie pauses briefly and looks at me with mortification. He must have heard her. She shakes her head and sucks in a breath. "Please tell me everyone didn't hear that. I keep forgetting you guys can hear a fish fart three miles away."

Samuel steps closer to her. "I only heard you because I was coming in with Patrick. So, he heard you."

"Yes, I did," Patrick says absently.

"The others are still talking. I'm sure they didn't hear you. Do what Kayla says; ask me out tonight. I'll say yes."

Patrick is doing a wonderful job of pretending he's not listening as he starts to pull the strawberries out of my bowl.

Samuel looks over the kitchen counter to me and winks. "In fact, I believe I'll ask you out."

"She likes almost all of the restaurants in Little Italy."

Samuel smiles and looks down at her. "Lettie, may I take you to Little Italy for dinner this weekend?"

She bites her top lip, clears her throat, and turns around to face him. "Yes. I would love to, Samuel."

Her voice cracks, and she looks in desperate need of a drink. As much as she ogles him, I'd think she'd be more happy than nervous. Aww, she really likes him.

Kerry comes into the room with danger in her eyes. "Kayla and Lettie, I forgot to tell you that I got you out of your lease at the apartment. Gerard, the pack leader in Maine, paid the fee to get you out of the contract, and Prudence is sending a check for three hundred and fifty dollars, your security deposit. When this is all over, I'm confident that you will get your apartment back, if that's what you want."

"Thanks," Lettie and I say in unison.

"Wait a minute. Why is Gerard paying the fee?" I ask Kerry.

"He takes responsibility for everyone in his pack, and as of last week, that includes Luke. He will be working it off until he has repaid Gerard. Until he feels that Luke is safe to leave the haven, he's under house arrest. More importantly, I'm going to send out an alert to all the pack masters—the Rogue Pack will be found, and I am charging everyone with their capture."

Lettie squinches her face. "Can we not move back

to the old apartment building? I'd like to move into an apartment where Luke can't find us."

Kerry gives Lettie a "poor human" look right before her face softens. "He won't be allowed to leave until Gerard deems him ready. You don't have to worry." She turns to me and Patrick as I poke his hand with my spoon to keep him away from my last strawberry. "You two are the ones that need to worry. I know that Patrick can work from home and so can you, Kayla. But school is what concerns me. Can you take a leave of absence?"

I shrug my shoulders. "My finals are coming up. I can't."

Mr. Levay appears out of nowhere. "I'll give you an exam here. We can go talk to your other professors and come up with some agreement. Maybe they'll let you take them early because of your family emergency."

"Is this what it's like when a human gets involved with a Were?" I keep looking at my bowl.

Mr. Levay walks closer to me and Patrick and sits on the chair across from us. "No. It's not. For some reason, they want you. They've killed nine wolves that have chosen to be with humans, and three of the humans were slain as well. Just a few months ago, in Texas, a werewolf named Jessica was killed, but her human husband was left alone. They had no children. Jessica was friends with a wolf named Alcott who is engaged to be married to a human. Alcott lived in a safe house with the Texas Pack leader. Alcott was left alone. He wasn't bothered because he was too close with the leader. At least that's my belief."

I eye the ice cream container and decide against it.

Emotional eating trying to rear its stupid head. "That doesn't make any sense. Patrick and I live here with Kerry, but neither of us can leave the manor without at least one of you with us."

Mr. Levay reaches for a banana. "Yes. You're correct. If you were just a normal human, I'm almost certain you would have been left alone. But somehow, Kayla, you are different. They're probably very interested in you. The letter said that they don't believe you've been Chosen. And if they do believe, as I suspect they do, they want to know why you're unique. We all feel it." Mr. Levay looks around the room.

Now everyone is staring quietly at me.

Patrick strums his fingers on the counter and then balls his hand into a fist. "You don't talk about her, but you all agree? Sounds like you've been talking about it." The knuckles on his hand are getting lighter.

I touch his shoulder. "Don't be upset. I get it."

"I don't get it." His voice lowers and he growls.

Kerry touches his shoulder. "Prudence said it first. There is something about you, Kayla, that is different. We feel it."

The silence is uncomfortable.

"All right, all right, stop gawking at her," Lettie orders. "Here's your ice cream." She puts the bowl in front of me.

"Thanks, Pix. I'm going to take this outside on the patio and eat it." Everyone, except Kerry, stares in different directions, not me. Her look isn't accusatory, just curious. As I begin to rise, Patrick pulls out my chair and follows me outside.

The rage roiling off Patrick is dense, like an oily film coating my skin.

"How the fuck is he doing that?" Samuel says as we leave the kitchen.

Doing what?

I turn around and see Kerry still looking at me. There is a hint of a smile on her full lips. "He's becoming dominant. And no, Kayla, that does not happen. One is either dominant or not." She lifts her coffee cup to me in a silent salute and winks.

Even outside the air is heavy with Patrick's fury. I'm usually able to ignore it, but this is different.

"Patrick, I know you're upset. Once they catch these people—"

"These aren't people, Kayla. These are hunters. Wolves. It's not like a crazy human killing other humans. They have patterns. Wolves are pack hunters, and they are getting away with killing. The only reason we know they are wolves is because they want us to know. The media doesn't know. The Rogues don't want them to know." He walks closer to me. "Your life is in danger, and I can't do anything to stop it. You can't imagine how that makes me feel."

I shrug. "You're right. I can't. You won't let me in. I can't help you. I can't help me."

"Kayla, you can't imagine the menacing hatred I feel right now. I want to kill something, rip something apart with my bare hands. My claws and teeth. And I want to taste their blood run down my throat. I can't let you in. You don't want that." He sighs and squats down, linking his hands behind is head in frustration. "Fuck! Go inside. I'm going for a run."

"Patrick, please."

"Damn it, Kayla. Can you just do what you're told? For once? I need…to kill. To fight. To fuck. But I don't want to hurt you. My wolf is fighting me to claim you with my bite and change you so that the whole fucking world knows you're mine."

"Okay." I turn toward to the door. "Be careful, and come back to me."

Before I can say anything, he turns away from me, taking off his shirt and draping it across the iron railing. The last thing I see before he disappears into the thicket are his pants and boxers falling to the ground and a hint of fur rushing through the trees.

Chapter Ten

"I'll be in my office finishing up some last-minute grading," Mr. Levay says, unbuckling his seat belt. "Patrick will be with me. Your class ends at three-fifteen," he points to me, "and Lettie's ends at three-thirty."

"Yes, it does," Lettie adds with a mock southern accent.

Mr. Levay looks at her, furrows his brow as though she confuses him, and turns back to me. "Kayla, Patrick and I will be there waiting for you when your class lets out. Then we'll wait for Lettie and head back to the manor. The campus will be filled with students and teachers. Too many people around for anything to happen."

I sigh and grab my book bag, "Got it. This sucks and seems more like a military operation than anything else, but I have it." I reach for the door to get out of Patrick's truck, step out into the warm breeze of May, and sneeze. "We need to stop off on the way back home so I can get some allergy medicine."

Lettie hands me a napkin from her purse and links her small arm around mine. "I'll walk you to class, Missy Kayla."

Patrick steps out and stands in front of us. "Steven and I will walk you both to class."

I nod my head and turn to watch Mr. Levay get his

briefcase out of the trunk. "Shall we?" he says, closing the trunk and walking ahead of us.

The three of us watch Lettie walk into the Cromwell Building where her class is, then Patrick and Mr. Levay walk me to Homewood.

Patrick kisses my forehead, pulls my book bag strap farther up my shoulder, and gives me a soft push toward the steps. "We'll be right here when you get out."

I turn to look at them both and smile briefly. "I know you will. Have fun helping Mr. Levay grade papers."

He frowns and shakes his head. "Yeah. Good times," he says stoically.

Aww, I think he's picking up my sarcastic ways.

One of my classmates sees me as I turn around to begin walking up the cement steps and holds the door open for me. "Thanks."

"No problem." She keeps in stride beside me. "Did you take the online quiz for class?" she asks as we walk down the hall to the classroom.

"Yup. I got an A. How'd you do?" I hold the classroom door open for her.

"When I pulled into the parking lot ten minutes ago, I remembered that I didn't take it. It was worth fifteen points, right?"

"No. It was worth five points. You turned in your extra-credit paper, didn't you?"

She looks a little more relieved. "Yes, I did."

"Well then, you're good."

She and I share more small talk as we wait for our teacher to get to class. Professor Summers is an older Hispanic gentleman who resembles the man on the

Monopoly box—he's short, keeps his dark graying hair cut so close he may as well be bald, and wears thin, wire-rimmed round glasses. He always wears some shade of dark tweed pants, a sweater vest, and a dark jacket.

It's already half past twelve, and he still hasn't arrived. Someone has already started a sign-in sheet to be taken to the English Department office. Everyone who signs the paper gets credit for being in class even though the teacher hasn't shown up.

My quiz-misser classmate is the last one to sign the sheet. "Maybe he posted something on the school website saying he wasn't going to be here. I'll slide this under his office door. See you next week during the final."

"Good luck on the quiz." I reach into my pocket to grab my cell phone to call Patrick and let him know to come get me. But someone bumps into me and grabs my left hand before I can get to my phone.

I look up, startled to see a man, a werewolf, staring into my eyes. His face is hard and angular with a square jaw that could almost resemble a snout if it weren't so flat. His eyes are pale green and glowing, and his hair is so light it almost looks translucent on his pale, pink scalp. He is a few inches taller than me, which puts him at about five foot eight, and his shoulders are so wide, I wonder how he made it into the building. Dark green pants, black boots, and a green shirt seem to be woven onto his fit body. His thick neck shows strained veins and skin. His face is calm. "Scream, and I'll break your fucking spine."

I close my mouth and let him push me back into the room, praying that someone is still left behind. But of course, it's empty. He kicks the door closed with his large, black booted foot.

He still hasn't let go of my hand, and when I try to pull away, he squeezes it and I let out a yelp. "Ah, ah, ah. No screaming. If anyone comes into this room and you signal them, I will kill them and then I will kill you. Do you understand?"

It's not really a question. He's letting me know what will happen if I react the only way my body is telling me to. "You're one of the Rogues, aren't you? And I'm guessing your sister doesn't live in our building, does she?"

"Mmm-hmm." His lips are pressed together so tightly there is only a thin pink line where his lips should be. "We're going to talk."

He squeezes my hand again, digging my nails into my palm. "Start talking so you can give me back my hand," I say, voice heavy with defiance and pain.

"I'm Gunther. I'm sure Kerry has had suspicions about me, and you're going to let her know that her thoughts were correct." He pulls me closer to him, puts his nose on my cheek and inhales deeply. I stiffen and fight the urge to pull away from him in fear that he'll squeeze my hand tighter. "You smell lovely. And different."

Eww. "Thanks?"

"You're not a wolf," Gunther says, staring into my eyes.

"That's not a question, Gunther."

He squeezes my hand. I hear my bones and joints cry under his pressure. "Don't be a smart-ass. Do you have wolves in your family?"

"No." My voice is strained. "Please, let go."

"Have you really been Chosen, Kayla?"

"Yes."

"Tell me about it."

Patrick. Patrick, please hear me. Patrick. "When we first met, we touched and there was a spark. Everyone in the room felt it." Patrick, please help me, but don't come alone. "I passed out. We can feel one another. We can sense what the other is feeling."

I smile as his face falters and he squeezes my hand even harder. I stifle a scream. I won't give him the satisfaction.

"So, he should be here shortly," he says, giving my hand a hard squeeze. I cry out as I feel my nails pierce my palm. Warm blood flows slowly down my hand onto my wrist. I look down and see the blood seeping between my fingers on to his.

"You know Kerry is going to kill you, right, Gunther?" I say through clenched teeth. "Not only is she going to kill you and the rest of your compadres— Ahhh." The snap of two of my fingers doesn't surprise me. I knew it was coming when I told him of his impending death. "But she has the Line involved. So, you've got everyone looking for you, you piece of shit. You'll have no peace, and you will die." My voice is shaky. False bravado. I'm pretty sure he's not here to kill me. He would have done it already.

He snarls and yanks my body against his by my hand. "We're not the only ones, you know. Your kind is polluting our blood. It's been happening more and more over the centuries, and I won't have it. We won't have it!" He sprays spittle onto the side of my face as I turn away from him. "I'm not the only one. There are many others who don't run with my pack that won't have it either. The day will never come when my kind are just as weak as yours. But we've been looking for you, Kayla. You, you were Chosen and—"

"Let her go, young man." Neither of us noticed Professor Summers steal into the room. He has a letter opener in his hand, and he's inching closer to us.

I turn back to Gunther and smile. "Getting a little slow, dog-boy? You didn't hear a weak human sneaking up on you?" I whisper so that only he can hear me. And then I feel Patrick getting closer.

Gunther lifts his head and cocks it to the side, sniffing. "Here comes your boy." He lifts our blood covered hands to his mouth and takes a long lick. "Mmm, the better to taste you with, my dear." He lets go of my hand, runs to the window, raises it, and jumps out.

Professor Summers follows him to the window and looks around. He closes it and then comes back to me. The fear and determination that were on his face give way to relief. Something tells me he wasn't sure whether or not he could have stopped Gunther. He would have been creamed, but he gets awesome points for trying. "Are you all right, Kayla?" He pulls a handkerchief from his right pocket and examines me to find out where the blood is coming from. I let out a yelp as he touches one of my fingers.

Tears break loose and start a fast track down my face. "He broke my fingers."

When Patrick and Mr. Levay burst into the room, my head is on Professor Summers' shoulder, and the sobs finally break through as Patrick touches my arm.

Professor Summers looks at them. "Steven, call the police. Someone attacked Kayla."

Patrick and Mr. Levay exchange wary looks. I sense from Patrick that they don't want to get the human police involved.

"Professor Summers," I say, lifting my head from his shoulder and turning to Patrick. "We can call them from the Emergency Room of Mercy General. It's the closest hospital. At least two of my fingers are broken." I look down and see that the bleeding hasn't stopped. "And stitches. I may need stitches."

Chapter Eleven

On the way to Mercy General, Mr. Levay makes a phone call while Patrick sits in the backseat with me. He's calling Kerry to make her aware of the situation and asking her to contact a physician who is a pack member at the hospital to treat me. They don't want the police to get involved. I should be bothered that we're not calling the police, but I understand. Even though he didn't kill or savagely beat me, this is still an attack against a human by a werewolf.

Humans don't know about the Rogue Pack. Your average human just thinks that werewolves are being killed for the simple fact that they are werewolves. If it went public that the Rogue Pack was killing Weres and humans because of their romantic involvement, it would cause undue tension to the human-werewolf relationship. People would live in fear of interacting with Weres more than they already do.

I sit up and tap Mr. Levay on the shoulder. "Tell someone to go get Lettie."

"Samuel is already on his way," he says quietly.

As we pull into the garage at the hospital, a tall thin woman in blue scrubs and a lab coat walks toward the car. She is handsome, if I would ever use that word concerning a woman, with shoulder-length brown hair and skin a little darker than my own. She looks no older than me. But when she speaks, the age in her voice comes through.

"If she needs surgery, I'll page a few other wolves to help." She peers into the backseat and eyes my hand. "But I think I should be able to set it myself."

"That sounds really painful," I say, pulling my hand from Patrick. He's barely said a word since we left campus.

"You'll be asleep during the setting. I'm Cybil. It's nice to meet you, Kayla. Congratulations to you both on your being Chosen by the Goddess." Goddess sounds like two separate words when she says it. "Come on. I have a room set aside for you all."

Mr. Levay gets out of the driver's side door and opens the back door for me and Patrick. "Do you need a wheelchair?"

I shake my head. "Nope. I'm good."

"I'll carry you." Patrick leans down to grab my legs.

"I'd like to walk, thank you."

We follow Cybil into the Emergency Room through the emergency exit. She leads us down a long white hall that smells clean and medicated, as if the hall itself has taken on the persona of what an Emergency Room should be like.

The cold, sterile, beige floors blend in delicately with the white walls that lead to the bitter and blinding fluorescent lights. It gives me the impression that once you come into this place, you don't leave. Every step I take somehow causes pressure on my fingers, which are throbbing and numbing at the same time. I use my right hand to cradle my left, protecting it from the slightest bit of wind that would sneak down this sealed-off hall just to cause me pain.

Cybil turns in to an open room being held open by a teenage boy in dark blue scrubs. His badge says Ronald Molin, Nurse Technician. "Blessed be, you two."

I nod my head and keep walking. I don't even bother to see Patrick's reaction. I'm in too much pain to make new friends.

"Lie down right here." Cybil points to a gurney in the far-left corner of the room.

Before I can walk any farther, Patrick picks me up as if he is carrying me to our bridal suite. He keeps avoiding my gaze.

Cybil takes a deep breath and then rolls her head to the side, baring her neck to him. "If you want to stay in here, you're going to have to dial down the dominance play," she says, looking at the floor.

Mr. Levay shakes his head and shows his neck, too. "How the hell are you doing that, Patrick? You've never—"

"Knock it off, Patrick. I don't know why you feel responsible, but I don't need you to feel that way right now. It's making me feel...heavy." It's the only word that comes to mind when I try to tap into his thoughts. He feels guilty.

Patrick takes a deep breath and closes his eyes, the dominant atmosphere in the room getting lighter. "I shouldn't have left you," he says, moving away from the gurney to let Ronald come stand next to me.

"You couldn't come to class with me. It would have been inappropriate and weird. This happened, but at least I know what that son of a bitch looks like. And his name. Gunther." I spit out his name as Ronald touches my hand.

Cybil interrupts. "Not now," she says, looking at Patrick. "I'll pull out the bed so you can go on the other side and hold Kayla's other hand."

"Yeah, Patrick," I say, slightly irritated. "That would be more helpful than feeling crappy about something you couldn't control."

"Now you knock it off, Kayla." Cybil wears an amused and irritated smirk. Good combination. "I'm going to give you a strong sedative, and when you wake up the two middle fingers on your left hand, will be taped and held together by a splint. Those seem to be the only ones that are broken. Ronald is going to get the portable x-ray machine."

Ronald hands her a syringe with a white, cloudy liquid in it while Mr. Levay stands at the door, concentrating on the Heimlich maneuver poster on the wall. Cybil ties a rubber tourniquet around my left arm just above the elbow, and I welcome the light prick of the needle. I want to apologize to Patrick for being snarky, but the sweet rush of drowsy pain relief sets in and my eyelids are weighted down.

"S-sorry, Patrick," I hear myself say dreamily.

"Not as sorry as they will be."

A still quiet takes over, and Gunther's voice is the last thing I hear reverberating in my head. We're not the only ones, you know, his voice says angrily.

We won't have it!

Chapter Twelve

"—seven-day supply of painkiller and then you can give her an NSAID after that. Since you two are Bound, you may be able to assist in the healing." Cybil's voice fades in and out, and I feel the sensation of being moved. "I'll come to the manor in a week to check on her. Call me directly if she develops a fever. Blessed be."

"Blessed be," Patrick responds quietly, and I feel his gentle touch on my shoulder. "Kayla? Cybil, she's waking up. Is this too soon?"

"No, not at all. Kayla, are you in any pain?" Cybil's voice sounds far away.

There is only numbness in my hand and heaviness in my head. I try to answer, but my words sound slurred and vacant.

"She's fine. Take her home and put her to bed. See if you can help her heal a few days a week," Cybil says as someone, no doubt Patrick, picks me up.

He lays me across the back seat of the car. There's a pillow for me to lay my head on. I feel Patrick slip into the back seat of the car and put the pillow and my head on his lap. The car starts, and the steady sound of the engine and the feeling of motion lull me back to sleep.

****

"What the hell happened to her?" Lettie's voice is

high and worried.

"Gunther. A Rogue is what happened to her." Patrick sounds as if he's trying to keep his patience with her.

"Well," she says. "Did you kill him?"

"No, Lettie. I didn't. It happened before I got there. Her class was cancelled and…Let me put her to bed, and then we'll talk." He sighs, and I feel the bed beneath my body. "Can you get her pajamas out of that drawer so I can get her ready for bed?"

"I can change my own clothes, thank you both very much." It took every bit of concentration to talk to them with a steady voice. The sedative is slowly wearing off, and I refuse to let them change my clothes.

"So very happy you're awake now and I don't have to take off your shirt," Lettie says. "You're ta-tas are bigger than mine. Makes me jealous."

"Very funny, Pix. Can I have some water?"

"Sure, honey. I'll be right back." I hear Lettie's soft footsteps trailing away from us.

"Patrick?"

"Yes."

"I'm sorry if I was mean to you earlier. My fingers were the ones being rude to you, not me. They were speaking from their pain." I reach to touch his face, but the throb in my hand makes me pause and I pull back.

"I deserved it and more. I'm supposed to protect you, and I did a piss-poor job of it." His face is unreadable, and his emotions are filling the room like some dark perfume diffusing through the air.

"You're supposed to be there for me, and that's not what you're doing. All you see is what you didn't do and what you had no control over. Just stop it." I clear my throat and soften my voice. Both of us getting angry doesn't make this better. "This won't go on for much longer. We know who he is now. I'm sure that helps. And once Kerry finds him, it's over." I try to sit up, unsuccessfully, and he grabs my arm and pulls me up. "You and I will get to go out together. Alone. And we won't have to worry about this anymore. But you can't let your anger get the better of you."

He leans in and gives me a lingering kiss on my forehead and then looks down to my splinted fingers. "You're right." He sighs. The right side of his lips curves slightly. "You're quite helpless. Bathing and dressing are going to be a problem. I'll have to help you do that." He comes closer and gives me small pecking kisses all over my face.

"You'll have to help me bathe?" I whisper into his mouth.

"I'm sure you're very dirty right now." He pulls my left leg over his waist so that I'm straddling him. "You have to take your clothes off."

I suck his bottom lip into my mouth and bite it. He moans quietly and uses one hand to cup my bottom. The hard bar of his cock is thick beneath his pants. "I have to close the door."

He pulls away from me to stand, and it's my turn to moan. I latch on to him, locking my arms around his neck and my legs around his waist. "I'm a koala bear, and you're the tree. Where you go, I go. Put the lock on so Lettie won't come in."

He cups both of his hands under my bottom and carries me with him to the door. "Should we wait until she brings the water and leaves?"

"Nope. Lock it. She'll get the message."

The back and forth movement of Patrick walking us to the door and then to the bathroom vibrates through my hand, but I fight to keep a straight face. He already feels like crap, and I don't want him to think he's causing me any pain.

"Do you know how fucking beautiful you are?" Patrick asks as we cross the bathroom threshold. Hunger is in his gaze as he looks at me.

His brown eyes flash reflectively when he turns on the bathroom light. I lean in and kiss his nose. "Do you know how big my head is going to be if you keep saying things like that?"

He lowers my feet to the bathroom floor and then cups the back of my head, bringing me close for a kiss. His lips are soft against mine. I let out a soft moan as his tongue brushes against mine. I don't think I'll ever get used to how soft and gentle he can be even though he has a massive wolf inside him.

His eyes are on mine as he unbuttons my shirt, and he's careful not to touch my hand when I pull my arms through. Lowering himself before me, he kisses a fiery path from my neck to my belly button. My body jerks as he bites the sensitive flesh at my waist.

"Can I have these?" he asks, motioning toward my pants.

I shrug and shake my head, and I can feel a playful grin tugging at my lips. "I don't think so. What are you going to give me in return?" This is fun.

He pops open the button and uses his teeth to pull down the zipper. The sound echoes through the room. The heat of his warm mouth blows across my belly, and goose bumps erupt all along the skin of my stomach and chest, all the way up to my arms.

"Hmm," he says, using both hands to pull down my pants and panties. He scratches his nails along my legs, and the sensation shoots heat directly to my core. "What am I going to give you?" He taps on my leg and points toward the ledge of the shower. When I lift my leg and place my foot on the ledge to give him better access to my already aching pussy, he says, "For starters, my mouth."

With his eyes still locked on mine, he parts my folds with the tip of his tongue and licks up my cleft. I let out a steadying breath as his tongue is about to reach the apex of my slit, but he stops and kisses the inside of my thigh. He does this over and over again, licking me but avoiding the now throbbing bundle of nerves that yearns for his kiss. When I try to move my hips forward, he grabs my legs to keep me in place.

"Patrick." I hold on to the shower curtain with my good hand. I should probably find something else to hold on to. If I go tumbling down into the shower and hurt myself, Patrick may decide to stop touching me. "Are you teasing me?"

"Yes. Are you going to be a good girl and keep your hand out of the path of the water when we get in?"

Right now, I'd do just about anything to have him make me come, to feel him move inside me. I nod my head and bite my bottom lip to keep from growling in frustration. I want him now.

He smiles and rewards me by pulling my clit into his mouth and flicking it with his tongue.

My hips buck forward, and I let go of the shower curtain and grab onto his head, pulling him closer to me and grinding my pussy into his mouth.

"Please," I whimper. "I want you inside me."

His hands glide over my thighs and up my legs as his tongue laps at me, as his teeth nip at my flesh. He flicks and laves, faster and faster, rushing me closer and closer to orgasm.

I massage my hand over his face and neck, watching him as he watches me. My panting and moaning, and the slick sounds of him eating me fill the room. He slides two of his thick fingers into my empty channel, curving his fingers perfectly to hit that sweet spot just inside.

A low growl works its way up his chest and through his mouth, and the vibration against my core sends me over the edge. "Patrick!" He keeps nipping and tasting.

When he finally wrings every ounce of pleasure from me, I grab him by his shirt and pull him up to stand in front of me. With one hand, I tug his shirt over his head. I pause to look at him as he slides his pants down his legs. His cock bounces free and seems to point right at me.

"Come here." He steps into the shower and then brings me with him.

I can taste my lust on him as his lips crash into my lips and his tongue strokes roughly against mine, his hands touching every part of my body. He reaches over and turns on the water and pulls my body away from the falling spray until the temperature is just right.

"Turn this way." He grabs me by my waist and turns me around so that my bandaged hand is sticking out of the curtain.

His warm tongue trails up my shoulder and then up the side of my neck. There is a lovely lick of pain as he bites my ear, and it sends a rush of liquid warmth between my legs. Patrick uses his hand and angles my hips toward him, and I feel the hot length of his cock against me.

I am completely open to him. My body, my heart, my mind. He is in every part of me. A slow smile stretches across my face with the realization that he is mine. No matter what's going on in the world or who is trying to find us, Patrick is mine. And I am his.

His cock slides along my waiting entrance, teasing me. He rubs himself against the wetness of my slit, coating himself with my passion. With gentle and slow ease, Patrick begins to slide inside me, and I can feel my body stretching to accept him.

"*Fuck*," he draws out, as he fully buries himself within my sheath. "You feel so good."

Running his palms up my torso to cup both my breasts, he pinches my nipples as he slowly, torturously pulls out of me and then slams back into me.

I try to reach back and grab his hips to make him go faster, but he says, "Pull that fucking hand back into the shower again, and I'll stop. Do you want me to stop?" He makes slow circles with his hips and grinds against my ass.

"No," I say in a low, trembling voice. "Please don't stop. Faster. Go faster."

His hips start to piston against mine, and the sound of his wet skin slapping against mine fills the bathroom. I close my eyes as he tweaks my nipples with the rhythm of his taking me.

"Good girl." He moves one of his hands down to where our bodies meet.

He starts to rub firm circles around my clit, and he leans forward and clamps his teeth on my shoulder blade. The thought of him sinking his teeth into me and claiming me forces me to orgasm. His body is pressed against the length of my back, but his hips are still thrusting. A low feral snarl rumbles in his chest, and his cock begins to swell within me.

I call out his name as his hand cups my sex, his seed pouring into me and warming me from the inside out. My whole body is trembling. He kisses along my shoulders and neck, adoring my body.

"Kayla," he whispers. "When this is over, will you let me claim you? Fuck the ceremonies. I want to claim you as mine."

I'm already panting from our lovemaking, but my breath catches in my throat and my heart trips over itself. I hadn't really thought of being Changed. It occurred to me, but I never really and truly considered it.

"Don't answer now. Just know that I would be honored if you were to bear my mark."

With my back still to him, I smile and nod. "Yes, I'll think about it." I glance at him briefly over my shoulder and see a line of worry between his eyebrows. Was he nervous to ask me?

"Come on," he says, pulling his semi-hard cock out of my now-tender entrance. "Let's get cleaned up and dressed for dinner."

****

Kerry takes a sip of her water and stares at me with unblinking golden-yellow and pale blue eyes. "What did Gunther look like?"

"A 'roid-monkey, boot-camp drill instructor." I feign a smile. "By the way, he says hello." I sit down and reach for my water. It's time to take a pain pill.

"Professor Summers came out of his house to find two of his tires were flat," Mr. Levay adds when I finish the story. "He called the school, but the English Department office is closed on the weekend. No doubt Gunther, or one of his lackeys, was responsible for the flat tires. He must have really wanted to check you out."

"That's frightening." I point at the iced tea pitcher. Lettie pours a glass for me.

"This may sound strange," Kerry begins, "but did he say why he came for you and not Patrick? With the other slayings of wolves seriously involved with humans, the wolves were targeted. Did he say anything?"

I think about the question for a few moments, but nothing comes to mind. "No. He just went on about not having the bloodline polluted. Wait." My voice rises. "He licked the blood from my hand which really added to his 'I'm creepy' effect."

The better to taste you with, my dear.

I shudder and look at Kerry, who's still staring at me. "Sorry, Kerry. That's all I have."

She sighs. "Well, at least we know who he is. I'll call the rest of the Line this evening. Everyone will be alerted, and we will find them." Her words have a sense of finality.

"Guess I won't be typing for a while," I say, trying to fill the uncomfortable silence.

"Cybil called a little while ago and suggested using your bond to heal. She said that the first time may be a little uncomfortable for you. It should get easier each time. It may not even work, though I am interested in seeing if it does."

Oh, goodie. I get to be a science project. Patrick reaches into his pocket and hands me one pain pill. "Thanks."

"You sure you don't want two?"

Kerry holds up her hand. "No. She'll need to concentrate with you." She looks at me. "We want you to be alert, not fighting to stay awake."

I shrug and take another sip of water. "We'll meet you on the back porch when you're finished making your phone calls. I want to stretch a little."

Patrick and I step outside, and he hands me a packet of tissues.

"Just in case you start sneezing." He laughs and then grows quiet as a cool breeze flows by and tickles our faces. Patrick smooths a few strands of hair from my face. "After we try healing your hand, I'm going to shift and go for a run. Interested?"

"Not so much. Don't want my hand bouncing around just yet. And since mending bones sounds painful, I may not feel up to it later. I'll be waiting on the porch when you finish." I take a step toward him and put my head on his shoulder.

"If this doesn't work—"

"Then it will be just fine. Cybil was doubtful that it would work with me. I'm only human," I say, teasing him. "Kerry's doubtful too, but she's so interested in it because she's not even sure anything will happen. I'm kind of curious myself."

The screen door squeaks open. "I've made the phone calls," Kerry says, walking toward us. "By tomorrow morning, Gunther and his Rogues will have nowhere to hide. He should be in custody very soon." The look in her eyes is almost malicious.

"Sounds awesome," I say, pulling away from Patrick. "I'd like someone to break a few of his bones."

"Come," Kerry says. "Let's walk a little way from the house where we won't be interrupted." Kerry leads us away from the house and points to the ground. "Please, sit. You're going to be pulling energy from the earth through Patrick. The ground is firm, and the dew is gone."

"Sounds good." I plop down with a thud on the not-so-soft grass.

Patrick sits down across from me and lifts his nose to the sky. "There's going to be a thunderstorm tomorrow. It could wash some of the pollen away. Your hay fever should calm down after that."

I look at him and then to Kerry. Until now, it never occurred to me how comfortable they look outside. All the werewolves. Their bodies seem to spread out and relax when they are outdoors. Kerry's limbs seem more graceful, if that's possible, and Patrick looks like a child sitting in the grass, marveling at the new growth and the fresh smell of the coming summer.

Kerry stretches and then comes to kneel beside us and takes off her shoes. "Patrick, hold Kayla's right hand in both of yours." She leans toward me and presses her right forefinger to the center of my forehead and for some reason, I become calmer. Kerry then begins to take the splint and bandages off my hand. Thank God the painkiller is working. "Kayla, lay your hand on the ground."

I turn my palm to face me and see the dark sutures in the center of my hand. The two broken fingers that are still taped together look odd. I know they're broken, but they just look...helpless. That's the only word I can use to describe my broken fingers. The same way I felt when Gunther was holding my hand. The bastard.

Even though the painkiller is working, my hand begins to throb as I lay it on the ground. "I'm not going to be able to lay them like this for long. I think the splint keeping my fingers straight makes it feel better."

"Do you want more pain medicine?" Patrick asks.

"Nope. I've already had enough. Kerry wants me alert, not drooling and falling asleep." I squeeze his left hand with mine and smile.

Kerry interrupts by placing her hand on the tops of ours. "I'm not sure if this is going to work, but it's worth trying. I want you both to close your eyes and imagine the light of the earth beneath you. The world is alive, and the energy of it swirls through the earth. Imagine the light of the energy being pulled up through Patrick, into your right hand, and then focus that energy to your left hand." Her voice sounds melodic. "Visualize that power of the light working through your broken fingers, mending them. See the light heal the wounds on your palm. Envision that scene and concentrate on it. Patrick, feel the warmth of the earth flow up from the ground, through you and into Kayla. Breathe deeply."

Kerry's voice is soft and steady. My eyes are closed, but I can feel her gaze on me. "Do you feel anything?" she asks.

Patrick's grip on my right hand tightens briefly and he exhales deeply. "I don't feel anything. Do you, Kayla?"

I keep my eyes closed. "Nope."

"Keep concentrating," Kerry says.

Kayla.

"What? I'm sorry," I say to Kerry.

She shakes her head and motions for me to close my eyes.

Patrick's hand is warm on mine, but I don't feel anything coming from him. I squeeze my eyes together and try to picture a green light pooling beneath us and flowing through his body.

Let me in, Kayla.

Wow. That pain medicine is something. I open my eyes and look at Patrick. He's still concentrating. Kerry is staring at us, and when she realizes that I'm looking at her, she shrugs her shoulders. It was worth a shot.

"It's okay, Patrick," I say pulling my hand from his. "We kind of figured it wasn't going to work. No harm."

He opens his eyes and smiles briefly. "I know. Still don't like it when you hurt."

I lean back, placing my right hand behind me on the ground, and look at my stitches. "It looks funny. The stitches. They look like they don't belong. Like they're angry to be in my hand." I stare at the thick black thread interrupting the natural look of my palm and the white tape wrapped around my two middle fingers.

Kerry stands up and looks at the sky. "Cybil will be over next week to take them out. You'll be wearing a splint for a few weeks though." She reaches out her hand and helps me off the ground.

"I'm going to stay out here and go for a run. Interested?" He motions to Kerry.

She clears her throat and points to the house. "Samuel and Easay had planned on a hunt when we were finished. Let's head back to the house, and then we can all go."

"Let me get my bandages off the ground," I say, stooping down to collect the white material. "It would have been nice to not have to wear the splint for the next few weeks." As I try to stand up, my head swims, and I fall to my knees.

Come to me, now.

"Too much painkiller. I need to lie…" I begin. And then, somehow, the grass starts growing really fast toward my face.

****

Do you feel the light, Kayla?

"I don't know. Is it supposed to feel warm?"

Yes, it's supposed to feel warm.

Her voice seems to be a part of this place. It comes from everywhere. Even from my insides.

I breathe deeply, feeling my lungs expand. "I like it. It feels nice. This is good."

You can rest here, for a while. But not too long, she says sweetly.

"Why? Because he's not here?"

No, child. You know why.

"Yes. I know," I say with disappointment. "Because if I stay too long, I won't want to leave. I won't want anything but to be here. With you. This is the place that Father made for you, isn't it?" I already know the answer.

Yes.

I feel her caress my face. "It's coming, isn't it?"

Yes, Kayla. It's coming. That's why I couldn't wait for you any longer. I had to bring you here. All will be made clear to you. She kisses my forehead.

"Will I be ready?" Maybe if she tells me that I will

be ready, that will make it so.

You will be strong.

I furrow my brow.

She laughs. It sounds like a wind chime dancing in the wind. *Strength is all you need, Kayla. And your family. You know the Father is always with you.*

"He's always been with me. And you are too, now, aren't you?" It's all becoming clear to me. Everything is clear in this place.

I can feel the warm grass beneath my body, but the light that comes from everywhere doesn't allow me to see everything. To see her.

Yes. I've always been with you, too. Her voice is carried by the wind. It whispers and embraces me.

"Please, don't make me leave. I want to stay with…"

****

I sit up straight with a snap and hear a soft "oomph," as I connect with someone sitting too close to me on the bed. It's Lettie. And I've knocked her on the floor. "Oww," I drone. "My fingers."

"They're broken, genius," Lettie says as she gets off the floor. "Kayla, are you all right? I was standing on the porch when you went down like a ton of bricks. I thought you might have broken your nose."

"I need to talk to Patrick and Kerry." I get off the bed and look for my slippers. "Sorry for knocking you down, Pix."

She follows me as I open the door and find Patrick already standing there with his hand reaching for the knob. "Are you all right?"

I grab his arm. "I'm great. Let's get Kerry and head back outside. Has she left for the run yet?"

Curiosity and unease blanket his face. "Kayla, that was yesterday. You've been asleep since yesterday. It's Sunday morning."

"What?" It's not possible. "We were just outside. I couldn't have slept the whole—What am I talking about? Of course, I could have. It doesn't matter."

I pull him toward the stairs. Everything makes sense now. Well, more sense than it did yesterday.

"Kayla," Kerry says as she meets us at the bottom of the staircase. "What's going on?"

"I'm going to try to explain it, but I have to show you something first. At least, I hope I do."

I lead Patrick, Lettie, and Kerry out of the back door through the kitchen. Patrick's arm is still in my hand, and once we're about thirty yards from the house, I stop and plop down on the grass bringing Patrick with me. I thrust my splinted hand at him. "Take this off." He doesn't protest.

I look at Kerry. "You wanted to tell me something yesterday. What was it?"

She shrugs and sits down on the grass across from Patrick and me. "I was going to tell you that I wanted to have DNA testing done on you. There has to be a reason for you being Bound to Patrick. Maybe one of your ancestors could have been a Were. I didn't want to pry, but I have to appease my curiosity. If you don't mind."

Lettie pulls her short purple skirt close to her legs and sits down. "No disrespect, Kerry, but that's kind of weird."

Kerry looks reluctant. "Saying it out loud, it does sound a bit intrusive. I'm sorry, Kayla."

I shake my head and shrug it off. "It's fine. I would

have let you. I was interested myself. But now, I don't think you need to do any testing." I smile at her and turn to Patrick. "You ready?"

"For what?" He smiles.

"I don't know," I say quietly as I lean forward to kiss his lips.

"You seem funny," Lettie says, eyeing me cautiously.

I smile and shrug.

The stitches protest as I lay my hand on the ground and they are stretched tightly against the cool grass. I inhale deeply and close my eyes, picturing a light beneath us all, pooling in the earth. "Heal."

And with that one word, a jolt of energy hits my hand from the ground beneath. I scream out in pain and shock as the bones in my hand instantly mend and the tight stitches are ejected from the skin of my palm. "*Ouch!* My fingers!" I yell, yanking them away from the ground and pulling my hand to my chest to cradle it. Like that'll make it better. I wiggle the fingers, all the fingers, of my left hand and then ball my hand into a fist.

"Dear Goddess," Kerry says with wide eyes.

"What the fuck was that?" Lettie screams as she jumps up from her seated position. "I just felt…"

"Power," Kerry answers in a low voice. "It's pure earth energy." She shakes her head violently. The tears that have begun to stream down her face make a zigzag pattern on her sharp cheekbones. "Not even the strongest witch can do that. My—Kayla, are you Lilith? Are you our Goddess?"

"No, Kerry, I'm not Lilith. I'm her daughter."

Chapter Thirteen

"Why are you looking at me like that?" I ask Patrick.

He's staring at me, and I can sense the butterflies zooming around inside him. A line between his eyes keeps fading in and out as his curious nature appears not to know whether to grab me and fuck me or bow down and worship me.

He averts his eyes and I can't see his expression, but his emotions are rolling off him in colorful waves. "Because I love you. Because you are fucking amazing and I need to touch you, but I don't want to make you uncomfortable in front of everyone."

"Patrick—"

"Because you are the living child of our Goddess and creator, and you're mine."

"And I'm still me."

"And you're still you. And you have no idea how powerful you are, do you? The same you that you were yesterday, but between yesterday and since you woke up, your power has…You feel bigger and heavier than Kerry." He smiles, and his head cocks to the side like a curious animal.

I swallow, trying to figure out whether this is a good thing or a bad thing. "Does that bother you?"

He shakes his head, and that small smile turns into a wicked grin. "No. It makes me want to drag you into the middle of that field over there and claim you. I can see it. Just like I saw it when we first touched. I want to fuck you and tame you. I want to sink my teeth into your shoulder and make you more mine than any ceremony could ever do."

The screen door slams from the house. I jump. Letting out a shaky breath, I watch as everyone in the house files out behind Kerry. When I look back to Patrick, his eyes shine bright as the stars. I fight everything inside me to crawl closer to him, on top of him, and let him make good on what he wants.

"I'm patient," he says. "I'll wait until you beg me to claim you with my wolf, but I'll settle for fucking you until you can't see anything but me."

Holy crap. That was freaking hot.

"Well," Lettie says as she reaches us first. "I can't wait for you to tell me what the hell is happening." She sits down and then pulls blades of grass from the dirt and throws them at me.

I glance at Patrick one more time and try to tamp down on my need for him. "Don't worry, Pix." I clear my throat. "As soon as everyone sits down, I'll tell it all." I close my eyes for a moment and imagine the place of light I was in. With her. My mother.

And then I see me and Patrick in the field. Him taking me from behind as blood from his bite pours from my shoulder between my breasts. My eyes snap open, and I look at him. No raging pheromones around everyone in the house.

Samuel gets close and then slams to a stop. "How the fuck are you doing that?" he says, baring his neck to Patrick.

Kerry comes closer, walking past Samuel with a

smirk, and sits down next to me. "You made him dominant. You are making him an alpha. I don't know how, but I have a theory." She looks at me and nods her head once. "Only an alpha could be the mate of Lilith's daughter."

I shrug and look around at everyone. She's got a point.

"What's going on?" Mr. Levay asks as he takes off his shoes and socks and then sits down, pressing his feet into the grass.

Easay lies down on her stomach, cradling her cheeks in her palms. She motions her head toward me. "You're not wearing your splint."

"Yeah." I sigh.

Everyone sits in silence as they wait for me to speak. Their gazes are trained to me, but right now, I don't mind. "This is going to be a lot. So please, no one interrupt me. I don't want to lose track of the story myself.

"You all know the story of how Lilith was ejected from the Garden of Eden because she was too headstrong for Adam. He loved her, but he couldn't deal with her. She was too much like him, and he needed someone to help him, not be his equal. But what no one knows is that Lilith was with child when she left Eden. Lilith knew she didn't need or want Adam, but she coveted the child he'd given her. He tried to stop her from being who she really was. Lilith also convinced herself that she didn't need God. God didn't turn away from Lilith. She turned away from Him. And in doing that, she turned away from His grace.

"When her daughter Lila was born, Lilith did all she could to take care of the little girl. And she loved that child more than anything in the world. So much so that she gave her up. Lilith couldn't take care of Lila. She was alone in the world and fought for the little bit of food and resources she had. So, when Lila was a few months old, Lilith took her back to the Garden of Eden and begged the angel who guarded the gates to bring Eve to her. Lilith appealed to Eve as a woman, as a mother to be. And Eve took the little girl and promised to take care of her as if she were her own. To ensure that Lilith would live and one day return to claim her child, Eve gave her fruit from the Tree of Life."

Lettie raises her hand. "I'm sorry to interrupt, but I thought that the Tree of Life was forbidden?"

I shake my head. "No, that tree wasn't. You're confusing it with the Tree of Knowledge. God told them that they could eat from the Tree of Life but that they had to stay away from the Tree of Knowledge, or they would know the things that He knew. God intended for us to live in harmony with Him forever. But the wonder of woman was too strong, and she fell prey to the whispers of the serpent, and that's when all hell broke loose. But that came later.

"While Lila, Adam, and Eve were still living happily in Eden, Lilith struggled, and her hatred for God grew. So much, that it infected her entire being. For hundreds of years while Adam and his family were happy in Eden, Lilith thrived on hatred and let it consume her. The Devil fell in love with her abhorrence of God and imbued her with gifts to sway her to his side. He gave her the gift of the craft, which she later used for the good of humanity. And from that craft came the knowledge of potions, being able to move through space and dimensions, shape-shifting, foresight, and the Power of Spoken Word, which I just used to heal myself. This is where witches come from. They are descendants of Lilith. Just like werewolves. And just like vampires."

"Fucking vampires!" Lettie screams. "Are you serious? There are fucking vampires?"

Kerry interrupts before Lettie starts screaming more obscenities. "There are many things in this world humans don't know about. We were the only ones who chose to openly live among humans."

Patrick and Mr. Levay nod in agreement.

"Can you please finish?" Easay asks with impatience.

"Anyway," I continue, "once the Devil had given her these powers, she still didn't join him. But by the time he figured it out, she had found a way to bind those powers to herself. He couldn't take them away from her. But she continued to suffer. And that's how Cain, son of Adam, the first vampire was made. I know I'm drawing this out, but you have to know everything to understand where I fit in.

"Lilith was wandering looking for water when she came upon a man. He had an animal skin full of fresh water, and Lilith saw him drinking it. She pleaded for some of his water, but he laughed at her." I close my eyes and see the scene play out before me, as if I were there with them. "He took the satchel to his mouth and drank the water, all of it. It ran down his beard. Cain was angry because he felt that God loved his brother, Abel, more than He loved him. But he took it out on the wrong person. He threw the satchel to the ground and called her terrible names, and she attacked him.

"She was so thirsty that she jumped on him and

began sucking the water from his beard. But when they both fell to the ground, because of her momentum, he hit his head on a rock and was knocked unconscious. But she still continued to suck the water from his lips and in doing so, she nicked his lip and began drinking his blood, along with any water that was left. Lilith realized that the warm taste of his blood was almost as satisfying as the water. So, she bit into his neck and began drinking his blood. He woke and tried to scream, but Lilith covered his mouth with her hand to quiet the noises. He bit her, deeply. He didn't mean to. But as her blood began to pour down his throat, he became polluted with her hatred.

"Cain lay still as her poison infected him, taking over his body. She thought she'd killed him, so after draining much of his blood, she ran. She was ashamed of what she'd done. And when night fell, Cain arose. He was no longer just Cain; he was something tainted by Lilith's detestation. He also had the nectar from the Tree of Life that was running through her veins, now running through his. And he was ready for a kill. He didn't yet know that blood would sustain him; he just knew that if his brother Abel were dead, he would be loved most. That hatred that she felt was the reason for the first murder ever in history.

"Even though she hated so much, she still had humanity left in her heart. That's why she didn't try to get her daughter back. She knew that she wasn't fit to raise a child.

"Anyway, time went on, and as she scavenged for food, she fell in with a pack of wolves. They took pity on her and helped her secure the food and water she needed. And when it was cold, they let her sleep with them for warmth. The wolves are what softened Lilith's heart—their love and loyalty to one another. And to her. To reward them, she shifted herself into a wolf and lay with the leader of the pack whom she called Rovosfeld, to make the wolves more than just beasts. She ran with the pack in her wolf form until it was time to bear her children. She even turned some of the female wolves into women so they could breed with men. After the women got pregnant, she turned them back into wolves."

Werewolves. They were not like werewolves are today. But that was all that was needed to start a new species.

"There are many more stories of her offspring, but that's not important now. She finally saw that she had been wrong to turn away from God, so she went to Him and begged for His forgiveness."

"And of course, He gave it to her," Patrick says.

I smile and touch his hand. "Of course. He told her that it was all she needed to do. That everything that had happened to her happened according to His will and His plan. Eve was to be the mother of all humans. Lilith was to be the mother of all supernatural beings, but Lilith's one human offspring would help unite the supernaturals. As a reward for her return to grace, He gave her a bite of fruit from the forbidden Tree of Knowledge and she saw what was to come—a war between supernatural beings that would destroy most lives on this planet. He also gave her fruit from the Tree of Life that would blossom in a dimension that He had made just for her.

"Lilith went back and found Adam and Eve, to take back her daughter. It took a while to find them because they were no longer in the Garden of Eden. And when she found them, she learned that Lila had died sometime before Lilith came for her. But Eve did a wonderful thing—she kept Lila's body and asked God to bind her life force to that body until Lilith's return so that she could give a final farewell to her only human child. And He did. God allowed Lilith to take Lila's life force with her, to keep until the time was right." I pause for dramatic effect. I'm so tired of talking.

Kerry speaks up before a full five seconds have passed. "Time for what? That can't be the end of your story."

"Nope, it's not. When God gave Lilith a bite of the fruit from the Tree of Knowledge, she saw what could happen if everything was timed just right. When the time came, Lilith was to bear Lila back into the world through a mortal host. That child would align herself with Lilith's most powerful and most favored group of supernaturals, so that they could stand behind her and unite all the offspring of Lilith and stop them from having a power struggle that would bring this planet, this Paradise that God made for us all, to its knees.

"And apparently, werewolves are her most powerful, loyal, and headstrong creation. You are her most favored handiwork because of your characteristics, that have been a part of you since the beginning of time. Your ancestors taught her what it was like to have a family. What it was like to have a leader that did what was right for you, even if you didn't see it that way. The wolves showed her that God didn't love her any less than Adam or Eve. He guided her steps from the beginning to bring her where He wanted her to be."

All the Weres look as though they were treading a thin line between confusion and pride. Lettie just looks confused.

"How do you know all of this?" Lettie asks.

"After I passed out last night, Lilith pulled me into her dimension."

I can see the question on Kerry's face before she even gets a chance to ask it.

"I don't know what it looked like. I don't know what she looks like. It was so bright and warm. I couldn't see. I've never felt so close to God as I did in that place. This world has been changed so much by human hands. Her dimension was pure, fresh. Untouched." I close my eyes and try to bring her voice back to me. "She sounded like children laughing. She smelled like the freshest air mixed with the wildest of wild flowers ever imagined. I wish you could have met her, Kerry."

Kerry wipes away the last of her tears and runs her hands through her short brown hair. "I don't need to see or hear Lilith to know her presence. But nonetheless, I thank you for the thought. To know that I support and protect her child is wondrous enough." She stands and walks toward me, placing her hands on my shoulders.

Everyone stands and stretches, looking somehow renewed in the long-forgotten knowledge they've just learned.

Lettie stands very close to me and wraps her thin arms around my waist. "I know this may sound inappropriate, but do you think that's why the relationship with your parents has always been strained? You're not really their child."

"Leave it to you, Lettie," Easay says, shaking her

head and wrapping her arm around Lettie's.

I shrug. "It's fine. I was thinking the same thing." I take a deep breath and shake my head. "I'm done thinking about it now." I'll tackle that later.

Lettie hugs me tightly and then brushes my hair from my eyes. "You smell different," she says sniffing me.

"Ew, Lettie. Knock it off."

Patrick leans in and sniffs me. "You do smell different."

I use my newly healed index finger and push him away. "Don't you start." I lean in to my underarm and inhale. "What do I smell like?" I ask with a grimace.

Patrick kisses the sensitive spot below my ear, and it sends a delicious chill through me. "Like wildflowers."

Chapter Fourteen

"Kerry, may I speak with you for a moment?" I ask as I walk into her office and close the door behind me.

"Of course. Is everything all right?" Her face tightens, and she chews the inside of her lip.

"Oh yeah, everything's good." I sit down in the chair across from her desk. "You're going to call the Line and fill them in, aren't you?"

A brief smile crosses her face and she nods. "You don't think I should?"

"Not so much. Not right now. I don't know why but you should invite them here when this is all over. I need to tell them the story and I need to see their faces when they hear it. It's strange but—I don't know." I shrug and sit back in the chair.

Kerry clasps her hands in front of her chin and begins to chew on her thumbs. "I knew I hadn't called them for a reason. It's not that I don't trust them because I do, completely. But they need to meet you and feel what we all feel." She rests her chin on her hands. "May I ask you something, and if it makes you feel uncomfortable, I will understand if you don't answer."

"Ask away."

"I heard what Lettie said to you about your relationship with your parents. And I believe she is correct. Will you tell them?"

I inhale deeply and hold my breath for a moment and puffing out my cheeks. "I don't know. I really don't know. I think I'm afraid of their reaction. Would my mother take pride because of her role in this and make it about her? Will my father become more distant because he knows I'm not really his child? I mean, I am their flesh and blood, and that's what should matter. But I'm not of them. They were pawns chosen, maybe at random, and…I just don't know." I shake my head and sigh.

"Kayla, from what you've told me of your parents I believe your mother would make this about herself. She would tell everyone, and right now I don't think the world should know. And your father seems to have cared for you, even if he didn't know how to show it. If you tell anyone, it should be him."

I wish I could tell Craig. He'd know what to say.

I shrug. "You're right. But not now. There's other stuff going on and I don't want to add to it." I stand up, walk toward the door, and grab the knob.

"Kayla, I value your opinion," Kerry says in a strange voice. "And just in case you have any doubts, rest assured, I won't tell the Line until you think it's appropriate. We'll invite them here for a few days and you can tell them. I don't know if you were worrying, but I just wanted to reassure you."

"I never doubted your word. And I never will. I think Lilith sent me here, to you, because she trusts you with me. She trusts Patrick and me to be safe here with you." I turn toward her and look her in the eyes. "Trust your feelings. That's how she speaks to us. This probably sounds like mystical crap and it doesn't all make sense to me either, but know that not everything is in your power to stop. Something is going to happen, and you're going to feel like you've failed, but you didn't. You'll be helping things along as they should be. Always know that. Trust in that. I'll see you later."

I turn back to the door and walk through it, feeling that everything Kerry and I have just said to one another means more than we know right now. There are no feelings of confusion anymore. The time spent in my mother's world, realm, dimension—whatever, has brought me a sentiment of serenity and strength that I can't explain. And I don't need it to be explained. Everything makes sense even though—

"Ow, Lettie," I scream out as Lettie shoves me as I round the corner from Kerry's office. "Haven't we talked about this before?"

"Yeah, yeah, communicating with my hands isn't necessary." She slaps me on the bottom.

"Lettie, why are you wet?"

"I've been looking for you."

"And that's why you're wet?"

"No! Samuel and I went swimming in the pond and…"

"There's a pond on the property?"

"Focus!" Lettie says, snapping her fingers together too close to my right eyeball. "We didn't have sex, but let me just say, buddy-boy can sure hold his breath cause…"

I grab her lips. "No! No. Are you trying to make my eardrums explode?"

She slaps my hand away. "That was the best orgasm of my life! I thought I was gonna snatch his ears off. Aww, I really like him, Kayla," Lettie says with an odd look on her face. Eww. I think it's satisfaction.

"Um, I really hope you like him since you're considering de-earing the poor man in the name of passion." I exhale deeply and hate myself for what I'm about to say next. "Damn it. Tell me everything that happened."

****

"You are the daughter of our maker," Patrick says as he settles into bed next to me.

I nod my head. I look at him and try to read his expression. "Yes, it would appear so. Does that make you feel awkward?"

He seems to think it over for a moment. "It should. Maybe I should feel intimidated."

I laugh and turn on my side to face him. "Why? I'm one of only two humans in this place, remember?"

"Mmm-huh." He smiles. "And you healed your broken hand, and your skin spontaneously spit out your stitches. Yeah, sounds just like what a human would do."

I change the subject. "Lila. I keep thinking of that name. It's pretty."

"So are you. It's very similar to your name."

"I noticed." I shift and rest my palm on his chest. What am I going to do? I don't know what I'm supposed to do. Everything seems to make sense, but at the same time, I have so many questions. I can't do what Lilith says I can. Unite humans and supes? Shyeah.

"Apparently you can," he says, answering my thoughts aloud. "After everything you went through today, you don't think you can do what She asks?"

"Patrick, I want to believe it, but I don't know

how." I sit up on my elbow and drape my torso over his.

Up until a few days ago, I didn't even believe in her, never really considered her. I'd seen television shows about her and listened to the Weres give thanks in her name. It never occurred to me that she might have actually existed, and now I find out that she's my mother. And even after all this time she still loves me.

Earlier today, I thought that her love should lessen the blow of my parents' lack of something for me. Shouldn't they feel something? To them I was still their daughter. Or maybe they knew deep down that I didn't really belong to them. But my mother still carried me in her belly and kept me safe. Shouldn't that make her want to be a part of my life?

Patrick leans over and runs his lips along my cheek, pulling me from my thoughts. "You'll figure it out. She'll show you. And I'll be right here to keep you safe."

"I know you will." I turn my head and let his lips meet mine in a lingering kiss.

He slips my nightgown strap down my arm and bites my shoulder. "I'll always keep you safe," he says forcefully.

"And I'll keep you safe, too. Once I figure out how."

"You don't have to do this alone, Kayla. Not while I have breath in my body."

His blazing gaze rakes down my body. He hesitates for just a second and then he lifts his head, focusing on my lips before his come crashing into mine.

Patrick pulls my nightgown over my head and flips me over so fast that my stomach dips. He pins my hands above my pillow and kisses me, hard and deep. He kisses me until I can't breathe, until nothing else but us seems to matter. His tongue explores every inch of my mouth, moving in and out between my lips. I want him inside me so badly, moving his cock in and out of my slit, penetrating me from both ends.

Patrick breaks the kiss and sweeps his head down to take my pebbled nipple into his hot mouth and grinds the hard length of his cock against my warm center. I close my eyes and see stars, my body teetering on the verge of an explosive orgasm from his lips suckling me, but then he bites down. It shoots a lightning bolt of pleasure straight to my waiting channel and dumps liquid heat to my core. Never have I imagined the delicious and welcomed feel of pain, his teeth on one of my most sensitive areas.

"That hurt," I say through gritted teeth.

Shifting my hips and opening my legs wider to make room for him, I whimper into the top of his head as he sooths my aching bud with his lapping tongue. He rolls his hips and the instant pressure makes me insane.

"I want you inside me," I say as I fight to pull my wrists from his strong hands. I want to touch him, scratch my nails against his skin as payback for the bite.

He uses his free hand to glide his fingers down the length of my body and right through my sensitive folds. I shudder as he zeros in on my clit. He slides his finger inside me and then pulls back out. I raise my hips to encourage his touch, but he keeps my hips pinned down with his. He's so warm against me, inside of me, and my body longs to have that warmth deeper. He surges two fingers into my saturated entrance and presses his palm against my clit.

My heart is in overdrive, my breath comes in pants, and I want nothing more than to be closer to him. "Please, Patrick. Make me come," I beg.

His fingers speed up as he places sucking, biting kisses from my breasts to my lips, leaving a trail of goose bumps along the way. "How? On my dick, my hand? Tell me what you want."

I thrust my hips up, meeting his torturous fingers over and over again. "Doesn't matter. Just you. I want you."

I look down and watch his bicep flex as he strokes into me, and just as I think I can't take anymore, his fingers hook and focus on that precious spot inside me. I groan out a wordless sound of thanks as the orgasm explodes from me, my pussy clenching around his fingers as he continues to work me over.

He whispers sweet, filthy words into my ear as he continues to draw the pleasure from me. "You're always so fucking wet for me. So responsive to me. You ready for my cock, Kayla?

A tremble works its way through me as he withdraws his fingers from me, bringing them up to his lips to suck my passion from his fingers. "So fucking sweet," he says.

His tongue toys with my nipple, and when he bites down this time, it sends a delicious jolt through me. My back bows from the bed as I push my hips toward him, seeking a release that only he can give me.

I gasp at the feel of his cock against me and roll my hips until he is hot and hard against my opening. In one strong thrust, his cock slams into me, and we both cry out in relief. I wrap my legs around his waist to keep him buried inside me, giving my channel time to adjust to his welcome invasion.

"You feel so good. So tight," he says, his hand loosening from my wrists.

The firm muscles of his chest beneath the velvet softness of his skin abrades my receptive nipples. His fingers entwine with mine as he starts to slowly, deeply piston into me, and I meet him thrust for thrust. I dig my heels into the back of his legs to keep the constant, delicious pressure against my clit to bring on another orgasm that's already coiling its way through my center.

He takes me, owns me, and doesn't let go until that sweet release comes barreling to the surface. His mouth covers mine as he drinks in my screams, and I lose myself in him. He groans into my mouth as he shoots hots streams of his seed into me, again and again. I smile against his lips, happy that my body can give him all that his gives mine.

Even after he is spent, he continues to grind his hips against mine, building another release from me.

I clamp my teeth together to keep from screaming as my body trembles, being forced over the edge again. "I don't think I can." My voice is almost a sob.

"It's okay. You don't have to come if you don't want to." He smiles.

My body pulses around him in pleasure. "Patrick!" I moan. My heart beats erratically, and my breaths come in pants.

"You're mine and I'm yours, Kayla," he says. "My body was meant to please you, to protect you, to comfort you." He pulls away from me, and the brightness of his eyes is almost blinding. "Marry me."

I never thought I'd get married. Even if asked, part

of me knew that I would always say no. My parents scared me away from commitment, from wanting to join my life with someone who could walk away with no notice. Someone who could break my heart into so many pieces that I would never recover. Who would want that?

I smile and nod my head. "Yes. I'll marry you."

Chapter Fifteen

"Uh!" I say, shaking my favorite pen up and down. "I think it just ran out of ink, dang it."

Lettie and I have been studying for the past two hours. It would have been three hours, but it took her some time to get over talking about Samuel. She finally shut her trap when she started eating candy. I guess I should be grateful.

She notices me looking at her and smiles. "Don't hate me because I have the metabolism of a race horse. Besides, munching helps me think."

"Munching makes me chunky and lazy. But it makes me feel comforted."

"At least we only have one day of finals left. Pretty cool how Mr. Levay got our teachers to help out, so you won't get assaulted again." Lettie says it jokingly, but I know she's happy about me staying here at the manor. I can't stay here forever.

"At least I didn't get killed. That would have really mucked my finals."

"Not even funny." Lettie puts down the colorful candies.

"Oh, come on. It's kind of funny." I stop fumbling with the textbook pages. I hadn't even noticed I'd started. "But since we're on the subject...if anything happens to me, I want you to stay here with Kerry and Samuel."

"Knock it off, Kayla."

"No, Lettie. If anything does happen to me, because it could, I need you to stay here and be safe. Patrick and I can't spend the rest of our lives staying on the grounds of the manor."

Lettie stands up and starts toward the door. "Shut up, Kayla."

"Stop being a child. You and I need to talk about this because it could happen." I walk toward her and push her out of the way to stand in front of the door where she's trying to make an escape.

"Then don't let it happen, Kayla. Look at you. Look at what you can do. You healed your fucking hand by pulling energy from the earth. I felt it happen; we all did. You are making Patrick a super-wolf. And maybe you can use that power to kick their asses."

What does she expect me to do? Use dirt and rocks to pummel them into submission? I don't even know how I fixed my hand. I walk away from the door and sit on the couch. "You want me to use my 'power' to grow a nice garden for them?"

"Damn it, Kayla. Use it to kill them."

Lettie's eyes well up with tears. It breaks something deep inside me to know how afraid she is for me. She could leave any time she wants to, but she's here with me. Not in the safety of her parent's home, under the watchful eyes of her brothers and father, but here with me. In the middle of this shit-show, inside this beautiful mansion that has become my prison, Lettie is here with me. All she wants is for me to survive. Even though she's annoying the hell out of me, I don't think I could ever love her any more than I do in this moment.

"You're right, Lettie. We'll figure something out."

"I know I'm right. Bury them alive. Pull the life force out of anyone who tries to hurt you and shoot it into the ground. God knows this Earth could use some healing."

"That's death magic, Lettie." I shake my head. I don't even know how I know that. "It would be murder. That's not what I do, and that's not who my mother is."

"Kayla, those sons of bitches are trying to murder you and the man you love. You and Patrick have to stay locked up here like prisoners because they are trying to kidnap and kill you. You think that's the life your mother wants for you? You wouldn't be committing murder; you would be defending your family."

She couldn't wait until finals were over to bring up this crap? That evil pixie!

She throws a handful of candy in her mouth while looking at me. "I want you to think about it."

"Lettie, shut up and eat your candy." I walk back to my place at the table and sit in front of my text books.

"I'm not letting this go. Somebody has to do something. I'm sure the bad guys are just waiting for you and wolf-boy so they can do whatever it is they do." She sits down on the couch across from me.

"Come on, Lettie. We have to study. We can fight about this tomorrow. Truce?" I throw a candy box at her.

"Screw you and your truce. I don't need your candy cast-offs. I have more in my pocket."

We study in silence for the next hour or so, only making eye contact when we look up from our textbooks and class notes to give our eyes a break. She seems pretty angry with me right now, and I completely understand. I just need her to understand what I can and can't do. What I will and won't do. It's not even a question of if I can kill them or not, because I really don't believe I could. But even if I could do it, would I? It doesn't feel right to think of me killing anyone.

The phone rings somewhere in the house, but since Lettie and I are temporary guests, neither of us moves to get it.

"Have you talked to your mom yet?" Lettie says breaking the silence.

I close my textbook and close my eyes. "Nope. Last message I got was her telling me her new boyfriend was taking her on vacation. You talk to your parents?"

"Yup. This morning. When you're free and we've all left Crazyville, Mom wants you to come to dinner. She's weirdly excited about you and Patrick."

"Did you tell her about you and Samuel?"

Lettie rolls her eyes and frowns. "I wouldn't know what to tell her. I don't know if this is a fling since I'm staying here or—"

"I'm not saying that Samuel is not your typical male, but he is a werewolf. They take their relationships pretty seriously."

She smiles deviously. "I don't think you can classify what went down in the pond a relationship." She giggles deep down in her throat like she's trying not to laugh.

"Ew."

Kerry opens the door with Patrick, Samuel, Osai, and Mr. Levay close on her heels. "Kayla, you have a phone call," she says, handing me the phone. Her expression is unreadable.

I shake my head. "It's my mom, isn't it? How in the hell did she find me?"

"It's not your mom, babe." Patrick looks pissed. "It's Gunther. He says he'll only talk to you."

My eyes widen, and I look at Kerry. She mouths silently, "I think he has Easay and Seeley." They left almost two hours ago to go grocery shopping.

I snatch the phone from Patrick. "What do you want?"

"To talk," he says innocently. "And just so that bitch of a protector would let me talk to you, I told her all about the run-in I had with your housemates. I'd hate to have to hurt Easay's pretty face. She'd heal, but I'd make it hurt pretty good. And pretty long."

"So talk and let them go."

"How's your hand? I'm sure your bones have almost mended."

"The hand is fine."

His laugh is an ugly sound that makes me afraid for Seeley and Easay. "I'm sure it is. Anything you want to talk about, Kayla?"

"Yeah, the fucking weather outside. It's kind of warm for my taste, but hey, it is summer time. What. Do. You. Want."

"Exactly what I've been looking for. You."

The way he says "you" makes me cringe. It doesn't sound like he wants to be my best friend. It sounds more like a dirty perversion of the word that only true sadists and psychotics can communicate. "What do you want with me, Gunther? Another dead human who got involved with a werewolf? Is that seriously your angle? It's pretty fucking pathetic."

He laughs again. "Do you know why we've been

killing wolves and some of their humans?"

"Because you're a psycho who needs to get laid? Because you need a life of your—"

"Because we've been looking for you, you bitch!" he screams. "I knew who you were before you or any of them knew."

I look at Patrick and Kerry. My throat is suddenly very dry. "What do you mean?"

"Oh, come off it!" he says, his voice tapering off to a growl. "Why do you think we were hunting you down, Kayla?"

"I don't know, Gunther. Why don't you tell me, because now I'm confused."

His voice quiets, and I strain to hear every word he says. "I knew the daughter of Lilith would ally herself with the wolves, even if she didn't know what was happening. Kerry didn't know either, did she?"

I close my eyes and hold my breath. How the hell does he know? "What? What are you talking about?"

Kerry gently touches my arm. I shrug. I don't think Easay or Seeley would tell Gunther anything about me. And if they're within listening distance of Gunther and conscious, they'll know I'm not sharing any information.

"I know Kerry can hear me. I know they can all hear me."

"Yes. They can. What do you mean, a daughter of Lilith? Are Easay and Seeley all right?"

"Yes. They are. And they'll stay that way. So, tell me, what do you know?"

My snarky comebacks have abandoned me, and I can't even begin to imagine the horrible way it would feel to lose Easay and Seeley. I begin speaking frantically. "I-I don't know anything."

"What?"

"I don't know anything!"

Gunther exhales, and I hear him move the phone around uncomfortably. He wasn't prepared for me not knowing anything. "Why do you think you're Bound to a werewolf? Why do you think you're being protected by the Line? You are Lilith's daughter."

"That's…I don't…" Actress of the year, here I come. "Is that how Patrick and I healed my hand?" I have to give him something to keep them safe. Everyone in the room is very quiet, listening to what Gunther wants and how we can get Easay and Seeley back.

"You don't know? Lilith hasn't revealed anything to you?" His voice cracks.

"No. We don't know anything. Kerry and Cybil said it was because of our bond."

The calm drill-instructor has left the building. "It's you. Your blood…we've been looking for you! As soon as I tasted your blood, I knew you were different!"

"Is that why you killed all those people?"

"Yes." His voice is low and full of anger.

"You didn't kill me. Why did you kill them?"

"Because it was fun."

Patrick grabs my hand to comfort me, but I snatch it away from him because I know it will only make me cry. I would hate myself for letting Gunther hear me be that vulnerable. I shake my head. "You're lying. You said you were looking for me. You knew I was coming, but you didn't know who I was."

"No," he says.

"But why kill them?"

"Because we didn't want the word to get out that we were looking for you. We didn't want the wolves we questioned to go back to the Line and tell them what we were looking for. I didn't want the Line to find you before I did. So, we killed them to shut them up. Some of the humans were just…casualties. They didn't know what was going on either way. Just like Craig."

No. He killed Craig. The air in my lungs whooshes out and stops my heart. A low hum sounds off in my head, and everything goes silent. "I knew it wasn't a robbery," I whisper.

"He wouldn't talk. Didn't know anything." He sounds triumphant. "Couldn't let him live after we talked to him about you. That was a good friend you had there," he says, his voice teasing and joyous.

"You'll suffer," I say, promising him pain. "And it will be because of me."

"You get one more minute, and then I have to go say goodbye to your friends."

He's going to kill them, too. "What do you mean? I have more questions. How am I Lilith's daughter? Are you going to let Seeley and Easay go?"

"Do you know why I want you?" His voice sounds different. It's still Gunther, but not.

I try to think quickly, but nothing comes to mind. "I don't know. I can't help you do anything."

"Do you know how powerful you are? Anyone who has you wields the power over every supernatural creature on this planet. You have your mother's gifts. That a good enough reason? You'll learn how to use them all. And I know the perfect teacher." Perfect teacher sounds vulgar and dirty when he says it.

That doesn't make any sense. "I'm not a toy or a

machine you can control. What you want is crazy."

He takes a deep breath and then yells, his voice sounding more like his own. "Stop fucking talking!"

"Me?"

"Not you," he says, his voice sounding foreign again. "You know, you should be asking me a question. Can you think of what it is?"

What the hell is going on? He's losing it. "Are you talking to me?"

"Yes, Kayla, I'm talking to you. Can you think of what that question is?" His voice trembles. He's either really freaking crazy, or really freaking scared.

The question I know he wants me to ask doesn't take long to form in my head. "How did you know about me when no one else knew?"

"And there's the kicker," he says, raising his voice as if he were a ringleader. "There are some supernatural beings who know more than they should. Tell Kerry to go check her email. Bye." He hangs up the phone.

"No!" I scream. What is he going to do to them? "Oh my God, he's going to kill them."

Without a word, Samuel runs out of the den and toward the front door.

"No," Osai says, looking at Kerry. "He's not."

"I don't understand," Lettie says with tears making steady tracks down her cheeks.

"Seeley's car just pulled up. They're home." Osai looks relieved as he follows Samuel to the door.

I run past Kerry and Patrick to make sure Easay and Seeley are alone and all right. Samuel is standing next to Seeley's green hatchback.

"What's happened?" Easay asks as she gets out of the car. None of us speak just yet. I'm just happy that they're home. And safe.

"What is wrong?" Seeley asks, as he walks toward the trunk of his car to start unloading the groceries.

Kerry walks toward Easay and hugs her, and then hugs Seeley. "Gunther called. He said he had you both. At least he implied it. We thought he was going to kill you."

Even in the failing evening light, I can see Easay's complexion go from its normal porcelain pale to a sickly yellow. "There was a guy in the market," she says quietly. "A Were that I thought I recognized. By the time I realized he wasn't who I thought he was, I had walked him outside to his car while he put away his bags. It was one of them, wasn't it? He could have taken me. Or killed me. Why didn't he?"

"Because he wanted to give us a message," I say walking toward her. "He wanted us to know that he could get to us if he wanted to." And Craig is gone because of it. Because of me.

Lettie walks toward Samuel, and he pulls her close to him. "He wants you to be scared," Lettie says. "And he wants you to know that it doesn't have to be him that attacks. It could be any of his lackeys. And it could be any of you that gets hurt."

Kerry inhales sharply and shakes her head. "I need to check my email. He said he would send me something."

Groceries forgotten, we all walk into the house and patiently wait as Kerry checks her email.

"It's just a message confirming what we already know," Kerry says, turning the computer around so the rest of us can see the email. We're all crowded in her office taking comfort in the fact that all of us are together. "He says his numbers are larger than we know."

Mr. Levay loosens his bowtie. "Is the Line any closer at finding the Rogues? Patrick and Kayla need more protection. Kayla needs more protection. Taking Patrick would just be a way to manipulate her. We need more numbers."

"To do what?" I stare at him. "Come to the manor and guard us for the rest of our lives? We need to actively search for them." This is ridiculous.

Lettie shifts in Samuel's lap. "I don't know how much my opinion matters, but I agree with Kayla. As much as I want them to be safe, they can't be guarded for the rest of forever."

Kerry smiles at her. "Your opinion matters just as much as anyone else's."

Lettie stands up and looks me in the eyes. "Are you ready now?"

"I wouldn't know what to do, Lettie," I say, avoiding her gaze.

"Yes, you do." Her words are firm.

"What do you mean?" Patrick asks.

"I mean is she ready to kill them. She's powerful, so powerful that a whole group of werewolves want her so they can use her. You heard what he said—the one who controls her controls you all." Lettie pokes my arm. "I'm going to start calling you The Precious."

Samuel shakes his head. "What does that mean?" he asks Lettie.

"Seriously. One ring to rule them all?" she says.

I shake my head and touch her arm. "Not now."

"Well," Samuel continues, "they can't control her. Like Kayla said, she's not a machine. There's no way

Kayla would hurt anyone willingly." Samuel pulls Lettie back down on his lap.

"There is a way," Lettie says turning to face Kerry. "All of us. We'd be your motivational kill switch."

Kerry nods her head. "You are very correct."

"Imagine what you would do if they had me and were threatening to kill me." Lettie has a faint smile on her face. "Or what if they had Patrick?"

"I'd kill them."

"You would kill them. How?"

"I don't know, Lettie." My voice is slightly raised. I don't want to kill anyone. I wouldn't even know how to get close enough to a freaking werewolf to kill them.

Lettie gets up from Samuel's lap and comes to kneel in front of me. "Then figure it out, because sooner or later, one of us is going to be vulnerable. That psycho fuck will go from talking about killing one of us to actually doing it. Fix it."

"I don't know how!"

"Figure it out!" Lettie yells. "How did you heal your hand?"

"I don't know. I just got a feeling."

"Then go take nap, talk to Lilith, and get another feeling! Ask her what you can do. Tell her to do something, I don't know," she says, throwing her hands in the air.

I try to calm myself so that she and I won't end up arguing again. "It's not that simple, Lettie."

"Oh, I'm sorry," she says sarcastically. "How do you know? Have you tried?"

"Kind of. I keep thinking of how much I want to see her." I don't think Lilith is one who comes for a visit when you beckon her.

"Well, start thinking about how much trouble we all are in and then call her. You're her kid, and I'm sure she held onto your soul for the past few millennia because she likes you and wants to keep you safe."

"That's enough, Lettie." Patrick hasn't said one word this whole time. He's been thinking, and he hasn't let me in. Whatever he's thinking of, he doesn't want to share. "Do you not believe that she doesn't know what to do? Or do you think she's bluffing? Ease up."

Lettie's face shadows an array of emotions. Anger turns to confusion. Confusion gives way to pity. And then she settles on confusion. She shakes her head. "You're right. I'm sorry, Kayla. But you can't die. You just can't."

"That isn't the plan, Lettie," Patrick says. "This has been a busy day. Kayla needs to rest."

"You're right. Lettie and I have finals tomorrow and—"

"Are you insane?" Patrick says, his voice getting higher. "You're going back to school? After all this?"

"I've worked too hard this semester to skip my last two exams. And I won't let him control my life. He already has plans to do that. I won't let him throw this semester away for us." I feel another argument coming along.

"She's right." Mr. Levay runs his hand through his already disheveled hair. "It's one more day. There are plenty of Weres on campus who'll keep an eye on her."

"Like they did when that bastard almost ripped her arm off?" Lettie asks.

"Exaggerate much?" I say, interrupting Lettie. "Let's not do this. That was my fault. I shouldn't have gone back into the classroom alone." And no one will let me forget it.

"I'll stay with her," Mr. Levay says. "There are at least eight werewolves who are campus police. I'll call them tonight and make sure they're all there tomorrow. We didn't know how big the threat was last time."

Lettie covers her face with her hands. "It's just one more day of school. And then you're a prisoner again."

"And then I'm a prisoner again," I repeat. And after tomorrow, I won't leave here until we make some kind of progress with finding Gunther. Or until he decides to storm the castle and take me by force.

Chapter Sixteen

"I am officially on my summer vacation," Lettie says, throwing her school bag on the couch in the living room. "No more finals for us and no more students to teach. How are you holding up?"

I point to my e-reader sitting on the cherry oak table. "I downloaded four more books today. In the past week, I have given myself a facial, manicure, pedicure, tweezed my eyebrows, and tortured myself for twenty minutes by waxing my legs and lady parts. I asked Patrick to help with the waxing, but he cringed and left me in the bathroom to suffer alone."

"See," she says sitting down beside me, "you're not a prisoner. Do prisoners get to have personal spa days?"

"No, but they do go bonkers every once in a while and start killing people. I think I'm almost there."

Lettie takes off her shoes and starts rubbing her feet. "You said almost. You'll be fine for at least another two weeks."

"I swear I'm tempted to go to the mall by myself and see how long it takes Gunther to grab me. At least that would be a way to draw him out."

"Uh-huh. Except you'd probably only draw out his lackeys. He wouldn't come for you on his own. Canon-fodder is expendable and that's who he'd send." Lettie looks around the room. "Where is everyone?"

"Not in this room, genius. Everyone except Easay is out for a run. She's finishing up a hand vacuum manual." I look down at my Peachy Pearl toes and click my tongue. "I finished typing up the last of Kerry's tapes yesterday."

"*Oh*, you finished the memoirs?" She feigns excitement.

"No, but Kerry hasn't been in the mood to record tapes. She's been talking to pack members about finding Gunther. She didn't tell them who I really was, only that Gunther was a threat to all pack members who entered into relationships with humans. And that she wants him dead for threatening her." I shake my head. "Kerry and psycho drill-instructor man have one thing in common. They don't want anyone to know who I am. He wants to use me, and she wants to…protect me? Make sure the Line don't want to use me either? I don't know. I get the feeling that it's in my best interest to go unnoticed."

I start chewing on my lip and Lettie smooths my eyebrows. "Kayla, this'll be over soon. I know you're stressed and worried. And I'm sorry for being hard on you. This will all work out."

"I know, Lettie. This too shall pass. And stop touching me. You just finished rubbing your feet."

She lifts her hands, sniffs, and then shrugs. "Want to go for a jog?"

I point to my toes. "Nope. I don't want to mess up my pedicure. Besides, I did that this morning when I woke up. Have fun."

"Tomorrow then? We can jog together and then do some free weights down in the workout room."

"Sounds good to me, Pix. I'm going to sit here and

let my toesies dry."

Lettie stands and stretches. "Good. I'm going to get changed and go jog. By the by, your left eyebrow is too short. Maybe next time, you should wait to go to the salon and get them professionally done."

****

Do you know why I haven't been able to come to you? There is regret in her voice. *I have been watching you.*

"I know. At least, I do now. I'm sorry I couldn't see it before." It's still so bright here, but now I can make out shapes and colors—trees, the deep green color of the grass surrounding us, the white and blue of the clear sky, the natural brown color of her long dress. My head is on my mother's lap, and I am turned away from her.

She sighs. *I'm giving much of myself to you. To make you strong. To make you see.*

"I know. Why is it all so clear here? Why don't I know these things when I'm there? Not with you?" I want to call "there" home, but this place with Lilith feels like home.

This is only one part of my world. She doesn't answer my question. *This place that He made for me. But there is another side to this beautiful place. I keep my other children there. The ones that would devastate all humanity. Not every one of my children is stable. Some were…unintentional.*

"I don't understa—Yes, I do understand!"

She leans down, kisses my cheek, and presses something sweet to my lips. A few drops hit my tongue and she quickly pulls it away. *It's time to go back, child.*

****

I wake up on the couch, and Patrick is sitting across from me reading my e-reader. When he notices me watching him, he smiles.

"Your toes are pretty."

"Peachy Pearl. How long have I been asleep?"

"At least an hour. I saw you when I came back in the house, and I didn't want to bother you. I showered and then came in to sit with you." He puts down the tablet, stands, and walks toward me.

"Where is your shirt?" I ask, noticing he only has on blue and gray gym shorts and white socks. The muscles of his body flex naturally as he walks toward me.

He bites his bottom lip and smiles. "Stop it."

"Hey, you're the one with no shirt on. We can go upstairs, and I can take mine off too."

"Please don't," Samuel says as he walks past the living room and into the kitchen.

"Thanks for putting the brakes on that." I say it quietly because I know he can hear me.

"You are so welcome," he replies. Samuel is becoming just as snarky as Lettie.

I look up to see Patrick standing in front of me. His nose twitches as he bends down to kiss the top of my head. "You smell different."

My first instinct is to sniff myself, but then I remember Lilith. "I was with her. With Lilith!" I jump up and quickly walk to Kerry's office, knocking on the door and opening it at the same time. Yes, it's rude, but she and I have lots to talk about. "Kerry, I was with her."

Kerry sleepily looks up from her computer and

gives me a toothy grin. "What? Dinner's ready?" She looks funny.

Patrick walks in behind me and I feel his body tense. "Kerry, what's wrong?"

"You smell like outside." Her voice is weird. "I'm hungry," she says, her words tapering off into a low growl.

I begin to walk toward Kerry, but Patrick grabs my arm and pulls me behind him. As soon as he touches me, my senses flair and I can feel the earth all around me. I feel the rabbits hopping across the field, the deer grazing near the pond, the insects scurrying through the dirt. And a sickly disturbing feeling that's resonating from the earth.

"Patrick," I whisper. "Do you feel that?"

I turn to look at him, and he shakes his head. I close my eyes and concentrate on the area surrounding the manor and I begin to whisper-scream. "Samuel, get Lettie!" As soon as I say his name, I feel Samuel, actually feel the weight of him on the floorboards, feel the disturbance of the air surrounding him as he runs through the house.

"What's wrong, Kayla?" Patrick asks.

"It's a spell. Someone is working earth magic, but that person is...tainted and the earth can feel it." I grab my chest, feeling as if my heart will crash through it, and reach my other hand out, feeling around us. "There's movement. Getting closer."

Even though my back is turned to the door, I feel Samuel and Lettie walk into the room.

Easay rushes in behind them. "What's happening?" she asks.

"No, no, no! Where is everyone else?" I whisper.

Easay's eyes are wide. "Steven, Seeley, and Osai left half an hour ago to pick up pack members from the airport. What. Is. Happening?"

"They're coming for me. They have a witch with them. Whoever it is, is good, but they can't feel the earth like I can. And the earth doesn't like what they are doing to it."

"You can feel the—I don't understand," Lettie says.

I'm giving so much of myself to you.

"Samuel," I say harshly. "Get her downstairs. If you're in the lowest part of the house, underground, I may be able blanket you."

He doesn't ask any questions. Samuel grabs Lettie as she protests and rushes her toward the kitchen. As they round the corner, I get a glimpse of Lettie's face. I've never seen her look more scared and pissed at the same time.

"I said I'm hungry," Kerry says, whining like a child. She slams her fist on the desk. It strains under her pressure.

"Take her downstairs," I say looking at Easay. "Patrick, help Easay, just in case Kerry starts fighting."

"I'm not leaving you," Patrick says.

Easay is already helping Kerry get out of the chair. "Come on Kerry. let's make you a sandwich," she coaxes.

A huge and terrifying smile spreads across Kerry's face, but she doesn't fight. "I'll kill the son of a bitch that almost ripped your throat out," she says, rubbing her hand down the jagged scar on Easay's neck.

Easay smiles and pulls her. "You already did, Kerry." Easay looks at Patrick as she and Kerry get closer to the door. "Patrick, you've got to come with me. They won't hurt her, but they might kill you."

"So be it. I will defend her with my last breath." His look is defiant.

"Patrick, please. Help them," I plead with him.

As we stand there looking at each other, I feel Easay grab a few things from the kitchen and take Kerry down into the basement.

"I will never leave you," he says. "How are you feeling this?"

It feels like a power dump from Lilith to me. We ran out of time, and she put all her eggs in one basket. Me. "It's Lilith." Everything is happening so fast. It feels like I've been in a darkened room and someone finally turned on the light. And the light is brilliant.

I'm giving much of myself to you. To make you strong. To make you see.

"What can I do?" Patrick asks.

I shake my head, realizing that I can't make him leave. "Besides go downstairs?" I give him one last pleading look. "Hold my hand. I feel stronger when I'm touching you. I'm going to cover the basement with magic so whoever comes in here won't be able to find them. They won't see the door leading to the basement. The witch who's doing this is using a...blocking spell? I don't know what else to call it. That's why none of you could sense the werewolves coming onto the property."

"How could you feel it?"

"I don't—" Someone knocks on the front door. And then the bell rings. I take a deep breath and grab Patrick's hand. "Let's go answer it."

Chapter Seventeen

"Hello, sweetie." Gunther stands on the porch, looking as psycho as I remember. Two men and a woman stand behind him. "It's good to see you again."

"Pleasure as always," I say.

The wolves behind him seem nervous. The man standing to Gunther's right is very pale with bright green eyes and a gangly body. He won't make eye contact with me or Patrick. His face is hard, and his chin is very prominent. It reminds me of a crescent moon.

The man on the left and the woman standing beside him look almost identical. Their olive skin is flawless. Eyes a brown so bright it's almost hard to look at. The woman's hair is just past her shoulders, thick and wavy, and looks soft to the touch. The man's hair is cut close, but the texture still looks the same.

The woman looks at me and nods. "Hello, ma'am." Her voice has the heavy twang of Louisiana.

I nod back and smile. Does she know what she's gotten herself into? Do any of them really know? When this ends, it's not going to go well.

I can feel Patrick tense. He wants to attack, but Easay was right; they would kill him.

Patrick's thoughts are strong. Our mental bond seems to be less fuzzy, and I can hear his thoughts clearly. He's thinking of attacking Gunther. I look at him and see that his eyes are beginning to change. The muscles in his jaw clench.

Patrick. There are at least five more Weres on the property, and they have a powerful witch. Please stay calm.

He takes a few deep breaths, but murder is still on his mind.

Gunther smiles and takes a step toward Patrick. "You owe me pain, don't you? I broke your mate's fingers. You must want to hurt me something good. Come on." He steps back and points to the open space in front of the house. "Let's give it a go."

Patrick takes a step forward, and I gently pull him back to me. I look at Gunther. "You didn't come here to fight Patrick. What do you want?"

He smiles again. "You, sweetie. And you're coming with me. You both are."

"Why? Why do you want him?"

A dark green, large SUV pulls up to the front of the house and comes to a slow stop. The person driving doesn't look at us. He just keeps staring forward. Gunther gestures toward the vehicle for us to get in.

"Answer me. Why do you want Patrick?" I've already started walking. There's no need to put up a fight. He might kill Patrick just to spite me.

"Because, we have a bond to break," he says. "Killing him wouldn't do it."

"A bond between a werewolf and his mate can't be broken. Even in death," Patrick says.

Gunther runs his large hand over his smooth, bald head. "That's why we're not going to kill you." He looks to me. "You are so powerful, and you have no idea, do you, Kayla?" Gunther shakes his head and then opens the door.

No, sweetie, you have no idea.

"Where were the rest of your housemates?" Gunther asks from the front passenger seat.

"Out getting reinforcements," I say. "This all had to come to an end. I convinced them all to all give Patrick and me some privacy." I can still feel them in the basement, though the farther away from the manor we get, the fuzzier they feel. The magic that was being used against everyone lifted shortly after we left the property. My spell worked.

Gunther laughs. "Maybe they felt like you were more trouble than you're worth."

I won't feed into his attempt at provoking me. Even though I'm not sure how all of this will work out, I won't allow him to make me lose my focus.

"None of us would ever feel that way," Patrick says.

The gangly man with the green eyes speaks for the first time. "So, what can you do? You're the daughter of our creator."

I turn around in my seat to see gangly boy and the twins staring at me, waiting for an answer. "I can't do anything. But imagine how pissed off my mother is going to be when She does something." I face the front of the car. "I have to say, every supporter of Gunther is definitely backing the wrong pony. You should try to fix things before it's too late."

Gunther scoffs. "She's been dormant for centuries. Lilith hasn't helped you yet, and she's not going to. I'm the one who's going to unleash your potential. I'm the one who's going to set things straight and stop the degradation of our bloodline. We will not be made as weak as humans."

"There are worse things, Gunther," I tell him, remembering my mother's words.

I keep my other children there. The ones that would devastate all humanity.

"Where are you taking us?" Patrick asks.

"To a place where we can have a nice sit down and discuss some things. Don't worry; we'll have privacy."

"How have you been able to stay off the radar?" Patrick asks, taking my hand in his.

"Magic. Found a nice warlock to cover us." Gunther sounds like he's attempting to be haughty. It's not working.

"Human or wolf?" Patrick asks.

"He is a wolf, of course. I'd never deal with anyone else."

"Is he the one who's been telling you stuff about me?" I ask.

"Yes. He came to us some time ago. I'd like to take all the credit, but he's the one who put this together. I just wanted to kill wolves that were breeding with humans. They produce inadequate offspring."

"So, you're his flunky, eh?" I say. Gunther doesn't respond. "Hmm. Are we going to get to meet him? Sounds like a real gem." Maybe I'm blaming the wrong person for all this violence. Scratch that; Gunther is to blame. Now, he just has someone to share it with.

"Don't worry. He wants to meet you, too. Find out what you've got. He's powerful, and he's going to help unlock your mother's magic."

Warlock-were-boy isn't that powerful. If he was, he'd know that my mother has already given me a few things. And I have tons of things to show him. I hope.

After over an hour of driving, I'm anxious, nervous, and angry. "Are we there yet?" I ask for the fourth time trying to be a pain in the ass. The driver still hasn't said a word and the complete silence in the car is unnerving. "How 'bout now?"

Gunther clears his throat but doesn't say anything. A few more "are we there yet's" and he may be ready to punch me in the face. I'm pretty sure he won't though.

Patrick slides a little closer to me, if that's possible, and rests his chin on the top of my head. His mind is clear. He's trying to think of a way to get us out of this mess, but he doesn't want to put me in harm's way.

Sorry, sweetie, I think at him. *We're both in trouble.*

I pull away from him and look him in the eyes. He smiles and rubs his soft lips against my forehead. *I love you.* Even in his head, his voice sounds full of regret.

Damn it. I wish I had a tracking device on my phone, or something high-tech like that, so that Kerry can follow us. I wish I had my phone. That's still in my purse on the kitchen counter back at the manor. A thought hits me and I jump, but only Patrick notices.

What's wrong? he asks.

I'm going to try to send Kerry a message. I don't know if it will work, but...

My mother's voice reverberates in my head. *I'm giving much of myself to you. To make you strong.*

I don't know how strong I am aside from healing my own hand, which was pretty cool, but it's worth a try.

Patrick, just concentrate on me.

I close my eyes and take a few deep breaths. Even

though I have absolutely no idea what to do or where we are, I imagine a string of light from my mind all the way back to the manor, to Kerry's mind. The string is bright and starts with me. It curves and runs along the earth, seeking out Kerry. It knows where to go. Home.

The line finds its way to the gates of the manor, my home, and goes straight through the house to where Kerry sits on the phone talking to someone.

Kerry stops talking and looks around the room. "I'll call you back," she says into the receiver. She hangs up without waiting for an answer. She stands and I can see her face.

"Kayla?" she says out loud to the empty room. She closes her eyes and inhales deeply. "I smell your skin." She smiles. Kerry inhales again and tightens her eyes. "I see your line. I see you!" Tears stream down her face. "I'm coming."

I imagine the line running through the asphalt and grass that we've driven over. Only Kerry can see its light. It's a part of the earth now. I try to picture the line brighter so that Kerry can see it leading her to us. So that she can bring help to take down Gunther and the jerk that's playing him. The Line of Lilith will finally know where these douche nozzles have been hiding. Mother is giving me more than I bargained for.

I open my eyes and look at Patrick. He's smiling at me. I kiss him on the cheek and press my back toward him.

"Gunther," I say, but he doesn't answer. "Gunther," I repeat.

"What!" he says, finally breaking his cool.

"Are we there yet?"

Chapter Eighteen

"Damn," says an alarmingly deep voice from the back of the car.

My eyes widen in surprise, and I turn around to see where the voice is coming from. I look at the twins and gangly boy and try to remember their voices from when we first met. The voice that I just heard didn't sound like any of them.

"I'm sorry?" I say nervously, waiting to hear the voice again.

"That was pretty strong," says gangly green-eyed boy, but his voice sounds disconnected from his body. "I didn't think you had it in you."

"Neither did I," I whisper, staring at him. "I guess fear can push you to do things you didn't know you had in you." I've completely turned around in my seat to stare at him. He doesn't seem natural anymore, and his eyes are glazed over.

The green of his eyes is no longer vibrant and clear. They are now a dirty swamp color. The malicious curve of his lips frightens me. The twins have somehow shoved themselves into the other side of the car and neither of them are looking at him. They are scared. First show of a brain I've seen in either of them.

The car seems smaller now, and I fight everything in my body not to claw my way out of the steel frame of the vehicle. Only the feel of Patrick's hand steadies me.

"You're the voice from the phone? Gunther was talking too much, and you tried to stop him." I just thought he was off his rocker. This is so much worse.

"How long do you think it'll be before Kerry finds us?" gangly boy asks.

I feel my hands begin to shake as I look at him. "I don't know."

"Break the link, or I'll kill your wolf," says the voice. But gangly-boy isn't talking anymore. His eyes have gone foggy. The voice is coming from beside me.

I snatch my hand from Patrick and spin around quickly, almost dizzying myself to look at him. "Patrick," I whisper.

My Patrick winks a hazy brown eye and smiles at me. "Not so much," says a deep voice. It's not Patrick's voice. It's not gangly-boy's voice either.

"Gunther said he'd be fine. Let him go!" I scream.

The car is closing in on me, and I begin shaking my head back and forth bringing my right hand up to bite the knuckle of my thumb. It's a nervous tic I developed after my mother left me and my father.

Patrick oozes across the seat toward me. His movements are smooth at first, looking as if his body is fluid, but then the movements become fast as every muscle in his body jerks. I've never wanted to scream in my life more than I do right now. "Let him go. Please."

"Break the connection with Kerry, or I will kill him," says gangly-boy from back seat. "Let me show you how it's done."

I crane my head around in time to see gangly-boy go very still. He looks dead already, but he's not. His eyes begin to redden as blood pours from his tear ducts and frothy blood streams out of his mouth, nose, and ears. Even though he's not moving, I can see the panic and pain in his eyes. His gaze frantically darts around the vehicle trying to find something, someone to wrench him free of what has him. His gaze settles on me. The look is pleading and frightened. Even though I can't read his mind, the look he's giving me says, "You're the daughter of Lilith. If you can do anything, do it now." I wish I could. And then it stops. He closes his eyes and is no more.

I want to reach for him, to reach for the twins in the backseat and pull them up here with us. Why would they align themselves with this atrocity?

"I will not say it again." The driver speaks for the first time. But from the way his voice sounds, I know this still isn't the man in the flesh who's been trying to find me.

Patrick gasps and pulls me close to him. "I'm sorry," he whispers.

My eyes close, and I imagine the line between Kerry and me fading. It's getting dimmer, and it's pulling away from Kerry, making its way back to me. It's done. Our link is severed.

"Good girl," says the driver. I can hear the smile in his voice. He gazes at me through the rearview mirror and then the glossy look fades from his eyes as the driver puts his hands on the wheel and begins to drive.

I hadn't even noticed we had stopped.

The rest of the ride is in silence. Patrick holds me close to him, the twins sit even closer to each other, and the driver continues to drive with a blank stare. From what I can see of his profile, Gunther sits in the front seat with an arrogant look painted on his stupid face.

As the car begins to slow down, we pull up to a large shack in the middle of nowhere. I gasp. All the grass is dead in this area. The trees are sparse, and they look as if they never recovered from the cold winter. About fifty yards or so from us, the grass is green, and the trees are vibrant as they wave in the wind. Whatever magic Gunther's buddy has been using has killed all the life here. This is wrong. This place feels wrong.

The frame of the shack is a thin, blue metal material with a wooden roof. The fact that it's in the middle of nowhere only adds to its ominous effect. I knew that whatever Patrick and I were going to go through tonight would not be easy. But now I'm more afraid than I ever thought I could be. I'm afraid for the man I love, and I'm afraid that Kerry will never find either one of us.

The twins move swiftly to exit the car. Gunther gets out of the passenger seat and walks around to my door. He opens it and smiles.

"You said Patrick wouldn't be hurt. Let him go, and I won't fight."

"Like hell," Patrick says. There is no fear or panic in his voice. Only anger. Only murder.

Gunther lets go of the door and takes a few steps from the car. "Remember how you said fear could drive you to do anything? Well, you're going to sever the bond between the both of you, or he will be killed. And it won't be as pretty or pleasant as Beckett's death."

Gangly-boy had a name. I suppose it doesn't matter much anymore. Even though he was willing to side with Gunther, I will mourn him. I don't care if no one else will, but I will. Beckett's death was too horrible for someone not to mourn him properly.

"And here's the incentive," says Gunther. "Breaking the bond may kill him. So, whether he lives or dies is up to you, young lady."

I stare at him in horror but do everything I can not to react. He is a psychotic predator and to see me panic would give him joy. There isn't much I can do right now, but I can do that. I won't give him the satisfaction.

"Come on," Patrick says, running his strong hands up and down my arm. I think he's trying to comfort me. "Get out of the car. I won't die in here."

"What do you mean?" I whisper. "You're not going to die anywhere. Not any time soon." I climb out of the car.

He exits the vehicle behind me still touching my arm. "No matter what—"

"Come on," Gunther says, interrupting us. "Inside."

Neither Patrick nor I protest. We walk toward the large shack with no windows, trying to ready ourselves for what we will find.

I turn around to see the twins taking Beckett's body out of the car. They look as if they don't want to touch him. The girl squeals a bit and begins to wipe her hands on her shirt. She must have gotten blood on her. Her brother whispers something to her, and she backs away from the body. He picks up Beckett and begins to carry him into the grassy area. She looks up at us with an odd expression. She frowns and a line forms between her brows. The wind whips past her, throwing her hair into her face. She goes to pull it out of her face and then appears to remember that she touched the blood. Her eyes start to shimmer as the tears begin to build.

She's afraid. Both of them are, I tell Patrick. *I don't think those two are in it for the revolution. They just don't know how to get out of something they got themselves in to.*

I wonder how many more are in the same boat.

The driver of the vehicle is still in the driver's seat but is now hunched over the steering wheel.

"What's with the driver?" I ask, hating myself for allowing my voice to crack. I don't want any of them to know how afraid I am.

Gunther grunts and puts his hand on the doorknob. "Brison has used him so much he's pretty much just a vessel."

"Really, Gunther?" I stop in my tracks before he turns the knob. "You would side with someone who does this to werewolves? I knew you were narcissistic, but I didn't think you were downright stupid."

"Yeah," Patrick says. "Idiotic and insane, but not stupid."

"And by the way, Brison is a stupid name!" I say, frustrated. It's a poor comeback, but it's all I've got.

Chapter Nineteen

I don't know what I expected, but this isn't it. Once Gunther opens the door and ushers us inside, we see that it's exactly what it looks like on the outside. A shack.

"What, no operatives with earpieces attached to their heads? No wall of monitors checking on every werewolf who dates a human? This place kind of sucks." I look at the people standing in the room.

There are less than twenty people here, but they've all turned to look at us. Correction, they've all turned to look at me.

"This is all you've got? A handful of wolves in the middle of nowhere in a dusty room?" I shake my head feigning disappointment. "I expected more from you, Gunther."

I look around the room and see an array of emotions—pure dislike for me, interest, disgust in Patrick for being with a human, and fear. The men and women littering this room are people from all walks of life. I imagined insane commandos in green and black fatigues. They don't even look like maniacal rebels. One man still has on his work uniform from a local fast food spot. The name on his shirt says Scott. How normal.

"This dusty room is the place where I feel most powerful, most connected to the magic," says the deep voice again. Unfortunately, it's coming from Patrick. "I need to be in a powerful place to help you break the bond between you and your mate."

My brain screams at me to get away from Patrick, but I would never abandon him. And I will do everything in my power not to kill him. I don't want to break the bond between us, but I'll give it my all if it means he will live.

"Gunther," Brison says, through Patrick's lips. "Get the knife. I want everyone in this Pack to be a witness of what I can do. What we can all do. We don't have to conform. We will dominate. And you, little girl, will help us." He points at me. He walks toward me and touches my chin with my Patrick's hand. "You are powerful. You are the daughter of our creator, and with your power running through me as your mate, that power will make us the most dominant species on this planet. So, time to unbind you and your wolf."

"Why talk through everyone, Brison? Come and claim me, you sick son of a—" Wait, what? "Your mate?"

He ignores that last part. "Because I can't be present while the spell is being performed. The breaking of your bond could affect the bonding between me and you. Don't want to risk it."

"Then how will you help me break our bond? Why can't you be present? And I'm pretty sure you can't make me your mate." At least I hope not.

"I'm only giving you the incentive you need to do so. You love the boy. I'll kill him if you don't do it. I don't want your unbinding spell to affect me, so you're in this room with iron-plated walls. Magic can't penetrate iron. Now, do it or I kill him. I won't ask you again."

A low, guttural snarl makes its way up Patrick's throat, and I don't know if it's from him or Brison. I won't let him die, even if that means breaking what holds us together. Dear God, I hope with all that I'm good for that breaking the bond between us won't break us. There is more to us than just the bond. Damn it, I sure hope there is.

As blood begins to trickle from his nose, Patrick falls to the floor unconscious. I run over to him and pull his head and shoulders onto my lap. His skin is cool and moist. Whatever Brison is doing to Patrick is hurting him. Draining the life from him. Brison is going to kill him slowly if I don't start.

"What do I have to do?"

Gunther pulls out a terribly sharp knife and throws it on the ground beside us. "Just will it and bind it with your blood. We know you have the power of Spoken Word. Just like your mother."

I look at the knife. I can't do this. This can't happen.

God please, help me.

Mother, please, help me.

But no one answers. No great voice that tells me what to do. Only silence. Only every person in this room looking at me. I pull Patrick closer to me and kiss his lips. "No matter what, I won't let you die," I whisper in his ear.

I can't hear him. His thoughts are blank.

Neither one of us has much time left. I don't know what to do. I'm not a witch. I don't work spells and magic, and I don't know how to break our bond. But he says I have to will it for it to work. My will is to be with

Patrick.

Do I make up this shit while I go along? "My will be done," I whisper as I hold my lips to Patrick's. "My will be done." A torrent of tears running down my face blinds me and become all I can see. "My will. Be done. I bind your mind to you," I whisper. I grab the knife from the floor by its dirty green hilt and drag the razor-sharp blade across my left forearm. My blood wells from the cut. The knife is so sharp that I barely feel it slice my skin, only the piercing sting that it leaves in its wake. The thought of losing Patrick causes a pain in my chest and cancels out the sting of the blade on my arm. "I sever your connection."

"Yes," says Brison's deep voice from somewhere in the room. "Yes! Separate yourselves."

The earth makes me feels strong. Touching it has to be the only way to make this happen.

I drop the knife beside me and use my right hand to wipe away the blood falling from the thin, deep cut in my arm and touch the dry earth beneath us. "By my will, by my blood, and by the earth, I bind your mind to you." I rock back and forth holding Patrick's limp body in my arms. "By my will, by my blood, and by the earth, I bind your mind to you. May no other entity be able to enter your mind! I sever the connection." I turn to the direction that Brison's voice was coming from. "You will never enter him again, you son of a bitch!"

The shack begins to move and pulsate with each rising pitch of my voice. There is no wind that howls outside to shake the walls. Only my voice. The other people in the room begin to look around, glancing at the door as if trying to plan an escape or wondering if they should help. Help me or help Brison. I don't worry about them. My mother has made me strong, and I will not leave her weak with no purpose.

Energy surges through me, the sheer power of my voice pulsing around the room, bouncing off the iron walls and shaking them. My mother's words make sense to me now. I wipe more blood from my arm, squeezing to make sure I gather as much as I can to pull off my spell. Patrick begins to stir in my arms, and I lay his head on the ground.

My mother has prepared my mind and my body to fight until I have nothing left to fight with. To fight for. She was the first one of all to receive powers that were intended for evil. But by her love, by her perseverance, and by her forgiveness by the Almighty Creator, she has given me these powers to make me strong.

I stand up and begin to walk toward Gunther. "He's left you, you know? He's left you all. But I'll deal with Bris—"

My voice catches in my throat, and an explosion thrashes around in my head. My heart races and pounds as if it will beat through my ribs and through my flesh. I fall to my knees. I feel sick. I feel dirty and used. My entire body jerks against my will and I fall prone, gasping and unable to break my plunge to the ground.

Too much magic I don't know how to use? I try to stand but fall back down, breathing in the dirt that blankets the floor. "Oh, God." My words are forced and choppy. "Sto—Please, stop," I manage to choke out.

"Too much, too soon. And now you're weak, little girl."

The words bleed through my lips, but it's not my voice. They are not my words.

My body is unbending, and every nerve feels like

its own inferno, blazing with each attempted move.

"And now I'm going to bleed you dry," my distorted voice says through my lips. It doesn't bounce around in my head like my own voice would. No, the words that make their way up my throat and through my mouth are so foreign it tastes like poison.

Don't talk. Please don't talk. It hurts. It burns, I tell myself. You need me. You can't kill me.

"I've bled this whole place of its power."

The dead earth and grass and trees. He has leached all the natural power from this place to make it his own and twisted it into something nasty and unnatural. That's why nothing grows in this little circle around the shack. He has tainted the earth beneath it. And now he's going to drain my blood, my lifeline, into this stained place and take everything my mother has given me.

My hand moves of its own accord and reaches for the knife only a few inches from my face. I try to stop, to pull my hand away, but Brison has complete control of my body.

My hand takes hold of the knife even as I fight to stop it.

Mother, please. Please don't let him kill me.

My body rolls itself over on to my right side, and my arm pulls the knife way from me.

My mind screams and fights to control itself, but all I can hear are sobs. My sobs. No matter how hard I fight, I've lost all control over my physical body.

The blade plunges just beneath my ribs, slipping easily through my skin and muscles like a warm spoon through ice cream. I pull the blade out, feeling the sting of the metal against my skin, and I thrust it into my stomach. An instant, heavy, pooling feeling gathers, and within a few seconds my shirt is drenched in my blood. I can almost feel the ground soaking up my life.

Brison holds me long enough for my limbs to feel weak from the blood loss. When he lets me go, my head falls to the side and I see Patrick lying a few feet from me. He's beginning to regain consciousness. He hasn't noticed me yet, bleeding out in front of him.

I look over and see Gunther talking to a man and a woman. The woman looks triumphant, but the man next to her looks frightened.

Trying to picture light and life in this barren place, I lay my hands flat on the dirt floor as my body jerks from the rapid breaths that dry my dirt-covered lips. "Heal," I tell my body. "God, please, heal." Nothing happens. No instant surge of power. No green, healing light from the earth.

This place is dead. The only life that seems to be around me is in the blood that's draining from my body. I try to will it back to me, but it's already begun to seep into the ground.

I'm dying. And Brison is going to take everything that Lilith has given to me.

Except Patrick. He'll live.

He's alive. And he is my mate.

And we are Bound.

I slowly roll over on to my belly, wincing as a dull pain erupts from the deep knife wounds, and dig my fingers into the dry dirt. Concentrating on the energy that joins me and Patrick, I begin to draw power from him. I don't know if it's his power as a werewolf or the force that joins us, but a minute spark of life kindles inside of me. I dig my fingers deeper in to the dirt and focus on the living, breathing earth that lies far beneath this abomination that Brison has made.

The ground begins to shake, and dirt begins to turn in on itself, rattling the thin walls around us. Brown, decaying leaves and dead bugs give way to dark living soil and grass. The once stale air becomes fresh.

"Kayla?" Patrick says, as he fully becomes aware of what has happened to me.

"Stay back," I warn, praying that I can pull this off before I bleed to death.

Everyone in the room is looking at me. They look as if they are trying to figure out what's happening as the ground continues to turn and pulsate all around me. Patrick begins to crawl toward me once he sees my blood.

"Patrick," I say more firmly. "Stay back."

His beautifully, handsome face morphs into one of rage and vengeance. Electric butterflies take over the room as a shimmer clouds around Patrick. With a quick rush of snapping bones and ripping flesh, a massive brown and black wolf explodes from Patrick's skin. The ground beneath us shudders as his four dinner-plate sized paws hit the ground. With an almost calculated ferocity Patrick makes his way through the room, biting and slashing, tearing and clawing. He kills some but leaves others.

I smile at his carnage and focus again on healing myself. This is going to hurt.

Once I'm surrounded by living, vibrant grass that has sprung from the once dead earth, I think of my wounds, the sinews of flesh and muscles that have been torn apart by the blade. This is really going to hurt.

"Heal," I say calmly, feeling the cool, damp grass on my cheek. I can feel my body healing from the inside out, and I scream as the sheer force of power from the ground below me pulls me into the earth and then shoves me back out. With a loud *thump*, I land on my hands and knees, panting in fucking pain. "Ow, that hurt!"

I look over at Patrick and see him fighting three wolves the same size as him all at once. He's got this. For a brief moment, I see him in a new light. His housemates kept asking him how he was doing something or how has he changed. I see it now.

He is an Alpha.

Pretty impressed with my level of awesome, I look over to Gunther and smile. Uncalled for, but that was pretty awesome.

"You...you bitch...how did..." he whispers. "You're human. You're only a fucking human." He looks as if he wants to attack me, but his body won't move. But it's not Brison holding him. Not this time. It's me. Holding him where I want him.

The walls still tremble from the power, my power, filling the room. "There are worse things, Gunther, than being human." There is no anger or revenge in my voice. "And, by the by, my mother is not dormant, you bastard. She's been filling me with power. And you will meet her other creations."

Not every one of my children is stable. Some were...unintentional.

"I bind you, Gunther, and all of your sheep who follow you. Those who my mother chooses to take will be banished with you tonight."

He looks as if he's still trying to fight his way through my hold. Through my will. But my will is stronger than his.

"You will be hunted by our brethren that dwell in the darkness of our mother's world. I bind you, bind you all to your wolf form."

Before my eyes, Gunther begins to shift. The air around him becomes soft as his skin ripples and begins to sprout hair and nails. I turn around to see only a few others, the ones that Patrick hasn't completely annihilated, shifting into wolves with no control of their own.

My mother has made her pick, each of them being held in place by some force that I cannot see.

"By blood, by earth, and by my will, I bind you to your wolf form until you love and yearn to be human. And you will be hunted, just as you have hunted."

My power, my mother's power, fills the room with a thunderous throb that makes it hard to hear anything, even my own voice. I fall to my knees and see Patrick staring at me, eyes wide and brightly reflective as the moon. At first, I think he is afraid of me, but that's not it. The face of his wolf is smiling as blood drips down his chin and seeps from his fur. I don't have time to decipher what it means. I reach for the knife again and drag it across the existing cut on my arm. The blood has already begun to stop flowing, but I need blood to bind this spell. I drag the blade across my arm again and hiss from the pain.

"By my blood," I say, wiping my hand across the cut. "By the earth," I say, bringing my bloodied hand to the ground, "and by my will, I bind you all. I bind you all to that place, until my mother sees fit to bring you back!"

The air in the room feels as if it is being sucked through a vortex and the sound is being taken along with it.

The Weres who have been involuntarily changed into wolves begin howling and grunting. The others just stand there, among the dead bodies, in awe—watching what happens to their fellow wolves.

I feel Patrick grab me by the arm as the power in the room rises to a deafening pitch, and he pulls me to him. He wraps his body around mine, shielding me from the swirling haze of chaos. Does he realize that I'm the reason for this portal? That no one is going into that surging vortex that isn't meant for it? We could stand at the crest of it and still not be swallowed into the void.

And then there is quiet.

Gunther and his true followers are gone, and all that remain are a handful of wolves that look confused and scared. And Patrick still hovers over me, protecting me from a threat that no longer exists.

I look at him and smile. "You're naked."

He looks down at his half-hard cock hanging between his legs with no shame. Winking at me he says, "Yeah. I didn't have time to properly undress before I started killing, but I did take my pants off. They're somewhere in here." He looks around.

I lift my hand in a high five. "You kicked ass."

His large hand meets mine with a careful smack. "Not as hard as you did. My mate is fucking awesome," he says, proud as a rooster.

We both start laughing, catching everyone in the room off guard. They have no idea what we've been through. Both of us made it out of this crap storm unscathed. Even with Gunther, his douche bag buddies, and the bloodied bodies lying on the floor, Patrick and I deserve to laugh no matter how inappropriate it may be.

He walks off to find his pants, and I take a long steadying breath. Other than Patrick, everyone stands around looking at everyone else. What the hell are they waiting for?

"You fuckers got what you deserved," says a pretty voice in the room.

I look around and see a woman with heavily creamed-coffee skin, big coily hair, and huge dark wings looking at the discarded bodies.

"Come on, you douche bags," she says with a grin. "They handed your asses to you, and from what I heard you natches had it coming." She looks at me and stills. Her pretty brown eyes go wide with wonder, and she blows a stay hair that falls into her right eye from her face. "Can you see me?" She points to herself.

Who the hell is she? "Umm, yeah. I can see you. And your freakin' wings."

"Kayla," Patrick says. "Who are you talking to?"

I don't even try to break eye contact with her. She might disappear. "You don't see her?"

She's beautiful. Sexy. Shapely. And she stands with her hands on her hips like she knows how absolutely beautiful she is. With or without the wings, I imagine, she looks amazing. "No one ever sees me in this form. Child of Lilith?" she asks, pointing at me.

With my mouth wide open, I nod. "Yes. Her daughter. You?"

She gasps and then smiles. "Holy shit. I'm the Angel of Death, part of the Triad. You must be, too. I'm Per—"

With a barely audible pop, she disappears.

Angel of Death. Triad? I must be part of it, too?

"Patrick?" I say, running over to him. "I just saw the Angel of Death. Potty mouth, but hot as sin."

He shakes his head and looks in the direction I was looking in. "Is she still there?"

"No." I glance in that direction again. "She's gone. And so is Brison."

All that hard work, and he's gone. Dang it!

I look at Patrick. "I don't know if I got him. He wasn't in the room. Did I get him?" How the hell did I forget him?

"I—I don't even know what he looks like," says a red-headed woman. "Are you going to change us, too?" Her brow furrows as fear begins to cloud her eyes.

Patrick begins to speak to her, but I tune them out. He can explain things to them. I close my eyes and imagine the line leading back to Kerry and the rest of our family. The line is bright, and it's strong. Kerry feels our connection again, and I feel the relief flooding her mind.

"Kerry's coming," I tell him. My mouth is dry, and my head is starting to throb. How the hell did I forget Brison? "I need a bandage for my arm." Or not. "It's healing already."

A light touch caresses my arm as someone lifts it. "I'm sorry." It's one of the twins. The girl. "Many of us didn't expect anything like this would happen. And once it started, we were stuck. Brison and Gunther wouldn't let us leave." She ties a piece of cloth around my left forearm. "Where did my brother go?" she whispers.

"Did he turn into a wolf?" I ask her.

She nods her head silently and puts down my arm.

"He's with Lilith, in her world. I'm sorry about

your brother, but what was in his heart condemned him. He has a lesson to learn. I'm so sorry." And I mean it. "But you're still here."

"Are you all right?" Patrick asks, coming up to me, buttoning his pants.

"I'm good. Well, as good as can be expected. Are you okay?" I rest my hand on his cheek.

I look around the room to see scared and confused faces. "Those of you who weren't taken, why were you following them?"

The boy with the shirt that says "Scott" speaks up. "My dad brought me here. He said I could learn from Gunther, but—"

"Your dad, he's gone now, isn't he?" I ask.

"Yes," Scott says.

"And what did you learn?" Patrick asks.

"I—I never hated humans. My dad did. He thought they were weak. I never felt that way."

I sigh and lean back on my heels. "Do you have anyone to go home to, or was your dad your only family?"

"No." Scott shakes his head. "My mom is at home. She said she wouldn't have anything to do with this."

"Smart woman," says the redhead. "None of us should have been here with them. They were more than any of us expected. But once we got here, we didn't have a choice. Brison could possess any of us and make us kill. He doesn't speak for us, though."

"But you do dislike human and werewolf relationships?" Even though I try to sound neutral, I can hear the sarcasm in my voice.

"We don't hate it," says a dark-skinned man with the most beautiful brown eyes I've ever seen. "We just respect our blood, and we want our line to be strong. To last."

Many people murmur in agreement. These people were left behind because hatred wasn't in their hearts. Good for them.

"My father is human, and so is my wife," he continues. "Our son died last year when he experienced his first change. He had so much human blood in him his body couldn't handle it. We have a daughter that should start her change next year some time. We're afraid. That's what brought me here."

Patrick shakes his head in confusion. "Did Gunther or Brison know that? I thought they didn't approve of werewolf-human relationships."

The dark-skinned man begins to speak, but I cut him off. "They thought that your fear of losing another child would fuel your rage. That you would do whatever it took to help them."

"Yes," he says. "And when I told them I would leave because they were killing people, Brison took hold of me and made me kill one of the werewolves a few months ago. He said if I threatened to leave again and didn't follow through with this, I wouldn't have to worry about my daughter dying from the change. He would kill her."

My heart softens for the people left behind. "I'm sorry you had to go through that—"

"Jason," he says.

Patrick speaks up. "Jason, the Line of Lilith would never force any of you to do anything like this. You chose your wife because you love her, but I know plenty of Weres who stick to the old ways and only pair with other Weres."

"What Patrick and I have is different. I am Lilith's daughter, and I believe Patrick was made just for me." I turn and look at Patrick. "She knew what I needed, and he's it. You found your love in a human because you have the right. You all do."

As time goes by, many of the people gathered here begin to leave. A few people stay, waiting for Kerry to come get us. One man even bent down on one knee and swore allegiance to me. I told him to go home and think really hard about who he was and the decisions he has made. Some people are born followers.

The door is torn off its hinges, and Kerry steps through looking as if the big bad wolf just blew down the straw house and we little piggies need to find protection. Easay, Samuel, and Mr. Levay are behind her.

The one who has sworn allegiance to me goes to greet Kerry as she walks toward us, but she bats him away like an annoying fly. He soars across the room, crashing into the wall on the far side of the shack. The whole place shakes. "Anyone else move and I'll kill the whole lot of you," she says in a grim voice, eyeing everyone in the room as the air ripples around her body. It looks as if her body wants her to make the Change, but she's holding it at bay.

I tap her shoulder. "Umm…Kerry, these aren't the bad guys. Well, not really. They're gone."

"What?" She looks pissed. "That son of a whore got away?"

"Not so much," I tell her with a nervous laugh. "I banished them. Into Lilith's dimension."

"After she forced them to Change," the remaining twin adds.

Lettie peeks in through the missing door. "I told you that you could kick ass if you wanted to." She warily looks around the room and then walks quickly to me, throwing her arms around my waist. She inhales deeply and hugs me tighter. "Ahh!" she screams as she notices something behind me.

"What's wrong?" I pull away from her. I turn around, but I don't see anything.

"Look up," she says flatly.

I look up to a window in the ceiling of the shack and see Osai and Seeley looking through. "How did you get up there?" I ask.

They both disappear for a few moments and then come walking through the hole where the door once was.

Osai clears some dust off his pants. "Element of surprise. This place is surrounded by Weres in wolf form."

Seeley walks toward me and gives me a slap on the back that almost pushes my spine through my chest. "I doubted we would see either of you again."

"That's…so depressing," I tell him.

Twin interrupts us as Patrick and I begin to explain what has happened. "Can we take Beckett's body back to his parents?" she asks shyly. "It's not right to just leave him out there in an unmarked grave."

Patrick grabs my hand and kisses it. "You're right," he says to the girl. "He should receive a proper burial."

"Crap," I say, remembering the boy in the van hunched over the steering wheel. I run outside to the van and open the door. Twin is close behind me. "What's his name?"

"Allen. When we came here a little over a month ago, he was still getting around on his own. But Brison rode him these past few days, getting everything set up to come and get you. Sorry." She reaches in the van to pull him out.

Osai helps her pull him out and they gently lower him to the ground. His eyes are closed. He looks pale. The dark circles under his eyes make his face look like a zombie Halloween mask.

I lower myself to my knees and feel for his pulse. "His pulse is faint, and his breaths are very shallow. I don't know what's going to happen. If he'll wake up or—"

Allen's cloudy eyes snap open, and he begins to hyperventilate. He grabs my face and pulls me down toward him. He's kicking wildly and holding on to me so tight it hurts. "Where did you send us? I'll get us out of here, you bitch! You can't keep us here!" Brison screams through Allen's mouth.

I try to break free from his grip, but he holds me tight. Patrick reaches for him, but I yell, telling him to back off. "I won't let you do this to anyone else."

I grab both sides of Allen's face and stare into his eyes. His grip is hurting me, but I can't let Brison possess anyone else. Pushing my nose right up to his and tightening my hold to keep him from using me as leverage to get up from the ground, I push into his mind, Brison's mind through Allen's, and hold on. The strength in my arms surprises me. He's a werewolf, and he can't break free of my grasp. He's supposed to be the strong one.

I won't let this bastard continue to hurt my family. I see a thin, dark cord that stretches from Allen's mind back to Brison's, and I follow it. The cord transcends dimensions and leads me to Brison.

He is running in wolf form through a bleak, cold, darkened hillside. He's running from something. The cold from this something's body is what keeps his tired legs moving. Brison wants to look back, but he knows that if he does it will only slow him down. He is being chased by one of my mother's other creations.

Brison's paws are torn and bloodied by the rocky hillside terrain, but if he stops or slows down, he will suffer.

"By these words you will cross no more, Brison. By my will and my words, I bind you." I feel my lips move as I work my magic. My words resonate through his head and even though he wants to counter my spell, he can't stop to focus. He can only run. I begin to speak in another language, but somehow, I understand the words. It is the first language. The one that my mother and father spoke in the Garden to one another. Brison wants to fight, but there is no use.

Brison begins to speak, first cursing Allen for allowing me in, and then trying to force his way back into Allen's mind. But I'm in Allen's mind already, and there is no room for the both of us. I feel Brison's body jolt as something lands on him and begins to attack. By trying to push me out of Allen's mind, he has allowed himself to lose focus of what is hunting him, and it catches him.

I feel teeth and claws on his body as he fights and screams and begs. Even though I know I'm not being harmed, I scream out as I see what is tearing its way through Brison's flesh. Its chalk-white skin and rows of jagged teeth are nothing compared to its eyes. They are black and the iris is yellow with flecks of white. I scream again, fighting to get away, and then the connection with Brison, through Allen, is broken. I look up to see Patrick with blood on his hands. He has almost ripped Allen's head off.

I fall back and take deep breaths, trying to find something to focus on to let me know I'm not in danger. My breath is forced and fast. I look around, attempting to ground myself to this world. To forget the beast that I just saw.

Lettie is suddenly very close to my face. "Look at me, Kayla," she says, grabbing me by my hands. "Calm down. It's okay."

My breathing slows, but my heart still races. And then, I begin to cry. "They're all there, with those things after them." Did I do the right thing by sending them there? Will they suffer more than I even cared to think? How could I have done this to someone?

"You did the right thing, Kayla," Patrick says as he gathers me in his arms. He picks me up from the ground and cradles me close to him. "Lilith told you to send them there, right?"

She didn't say those words. I condemned those people to Hell, and I'll have to live with that.

"Young lady, what is your name?" Kerry says.

I look up and see that she is gesturing toward Twin.

"Sabrina, ma'am." She walks toward Kerry, her neck bared in a show of submission. She looks afraid. She should be.

Kerry steps closer to her. "If your intentions are true, Sabrina, you don't have to be afraid. Go find your friend that is buried and put him in the back of the van along with this boy here on the ground. Steven—" She looks at Mr. Levay. "—will help you. Take their bodies to their families, and tell them what happened. Let them know that I sent you and that I hold no ill will toward the young men or their families."

"Allen didn't have any family. I think that's why Brison used him the most," Sabrina says.

"Then we'll take him back with us and bury him properly."

"Yes, ma'am," she says as she walks off toward Beckett's body with Mr. Levay following her.

"The cars are about a mile and a half up the road. Can you two walk that far?" Kerry is speaking to me and Patrick.

"Do you want me to carry you?" Patrick asks.

"No, I'm fine. Are you okay?" I say as I wiggle to get him to put me down.

"I'm good."

Kerry steps toward me and smooths my hair behind my left ear. "I'm so happy you're both all right. Go on, start walking to the car. I'm going to have a talk with the people left over from Gunther's pack." Her face and voice are void of emotion, but vengeance and anger are roiling off her.

I touch her arm. "Please don't punish them. Most of them got a lot more than they bargained for. And the ones who knew what they were getting into are being punished." I look back toward the little doorless shack.

She smiles. "You must tell me what you did."

"I'll tell you in the car." I reach out a hand toward Lettie. "Come on, Pix. Get your boyfriend, and walk to the car with us."

Chapter Twenty

The car ride back to the manor didn't seem nearly as long as the ride to the middle of nowhere. I guess an hour flies by when you're talking constantly and don't feel threatened by a psychotic asshole and his buddies. I filled everyone in on what happened from the moment Kerry started acting like a scary drunk baby up until she ripped the door off the hinges of the wooden shack.

"How were you able to work magic the way you did?" Samuel asks.

I shrug and take a sip of water. "Beats me. Lilith told me that she was weak from making me strong. It didn't make sense to me at first, but then it all clicked when I thought I would lose Patrick." I look at him and smile. "Fear of losing the ones you love motivates you to do things you didn't know you could. If Lilith was doing her best to make me strong, I figured I had to give it my all. She was giving me everything she had. I think, and I could be severely wrong, that Lilith is giving me the gifts that were given to her."

"Like the gift of Spoken Word," Lettie says. "How did you know to send them to wherever the hell they are?"

"Right before Kerry went all wonky, I had a dream about my mother. She told me that there was a place in her world where she kept her children that were unintentional. A place where the troublemakers would go. Gunther and Brison were big troublemakers. They need to learn a lesson. It's up to them how long they stay there." I try to conceal a shudder and remember that they were the ones killing people.

"How are you?" Lettie asks.

I nod my head. "I'll be fine. They have to learn to respect life. All life. I understand that some of the Weres are fearful of what will happen to their children, but what they did was inexcusable. I mean, come on, humans and werewolves have been living together since the beginning of time. You're still here, and you're still strong."

Kerry stands up from the family room recliner. "You did good."

I smile. "Thanks. But there is more coming." I don't want to rain on the parade, but if what I know is true, the Rogue Pack was only the beginning. "Remember when I told you the story of Lilith and Eve making arrangements to protect both of their offspring and this planet? Well, I think this is how it starts. Or maybe it already started, and this is just where she decided to make me a part of it. Who knows? I don't know exactly how, but with you standing with me, we can try to prevent a war between supernaturals that will later include humans. And later lead to the extinction of humans. That is my purpose. That's why I was born back into this world."

"That sounds really hard," Lettie says, trying to lighten the mood. "Can we sleep first?"

Kerry sighs. "That sounds like a wonderful idea."

Everyone gets up from where they were sitting and begin walking toward the steps. These past few months have been hard on us all. A war isn't breaking out at this moment, so rest sounds awesome.

Patrick grabs my hand and pulls me to him. "I love you. You were wonderful." His face falters.

The tension in my body makes me hold my breath. "Yeah, I saw that look. Thought I could ignore it."

"Yes, I'll admit I was vexed for a moment. I'm just happy you're mine."

"Patrick's right," Kerry says as she turns around on the stairway. "You are of our Goddess, and she has put you here with us. That means a lot to me, to all of us. She has entrusted us with you." She smiles her little smile and turns back around to head up the steps.

"Hey." Lettie pulls on my hair from behind me. "You two actually get to go out on a date. A real date that doesn't include having dinner with the rest of us here at the manor."

Patrick stops. "I didn't think of that. Maybe you and Sam—"

"And maybe we can't," Lettie interrupts him. "We can double date later. Right now, you two deserve some alone time. And so do we." She begins to shimmy while Samuel walks ahead of her.

A thought hits me, and I stop walking. "Lettie, can I talk to you for a moment?" I look at Patrick and Samuel. "We'll be up in a few minutes."

Lettie follows me back to the sitting area while Patrick and Samuel begin a race to the top of the steps. It looks as if Samuel tries to throw Patrick back down the stairs, but their laughter continues.

"Werewolves sure can rough-house, can't they?" she says. "I want him to be rough with me, if you know what I mean, but he's afraid he'll break me."

"*Ew*. He should be afraid. And so should you."

Her face sobers as she sits down across from me. "What's up? Everything okay?"

"Yeah, Pix. Everything's good. I just wanted to run something past you." I clear my throat. Who knew I would even want this? "Do you want to stay here? Or do you want to get an apartment?"

She exhales deeply. "That's all you wanted to talk about? You scared me, Spock. Only use your serious face when you're serious."

"I am being serious. When we first moved here, I felt like I was taking something away from you. You pride yourself on being independent of your family, and because of me your safety was threatened. So, your opinion means a lot to me. This crap with Gunther is over, and I didn't want to bring it up until it was clear. You don't have to answer me now, but just know that if you want to get another place, I'll be coming with you."

Lettie bites the inside of her lip and looks around the family room as if the answer is painted on the walls. "I guess I didn't think of it that way. It's not like living at home. Even though everyone feels like family, I'm not being coddled. I like it here. And this is your family."

"You're my family too, Lettie."

"I know that. If Kerry lets us, I want to stay here. And not just because of Samuel. But because it feels good. It feels like a home to me, too. And we don't pay rent! That alone makes me very happy." She smiles.

"Okay. We'll talk to Kerry about it tomorrow."

Lettie and I stand and walk toward the stairway. I doubt Kerry will tell us Lettie can't stay. She was a little apprehensive at first, but Lettie has grown on her. In a completely non-fungi type way. It feels good to have my family here with me. And the fact that we're not being hunted by werewolves just makes it even better.

Once we get to the kitchen, I see that Patrick, Samuel, and Easay are making cold-cut sandwiches. Seeley is taking French fries out of the oven.

"Hungry, you two?" Easay asks. "We're always hungry, but it just seemed uncouth not to make you guys anything."

"I'm starving," I tell her.

Lettie opens the freezer door. "Anyone want some ice cream? I picked up some caramelized almonds, strawberries, and bananas yesterday. And some chocolate syrup." She winks at Samuel.

"*Ew*," Easay and I say in unison.

I open the cupboard to get some bowls. "Sure, Pix, I'll take one."

Seeley puts fries on all our plates. "I will as well."

Everyone nods in agreement to the sundae. This feels good. Those moments just keep on coming. My family surrounds me, and we're not being attacked anymore. This is pretty awesome.

****

"He's enjoying his freedom," Kerry says, watching Patrick in wolf form disappear between the trees. She walks down the three steps of the porch and comes to stand beside me.

"Yes, he is. It feels good to him." I sit down on the last step. "Why aren't you asleep? I had the feeling that everyone was tired."

Kerry exhales firmly as she gathers her long, billowing, brown skirt close to her legs and then sits down. "Not so tired. Just relieved. With all the worrying I've been doing these past few months, I think my body has to get used to not worrying." She looks at me, then rests her hand on my shoulder. "But it was worth it, Kayla. Don't you think?"

I consider the thought for a moment and then look up at the sky. "It was worth it. You all stood with me and protected me even when you didn't have to. Patrick is wonderful. And my mother…There are no words to express how I feel knowing that Lilith is my mother."

It makes things clearer for me. Not just because she's given me weird talents. Talents? Now I have a sense of why things happened the way they did when I was growing up. I'm not excusing my mother for abandoning me, but maybe she didn't feel a connection. Like she wasn't really a part of me, and she could feel it.

"Maybe that's what drove my mother away. She could tell I wasn't really her child."

"Or it could be because she's a selfish woman who left her child." Kerry's expression is dark. "There is no excuse for her treating you the way she does."

I still don't feel comfortable talking about her with anyone. Except with my therapist, and it took a really long time to get it out of me. So, I go in another direction. "My dad was good. He loves me in his own way. And now that I know I'm not truly his child, I admire him for it."

Quietly, we sit for a few moments and listen to the stillness of our surroundings. The cicadas have taken a break from their song and the only sound that can be heard is the rustling of the trees from the gently wafting wind. I look over at Kerry, and she has her eyes closed. She looks peaceful.

R.A. Boyd

"Well, Kerry, I'm going to go inside and take a shower. Goodnight," I say as we both stand.

We walk up the porch stairs, and before I open the screen door, Kerry grabs my arm and pulls me close to her in a warm embrace. "Dearest Kayla, we will always stand by you." She pulls away from me and looks into my eyes. The look of her golden-yellow and bright blue eyes appears grave, yet hopeful. "I heard what you said earlier, so please don't think that we will forget. It's not over, and we have much work to do to unite our brothers and sisters in Lilith. The war between the supernaturals will never come to pass." She winks at me. "You just let us know when you're ready to begin, but enjoy this quiet that we have now. You and Patrick deserve it. Oh, Lettie can stay." She kisses my cheek and opens the screen door.

I head to my room to get ready for bed, and Kerry walks toward her office. She has said everything that she needed to say, even though I knew it already. I don't stand alone. I don't think I ever really did, and I'm pretty sure I'll never stand alone again.

Chapter Twenty-One

You must secure my people from above and from below, my mother says, as we walk through a field with flowers that wave hello even though there is no wind blowing. *You must find the Sethians. It will be difficult to convince them, but once you earn their trust, they will be loyal.*

Lilith walks ahead of me. Her long, dark, radiant hair falls just above her waist. It's so thick that I only catch flashes of her arm as her mane sways back and forth. The earth tones of her long dress swing as she walks barefoot through the luscious field.

"Sethians? How did you make the—"

Not now, Kayla. You wanted to know what you needed to do and that's why I'm telling you. But rest first, my child. Do not let worries invade your peace just yet. There is a scripture about worrying.

I smile and stop walking. "Yes, I know it. So, I guess I shouldn't be anxious about tomorrow. Tomorrow will be anxious for itself."

She laughs, and it sounds like warm summer rain. *Yes. I am so proud of you.* She takes a deep breath and the entire landscape breathes with her. *There is something I need from you. The woman you saw, the angel. Don't seek her out. Not yet.*

I start to protest, but she quiets me with a soft *shhh. Trust me, daughter.*

I can give her that. "Okay. I won't look for her." She starts walking again and so do I. "So, what else can I do? I can wield magic."

You can wield elemental magicks, and you have the power of Spoken Word, she corrects me. *You are not ready for transmogrification. There's a book on its way to you. Be kind to it.*

I begin walking again to catch up with her. "Be kind to a book? I don't understand."

You will. Her head cocks to the side as if she's heard a noise. *Your mate comes to call.*

****

"Kayla?" Patrick slides into bed next to me. "Are you awake?"

I stretch to push the sleep away. "I am now. Did you have a good time?" I look over at the clock on the nightstand. Almost four in the morning.

He kisses my neck. "Yes. And you smell like wildflowers."

"That seems to happen after I wake up from being with Lilith."

"I'm sorry I woke you."

"No," I tell him as I roll over on my right side to face him. "Don't be sorry. I think she was about to push me out anyway. She seems to like doing that when I still have tons of questions to ask."

He laughs and snuggles closer to me, bringing my head to his chest and resting his head on top of mine. "I don't think she wants you to know everything at once. Maybe Lilith doesn't want to overwhelm you."

I inhale his scent. His clean, citrus scent is of fur and fresh dew on grass in the morning. "I think you're right. If she told me everything at once, I might be in denial."

We lie there for a few moments listening to the quiet of the still house. He kisses my forehead and then gets settled as if he's ready to go to sleep.

"I'm taking you to lunch tomorrow," Patrick says, breaking the silence. "Just the two of us. Alone. No one else."

I laugh and look up at him. "You sure you don't want to invite everyone in the house?"

"Keep being a smartass and I will." His look sobers. "What's wrong?"

"What do you know about Sethians?" The conversation with my mother isn't far from my thoughts.

"I've never heard of them. The Line is in direct contact with all supernaturals. They all kind of keep track of one another."

"So, the Line can help me find them?"

"If they're even still around. I don't think there's anything in the records about them. At least not in the past five or six hundred years. They may be extinct."

I exhale and look up at the ceiling. "Well, I think your records are wrong. Lilith says that I have to 'secure her people from above and from below.' And then she mentioned Sethians and a book."

"Are they from above or below?"

I shake my head. "I have absolutely no idea."

After a short period of silence, I hear the cadence of faint snores come from Patrick. I'm glad he can sleep easy. For the first time in what seems like forever, I think I can too. These past few months have revealed not only my true origin, but my true family—Patrick, Lettie, Kerry, and every other person who sleeps in this house tonight.

The complete abandonment by my mother and the indifference toward me by my father made the transition into my new family that much easier for me. I feel no remorse.

I have a feeling that whatever lies ahead will not be easy. There will be people like Gunther and Brison who want to use me or harm me. And what better way to hurt me than to hurt the people I love? It doesn't matter. Not really. I can keep them safe.

I'm strong enough to do that now, and with each passing moment, I'll only grow stronger. If my mother really is giving me the gifts she has, I know I'll be strong enough to stop this war from coming. My family stands with me. I draw strength from that. It's what I was born to do. Every supernatural on this planet who is in league with the Line of Lilith stands with me, and those who try to harm us will be brought to their knees.

This is going to be so much fun.

Blessed be.

About the Author

R.A. Boyd is a writer, and reader, of paranormal romance, horror, and urban fantasy. She lives in Maryland with her husband, daughter, and her massive collection of books.

She loves all things paranormal but dabbles in romantic comedies and hockey fights. When she's not writing at three in the morning, she's binge-watching Netflix or plotting random scenes from her novels in the voice of her characters. It makes her daughter giggle but worries her husband.

~*~

Visit R.A. at

http://raboyd.com

~*~

To chat with R.A. Boyd and other Wild Rose Press authors of erotic romance, join us at

www.groups.yahoo.com/group/thewilderroses.

Hunted by Angels
Line of Lilith Book One
By R.A. Boyd

Two sex demons walk into a church and get married in the sight of God, surrounded by their friends and family. Sounds like the beginning of a bad joke? Not so much.

All Perrian "Perry" Haines wants is to marry the man of her dreams—more like nightmares—and be left alone, but when Samael, a psychotic archangel, is out to murder her and all her kind, it puts a damper on her not so happily ever after. Submitting to Samael almost seems safer than her new husband, the seductive sex-demon O'Neil Haines, whose secrets hold the key to her survival and her humanity.

Instant snark-filled sparks fly as Perry and Haines discover the origins of her birth and the real reason Samael wants to end her destiny. What a way to start a honeymoon!

Sample Chapter of
Book One of R.A. Boyd's
Line of Lilith Series

Hunted by Angels

Chapter One

"I do," I say sulkily as the minister asks if I take this man standing next to me to be my lawfully wedded husband.

"You could at least muster *some* kind of joy over this," Haines says quietly as he squeezes my hand. "Your posture is disgusting."

"Shut-up," I snap at him.

For our friends and family attending our nuptials I have nothing but sweet smiles and kind words. But for this douchebag I have snark for days.

This is not the happily ever after either one of us was hoping for. And Haines is certainly not the man I wanted to end up with. But if I don't have a holy union —holy my arse! —with him all hell will break loose and blah, blah, blah. We're destined to be together. I despise him. He likes it. He's a demon. Figuratively and literally.

Haines is a full-blooded incubus, a male demon that feeds off the sexual energy of women. I am the female counterpart—a succubus. I also happen to be a cambion, a half-blood. *Perfect couple,* my parents said. *Marry him or you'll start murdering people. You won't hate each other forever.* Fat chance.

"Oh, my God," echoes the blubbering voice of my Aunt Rita amid the silence as the minister says the final lines of the ceremony. "She's. So. Beautiful!" She sure loves to be heard.

The minister smiles as he presents us to the crowd sitting in the church pews. "I now pronounce you husband and wife. You may now kiss the bride."

I turn to Haines and frown at him as he leans in and gives me a hard kiss on the lips. "Could you be more of a dick?" I say quietly while everyone stands and claps for us. "That hurt."

"Could you be happy about *something* for five minutes?" Haines says through gritted teeth, grabbing my hand as a show of affection. "Your parents should have let me train you years ago."

I look at him and scoff. "Are you insane?"

Haines is one of the yummiest men I've ever laid eyes on. He's just under six feet tall with broad shoulders, a narrow waist, and dark hazel eyes that complement his sun-kissed complexion perfectly. His chestnut wavy hair is cut fairly close but grown out just enough so that I can pull it when I get angry with him. Trust me. I've done it several times before. He pisses me off daily.

When my mother found out that I had inherited her demonic genes she contacted a soothsayer who did some witchy crap and found out that Haines was the man for the job. Again, we are fated to be together. There was a choice, though. Either marry Haines, apparently the only living, unattached incubus that has the power to help me control myself, or allow my need for sex and energy to take over. I loathe Haines, but I don't want to kill anyone.

Well, except Haines.

Bite Thy Neighbor
By Esmae Browder

Some neighbors suck...literally.

Quirky Maisy Harker spends her time daydreaming about her sexy husband, Jensen Helsing. Though their marriage is one of convenience, Maisy wishes the sparks of heat she feels around him were reciprocated. Sexually starved, she also lusts after her mysterious neighbor, Adam. True, his incisors do look a bit sharp, and he never seems to drink or eat anything—but hey, maybe that's how he keeps that yummy, drool-worthy physique.

Yet Maisy knows something's not quite right, and it isn't long before she learns Adam is a centuries-old vampire embroiled in a gypsy curse placed on the women of her family. All her female ancestors have been drawn to the vampire and bound by his desires, experiencing a terrible side effect of the curse and resulting in death.

It's up to Maisy to find a way to break the curse once and for all before she, too, falls under his spell.

Thank you for purchasing
this publication of The Wild Rose Press, Inc.

For questions or more
information contact us at
info@thewildrosepress.com.

The Wild Rose Press, Inc.
www.thewildrosepress.com

To visit with authors of
The Wild Rose Press, Inc.
join our yahoo loop at
http://groups.yahoo.com/group/thewildrosepress/

www.ingramcontent.com/pod-product-compliance
Lightning Source LLC
Chambersburg PA
CBHW051524260626
47170CB00003B/767